The Favored Son

The Gareth and Gwen Medieval Mysteries:
The Bard's Daughter (novella)
The Good Knight
The Uninvited Guest
The Fourth Horseman
The Fallen Princess
The Unlikely Spy
The Lost Brother
The Renegade Merchant
The Unexpected Ally
The Worthy Soldier
The Favored Son
The Viking Prince
The Irish Bride
The Prince's Man

A Gareth and Gwen Medieval Mystery

The
FAVORED
SON

by

SARAH WOODBURY

To Taran

Cast of Characters

Gwen – Gareth's wife, spy for Hywel
Gareth – Gwen's husband, captain of Hywel's guard
Llelo – Gareth and Gwen's foster son
Dai – Gareth and Gwen's foster son
Tangwen – Gareth and Gwen's daughter
Taran – Gareth and Gwen's son

Evan – Gareth's friend, Dragon member
Angharad – Evan's wife
Gruffydd – Rhun's former captain, Dragon member
Cadoc – Assassin, Dragon member
Steffan – Dragon member
Iago – Dragon member
Aron – Dragon member

Robert – Earl of Gloucester (deceased)
Henry Plantagenet – son of Empress Maud and Geoffrey of Anjou
Hamelin – Henry's half-brother
William FitzRobert – Earl of Gloucester
Roger FitzRobert – William's brother
Robert Fitzharding – Local magnate of Bristol
Cadwaladr ap Gruffydd – King Owain's brother
Stephen – King of England
William of Ypres – Stephen's spymaster

Stephen de Blois came to London,
and the people received him
and hallowed him to king on midwinter day.
But in this king's time was all dissension, and evil, and rapine;
for against him rose soon the rich men who were traitors.

Then was England very much divided.
Some held with the king and some with the empress;
for when the king was in prison,
the earls and the rich men supposed that he would never more
come out,
and they settled with the empress,
and when the king was out,
he heard of this, and took his force,
and beset her in the tower.

By such things, and more than we can say,
we suffered nineteen winters for our sins.
To till the ground was to plough the sea:
the earth bore no corn,
for the land was all laid waste by such deeds;
they said openly that Christ and his saints slept ...
–The Anglo-Saxon Chronicle

PROLOGUE

Westminster Palace
November 1147

King Stephen

The rap at the door was unwelcome, and for a moment Stephen considered not answering. But his attendants knew he was in his chamber—and alone—and they were likely to be persistent.

So rather than succumbing to his petty and uncharacteristic desire to hide, he said, "Come!"

The door opened, a bit more tentatively than usual, Stephen was pleased to see. His spymaster, William of Ypres, stood on the threshold.

At the sight of Stephen slouched in his chair by the fire, William put his heels together and bowed. "My king. We have received a message from Gloucester."

Stephen straightened, his heart suddenly pounding with a combination of dread and determination. "Just say it."

"Your noble cousin, Robert, has died."

Stephen let out wavering breath. "So it is over."

"Yes, my lord."

"He was more than a cousin to me. He was my friend, once."

"I know, my lord."

Stephen couldn't sit still any longer and stood to pace in front of the hearth. William knew better than to interrupt, though Stephen could sense his impatience growing. "You have something to say?"

"Maud hasn't moved from Devizes in months, and rumor has it she plans to return to Normandy soon. This could be the moment for which we've been waiting, my king. The empress is without a general, and who is she going to choose? Ranulf?" William scoffed. "Henry? You defeated him easily in the spring."

Stephen paused amidst his pacing. "You want to attack now? This late in the year?"

William stood his ground. "The weather hasn't turned yet. Our enemy is weak and leaderless."

Stephen chewed on his lower lip. "It would be unseemly."

William allowed himself a single tsk of disgust before swallowing down the rest of his arguments, though he did muster the temerity to say, "At least consider it, my king."

"What of our traitor in Gloucester?"

"He is prepared." William took a step forward, an indication of his surprise and anticipation. "You—you are considering my proposal?"

"I am."

"It is ... somewhat underhanded," William said hesitantly.

Stephen returned to his seat. As he studied William—and his options—his fingers beat a tattoo on the arm of his chair. "You are wondering why I won't take advantage of Robert's death to attack Lincoln or Devizes openly, but I am willing to seal Maud's fate by taking Bristol by deception?" With its high ground, moat, massive square keep, two concentric curtain walls, and three wards, Bristol castle was eminently defensible.

"Yes, my lord."

Stephen's eyes remained focused on William's face. He wanted his spymaster to understand that he'd never been more serious. "I will consider it because I want this conflict to end, and I must be the victor. Victory in this instance means not sacrificing more men at the foot of a castle I have been heretofore unable to take. But taking it from the inside because of my enemy's own weakness? That I can do."

Stephen could tell that William still didn't understand the difference and thought his king was splitting hairs. Perhaps he was. He knew in himself, however, that he hadn't moved against Bristol while Robert was alive because of their shared history and respect. He would and had taken his cousin in battle. He would have killed him on the battlefield had it become necessary. But he would not use subterfuge against him. Robert had been the very essence of honor, and in moments of self-honesty, Stephen could admit he'd admired him his whole life and as a youth had aspired to be like him.

But with Robert dead, William was right that a new strategy was required. Open warfare would serve only to tear England apart even more, but if he could take Bristol without losing an army, he would do it.

And end the war. At last.

William cleared his throat. "Henry is at Bristol."

Stephen's eyes lit. "Even better. I take him, and Maud is truly done."

"I should prepare?"

"Indeed."

William turned thoughtful. "We should send a messenger to Henry at Bristol with your condolences for Earl Robert's death."

"Of course." Stephen paused. "But—"

"But not a man you need at your side for the coming endeavor." William tapped his lips with one finger, and his expression became almost predatory.

Stephen knew that look. It sent a shiver down his spine, and he was more glad than he could say that William was on his side and not Maud's.

"Never fear, my king. I know just who to send."

1

Bristol Castle
November 1147

Gwen

"**I**'m so glad you're here. I was afraid you weren't going to come—" Henry Plantagenet, son of Empress Maud, broke off his greeting as he caught sight of baby Taran in Gwen's arms.

Gwen and Gareth bowed. By the time they'd straightened, Henry had come around the table that was serving as a repository for stacks of paper and halted in front of them.

Gwen smiled ruefully at Henry's evident surprise and said in French, the language he'd been speaking, "You said you wanted both of us, and both of us have come." She turned sideways to show him the baby, who was asleep in his sling in soft wool blankets. "Plus one."

Henry bent forward to look into Taran's face. "I never meant for you to put yourself or your child at risk!" With utter gentleness, he reached out a finger to stroke the baby's cheek and lowered his voice so his talking wouldn't disturb the child. "I would not have been so demanding had I known of his birth."

And then he amended, with a maturity not present the last time they'd seen him, "No, that's a lie. I would have wanted you to come regardless and resented that you could not."

"As soon as we received your message, we both wanted to heed your summons," Gareth said, "but Gwen and the baby would not have traveled such a distance if staying at Aberystwyth wouldn't have been worse. Croup."

The disease engendered such fear that Henry recoiled slightly. Gwen put out a hand, wanting to reassure him. "It has been ten days since we left Aberystwyth, and none of our party has fallen ill in that time. You have nothing to fear from us."

Croup wasn't as terrible a sickness as plague, but it invariably left dead children and broken families in its wake. When Gareth was five years old, his own parents had died of croup or something similar. He'd been too young at the time to know the difference between one sickness and the next. The disease was characterized by a swollen neck and a sore throat that eventually cut off a child's ability to breathe. It was an ugly and painful way to die—and horrific for a parent to have to watch.

Prince Henry regarded them. "I see now the reason for the delay in your arrival—and appreciate it."

What remained to be seen was whether or not anyone else did. Things hadn't started off well. Their entry into the castle had been further delayed by the need for the guard to write down every one of their names. Because they were Welsh, the construction and spelling had been unfamiliar to him. Just before Gareth himself had offered to write the list, the understeward had hastily finished it and sent them on their way, admittedly with his apologies.

"I am pleased not to take on an unnecessary measure of guilt. The weight I bear is heavy enough." Henry glanced over his shoulder as he walked back to his seat on the far side of the table. "Where are the rest of your men? Surely you didn't bring only one retainer with you?"

He was referring to their eldest son, Llelo, who'd put his back to the now-closed door. Gwen had never been to this particular castle before, but she recognized the room as a private office or receiving room. It was fifteen feet on a side, appointed with a long table, several cushioned chairs, and a window. Inside the confines of the castle, Gwen found herself all turned around, so she wasn't sure which direction the window faced, but it was letting in enough natural light that a few candles and the fire were sufficient to light the space. She could believe the room had once been Earl Robert's, but with his death, it had been given over to the next-highest-ranking magnate— not his son and heir, William, but Prince Henry.

Since it was only the few of them, Gwen didn't stand on ceremony and went straight to the hearth to warm her hands and Taran in his blankets. She didn't have Prince Hywel's condition, which caused his fingers to turn white when they grew cold, but this morning they'd woken to chillier air than they'd experienced in the whole of their journey. She'd been glad to reach the castle and find herself indoors. The hall had been warmer than outside, but it hadn't been as warm as this room.

Gareth followed Gwen to the fire, though he stood a pace closer to Henry with his back to the flames and his hands clasped behind him.

"We have a few more men with us, my lord, but we didn't fear for our lives in Bristol, knowing that it was within your sphere of influence, and we didn't want to impose on you with an army. We thought our son sufficient protection to enter your hall." Gareth gestured behind him. "This is Llelo, our eldest and my apprentice, if such a thing can be conceived, in investigating murder."

Llelo put a hand to his heart and bent his head. "I was also at Newcastle-under-Lyme three years ago, my lord, though I imagine you don't remember me."

Henry's eyes swept over Llelo in a quick assessment. He saw a tall young man, a year older than Henry himself, with dark hair and blue eyes that looked back at the prince with equal curiosity. "I'm sorry, but I do not. I won't make that mistake again." Then he paused. "How many soldiers did you say you brought?"

"I'm sorry if I wasn't clear," Gareth said. "We have a guard of six."

Up until now—except for the rueful laugh—Henry had appeared quite grave, but now his eyes lit. "Don't tell me you brought the Dragons with you!"

Gareth's eyes twinkled. "We did." He had felt some apprehension at taking Hywel's best warriors away with him, but left behind at Aberystwyth were Hywel's foster father, Cadifor, and Cadifor's sons, along with the entirety of the prince's teulu. They had to be content they were leaving their lord in safe hands—or as safe as could be arranged.

Gwen laughed to see Henry's enthusiasm. "How could you possibly know of them?"

"Who hasn't heard of the Dragons?" Henry sounded as excited as a boy whose master had just replaced his wooden sword with a real one. "They took down the Flemings' castle single-handed! What a blow they struck for my mother!"

The six men he was referring to, dubbed *the Dragons* by Prince Hywel, were each worth two or more average men. The decision to send only them with Gareth and Gwen had been deliberated upon at length, but in the end Hywel had decided not to send any more for the reasons to which they'd just alluded. In addition, though it hadn't occurred to Gwen until she'd seen Henry's face, the Dragons—of all the members of Hywel's court—were the most likely to be well received by English people. Their reputation, like Gareth's and Gwen's, had preceded them.

Gwen didn't mention—because to Henry it would have been immaterial—the rest of their retinue, which included their daughter, Tangwen; Evan's wife, Angharad; Gareth and Gwen's other adopted son, thirteen-year-old Dai; and four household servants: Tangwen's nanny, her daughter, and a husband and wife couple. These latter two were recent additions and a concession of sorts on Gwen's part. But with the new baby, basic daily household tasks were often beyond her, and Gareth was of the opinion that if he could afford to employ someone to help with chores, then he was morally obligated to do so.

Gareth had been smiling at Henry, but at the mention of the battle for Wiston Castle, he sobered. "I know; I was there."

He shot Gwen a meaningful look. The blow they'd struck at Wiston hadn't been in the slightest bit for Empress Maud—but for Wales, in the hopes of ridding their lands of the hated Flemings once and for all. That they'd attacked and taken the castle as allies of Gilbert de Clare, Earl of Pembroke, who'd recently abandoned King Stephen for Maud, had been of no importance to Prince Hywel. To Welsh eyes, there wasn't much to choose between these two cousins who were warring for the English throne. Either would both have conquered Wales in a heartbeat if one hadn't been too busy fighting the other.

Henry didn't appear to notice the glance, caught up as he was in the glories of battle. "I would have expected nothing less from you! I want to hear all about it, but it will have to wait until our business here is done."

Only a boy when they'd met him for the first time at Newcastle-under-Lyme (and saved his life), Henry was now fourteen and a man by Welsh reckoning. Though his freckled face was still rounded with youth, since they'd last seen him his hair had darkened to a reddish-blond. He'd grown stockier in build too, an indication of the martial upbringing that was required for the firstborn son of a claimant to the throne of England. Training in war was his birthright.

What remained to be seen was how much of the boy remained in the man. At Newcastle-under-Lyme, Henry had been a somewhat bewildered and unhappy child but fundamentally honest and hopeful. While he was reluctant to broach what had brought them here,

Henry's hesitation was out of grief, not uncertainty. He had approached them with confidence, certain of his own worth and authority. One could believe, looking at him now, that he really might one day become King of England.

Gareth dropped a cushion onto a chair and held it for Gwen until she sat. At the change in altitude, Taran stirred and pushed at his blankets, but she rocked him, and he didn't wake.

Henry folded his hands and rested them on the table. "Thank you for coming. I know the circumstances are unusual, and the request even more so, but I cannot rest until I uncover the truth—or you do."

He paused. "I believe that my uncle did not die a natural death but was murdered."

Neither Gareth nor Gwen showed surprise, since that had been the gist of the message Prince Henry had sent to Aberystwyth. Earl Robert had died three weeks ago, on *Calan Gaeaf*, or to the English, All Hallows' Eve, and the castle was still in deep mourning, as evidenced by the black drapery hung about the windows in the great hall.

"I understand Earl Robert had been ill for some time," Gwen said gently, trying to be diplomatic. Henry's suspicions could be misguided, and they needed to lay the issue bare immediately.

It didn't work.

Henry slammed a fist on the table. "I am not merely a grieving nephew who must be appeased! Nor am I a child any longer, and you are wrong to treat me as one. I am angry, yes, but it is because my uncle was hurried to his grave." At the sight of Gwen's stricken face—and Taran stirring in his wrappings—Henry immediately put up both hands in apology. "Please forgive me. Many others have said the same thing to me, and I am tired of hearing it."

"You seem very certain." Gwen rocked Taran back and forth. "Is that because you *are* certain or because you've had to defend your position to skeptical older men—or your mother?"

Henry bowed his head. "I admit I could be wrong." Then his chin came up. At Gwen's calm words and the baby fading back to sleep, his tension appeared to ease. It was no longer anger that had him clenching his fists, so much as determination. "But I don't think I am. I did not send for you on a whim."

Now Gareth hunched forward, his elbows on his knees and his hands clasped before him. The formality of their initial conversation had at last given way to a more casual practicality. "Say we believe it's possible. What makes you think your uncle was murdered?"

Henry blinked, perhaps stunned at being taken seriously at last. "Because he told me so with his dying breath."

2

Gareth

"My lord, before we say anything more, wouldn't you like to have one of your retainers here as witness?" Gareth said. "Perhaps Earl Robert's son William, if he is in residence?"

"He has taken himself off to Castle Cary, which he took from Henry de Tracy last summer." Henry was careful to keep his tone level, but his disapproval was impossible to mistake—though Gareth couldn't tell if it was William's absence that Henry disapproved of or the taking of Tracy's castle.

So he decided he had to ask the next obvious question. "Did he know we were coming?"

"He did."

"My lord, does he approve?"

"No, he does not, though after his first objection he has done me the courtesy of not saying so to my face."

Gareth glanced at Gwen to see how she was taking this. They'd known before setting out from Aberystwyth that many of the hours and days at Bristol were going to be uncomfortable. But now they were both thinking the same thing: bad enough to be investigating Earl Robert's death and doing it while Welsh. Far worse not to have the favor of the man in whose castle—and against whose father—the crime had been committed. They certainly didn't want to alienate the new Earl of Gloucester before they'd even met him.

"And your mother?"

This time Henry's pause was a bit longer. "I have not mentioned my suspicions to her." His eyes dropped to the table in front of him. "I will miss my uncle's wisdom."

"The Empress will as well," Gwen said. With the loss of Robert, Empress Maud had lost her general, and it had been Earl Robert's guiding hand that had kept the various barons who supported her together. "What is your mother going to do without him?"

Henry scoffed. "She never valued her brother as she should have, and I don't think she realizes what his absence means. I spoke to her last summer when I understood my uncle was seriously ailing, suggesting she begin to think about what she was going to do when he was gone. She dismissed my concerns." He waved a hand in direct imitation of his mother, which Gareth knew because he himself had met her.

"Perhaps she didn't want to think about his death," Gwen suggested gently. "It would not be an uncommon response to the loss of a beloved brother."

"Without his leadership in England, and without appointing a strong replacement, she has no hope of ever regaining the crown." Henry's response had no patience or understanding in it. In truth, it couldn't have been an easy assessment to arrive at and was a remarkable admission from Maud's son.

"If it is a lost cause, why stay in England? Why continue the war?" Until today, in fact, Gareth had thought Maud had returned to Normandy months ago, but an off-hand comment from a guardsman at the gate had informed him otherwise. Empress Maud remained thirty-some miles away at Devizes with her household guards and a small contingent of men. She had ridden to Bristol for her brother's funeral and then returned.

"Did I say the cause was lost?" Henry blinked as he refocused on Gareth. "It is not. *I* am the strong replacement. It is up to me to win the hearts and minds of the people. My mother failed in this regard, but I will not."

"You are also a man." Gwen wasn't just stating the obvious.

If Maud had been a man herself, she would have been crowned King of England without question after her father died, as the legitimate heir. The only reason Stephen had claimed the throne for himself was because enough barons in England were loath to bow to a woman and they disliked being coerced into doing so. Rumor had it Earl Robert too had considered putting forth his own name. Had he done so, many barons would have supported him, but in the end, he had rejected the idea because of his illegitimacy and had given way to his sister.

Henry dropped his head again, this time implying humility, though Gareth wouldn't have said the boy had a humble bone in his body. "I am learning every day how to be a king. In time, the barons will see it too."

But before the English barons would follow him, Henry had to convince them he was capable of leading—starting, without a doubt, with William. The last thing that Gareth and Gwen wanted to do was to come between Henry and his apparent destiny.

And yet, here they were.

"From what I understand, Earl Robert's death came as a surprise to no one," Gwen said.

"It is true that my uncle was dying, but who is to say when a man has truly breathed his last until he does? My uncle seemed better to me in the hours before he died."

Gareth didn't counter with what was obvious to him: what Henry had observed wasn't uncommon in a man at death's door. At the same time, Gareth wasn't inclined to be disbelieving—and certainly he didn't have enough incredulity to walk away and leave Henry to his own devices as William apparently had done. "What exactly did your uncle say?"

"He said he'd been betrayed."

Gareth raised his eyebrows. "That does sound definitive. But what did he mean by that?"

"I don't know." Henry's pain at his uncle's loss was clear in his voice. He had loved Robert like a father—perhaps more than he did his own father, who was known to be unbending and driven in much the same way as Henry's mother. On short acquaintance, the young prince appeared well on his way to embodying those self-same attributes, but that didn't mean he couldn't suffer from them at the same time.

"And he didn't identify the one he suspected?" Gareth said.

Henry shook his head. "He spoke no more words after that, and I was with him for every breath until the very end."

"Did anyone else hear these words?" Gwen asked.

"No."

"We are so sorry for your loss." Gwen's sincerity had Henry turning towards her again.

"Thank you." The prince stood abruptly and began to pace, unable to contain his emotions any other way. "I know what you're thinking. If I was with him when he died, how can I possibly accuse someone of murdering him?"

"That wasn't what I was thinking, actually," Gareth said. "Poison would be the obvious answer, and many of the symptoms of poisoning mimic illness like your uncle experienced this past year. And yet, I am uncertain as to what you want us to do. Your uncle is buried, and he was ill when he died. Whether or not he was poisoned cannot now be determined."

"He was only fifty years old and had never been sick a day in his life until this year. It's unconscionable that he's dead."

"That is grief speaking," Gwen said. "You know how certain sicknesses come upon a man and waste him away. Do you have any other reason to think he died of unnatural causes besides what he said to you?"

"In particular, do you have a suspect, someone to whom he could have been referring? *Betrayal* is a very specific accusation." Gareth was having trouble keeping the knowledge of how Henry's grandfather had died from the forefront of his mind—and the tip of his tongue. According to Abbot Rhys, the old King Henry had been poisoned by a dish of lampreys. To lay bare the truth to anyone, however, might not tear apart the kingdom more than it already was, but it would certainly cause dissension among Maud's supporters. And besides, Gareth had been sworn to secrecy. Normally, Gareth didn't have trouble keeping secrets. But all of a sudden, in the face of King Henry's grief-stricken grandson, the truth was eating away at him.

He had less trouble not telling Henry about the treasure belonging to Empress Maud that Gareth and other lords of the March and Wales had discovered last summer in the wake of the victory at Wiston Castle. The fact that Henry didn't know about it indicated that none of Gareth's co-conspirators had developed a guilty conscience either.

Henry returned to his chair and sighed heavily as he sat. "It would have to be a man he trusted."

"Or woman, surely," Gwen said.

Henry canted his head. "As you say." He paused. "I hate to put forth any name with no evidence."

Gareth was fed up with dancing around the issue. "Do you fear that the reason William has so adamantly denied your supposition of murder is because he was the one who hurried his father to his death?"

"Yes!" Henry burst to his feet, again unable to contain his energy. Gareth was becoming exhausted just watching him.

"That is the reason you didn't include any of your advisers in this conversation," Gwen said, not as a question. "You don't want them to know you suspect William or for rumor of your suspicions to get back to him."

"You haven't told us why you accuse him, however," Gareth said. "He is Earl Robert's heir, and I understand your mother has confirmed him in his holdings, even if King Stephen has not. Whether his father died last month or next year shouldn't have made a difference to his future."

"It would have made a difference if he was secretly treating with King Stephen and didn't want his father to overturn his plans. My uncle was too ill at the time to be the one who refused to pay the wages of my men. William forced me to grovel at Stephen's feet. If he'd secretly switched to Stephen's side, they could have planned that between them, to make me indebted to my enemy."

The accusation fell into stark silence, except for the crackling of the fire and a mew from Taran. Gareth sincerely hoped that nobody had his ear pressed to the other side of the door Llelo was guarding. Llelo still stood with his back to it, his hands clasped behind him and his legs spread. He was staring neutrally at a point on the far wall, not even startling at Henry's outburst. For a single heartbeat as Gareth glanced back at him, his eyes had flicked to his father's and then away.

"Do you have evidence of any such overtures?" Gwen asked gently.

"Not directly," Henry said.

"What does that mean?" Gwen said.

"We have intercepted two separate messages from Stephen's court, intended for traitors in Gloucester, though we are uncertain if they were meant for someone here at Bristol or another one of William's holdings." Those included Gloucester Castle as well as the aforementioned Castle Cary, or even Devizes, Empress Maud's seat in southwest England.

"And you think one of those traitors is William? Why?" Gareth found himself speaking to the prince as he would a nephew—or Llelo. In Wales, it would be his right, since he'd saved the boy's life.

"It is implied in the letters."

"May we see them?"

"Of course. The castle steward has them. He was one of my uncle's most trusted men, and it was his men who intercepted them all." Henry grimaced. "Whether or not William is a traitor to my mother, my uncle's death was the first of three suspicious deaths at Bristol Castle within a few days of each other, and William is best placed to have had a hand in them."

Gwen stirred in her seat. This was not the first time they'd heard these kind of rumors about William. "We will speak to the steward and to Earl William, my lord. With your permission, we will speak to everyone in Bristol if we have to. Please tell us more about these other deaths."

Henry seemed relieved at the change of subject and turned matter-of-fact, returning to his chair. "A maidservant collapsed while tidying the earl's room the day after he died, and then the next day, within hours of my uncle's funeral, his valet was drowned. It was after that, and after William refused to designate men to investigate or countenance my doing so, that I sent for you."

Now explained were the presence of the sprig of holly above the main door as they'd entered and the wreaths of blackberry bramble, ivy, and rowan on either side of the hearth in the great hall. Whether because holly was thorny or for another reason lost to time, it was thought that when an evil spirit passed under the sprig, the spirit would be caught and thus unable to enter. In turn, the ingredients of the wreaths were also thought to ward off evil. Whether or not something was amiss in Bristol Castle, there was no mistaking that its inhabitants were convinced of it and were afraid.

"And I suppose you only told William about it afterwards," Gareth said dryly. "Better to ask forgiveness than permission, eh?"

Henry had the grace to look a little sheepish, but then he lifted his chin, and the snap in his eyes was back. "I am the heir to the throne of England. I must follow my conscience. Besides, William took himself off, and I haven't seen him for more than a few moments in a fortnight."

"Is it your thought that this valet and maidservant were killed to silence them?" Gwen said.

"Why else?"

Gwen frowned. "Surely if they knew anything about Earl Robert's death—anything untoward, that is—they would have come forward."

Henry shrugged. "Maybe the murderer thought they knew more than they did or feared what they might remember."

"I'd be interested to know why you are the only one who is considering murder," Gareth said. "What explanation do others give?"

"They tell me it was the hand of God, every time, usually with a desultory wave and a look that dismisses me as a grieving youth. Is everyone blind or just in denial? I know people die every day. Of course they do. But Jenet was too young for a heart condition, not even thirty, and Bernard not much older."

Gareth was surprised Henry had learned the servants' names, seeing as how they were so far beneath him. But then, on consideration, Henry had made it his business to inquire into their lives. It was a little daunting, in fact, to have someone so young be so competent. "They are both buried by now as well, I assume, so we can't see the bodies?"

"She is buried. His body was never recovered."

Gwen perked up. "So how do you know he drowned?"

"His boots were found in the bottom of his boat, along with his fishing net. The boat was lolling in the shallows, and his hat was stuck in an eddy." Henry paused to consider. "He'd been made despondent by my uncle's death, followed immediately afterward by his wife's. It was only at William's intervention that the priest didn't declare him a suicide, arguing that it was as likely that he fell out of the boat as that he drowned intentionally. The body will eventually turn up downstream at the castle sluice gate, in a weir, or hooked on a log."

"Wait a moment—" Gareth put up a hand, having focused on the first part of Henry's explanation. "The maid who died was the valet's wife?"

Henry glanced from Gareth to Gwen, who was looking at him with her hand to her mouth. "Yes, of course. Didn't I say? They took care of my uncle together. Why does this change anything?"

"It changes everything." Gwen dropped her hand. "We are not overly fond of coincidences."

Henry's lip curled. "Obviously I supported William's defense of the valet, though not for the reasons anyone else thought. His death wasn't a suicide, and he certainly didn't drown on his own in the river. The man could swim. I asked around." He looked pleased with himself.

"You asked around," Gareth said, his tone very flat.

"You are not the only one who can investigate death."

Gareth glanced at Gwen, who was looking amused and alarmed at the same time. They'd often commented that investigating murder was like a disease—once you came down with the desire for knowledge, it was hard to throw it off.

No—" Henry was still speaking, "—I have no doubt. This was murder."

From behind them, Llelo cleared his throat. "If I may ask a question, my lord?"

Henry's head swung towards the door. He'd forgotten Llelo's existence. Gareth would make sure to compliment his son on his ability to blend into the background. It was a vital talent for men like them.

The prince waved a hand. "Of course."

"You have men for this, men who are better situated to ask questions and explore possibilities without standing out as we do. If you were going to go against Earl William's wishes anyway, why did you not ask any of them instead of sending for my parents?"

"My uncle spoke to me many times about what happened at Newcastle-under-Lyme. He was ever observant and watched you closely throughout your visit and subsequent investigation. He regretted that he had not taken the time to persuade you to stay in England and serve him."

Gareth blinked, not only at the fact that Earl Robert had spoken of the investigation many times, but at the unexpected accolade. Still, Gareth was glad Earl Robert hadn't asked him for his service. He would have had to turn him down and risk offending him in the process. It would be a cold day indeed before Gareth and Gwen lived in England willingly and served a Norman lord. Though, as the thought passed through Gareth's head, he immediately disciplined himself. To say *never* was to tempt fate, and they *had* come to Bristol when Henry had called—though their allegiance remained to Hywel.

Henry continued, "One of his comments about that investigation was how important it was that you had no stake in the outcome. You stood outside any lord's purview. I realized I needed that quality here as well."

In the silence that fell among them as they considered Henry's words, Gareth could hear shouts and running feet in the corridor outside. Hearing it too, Henry rose to his feet once more and flicked his fingers in Llelo's direction. Understanding the unspoken command, Llelo opened the door and poked his head into the corridor.

An aged retainer was just reaching the door, and as Llelo pulled it wide, he stumbled into the room. "My lord, I have grave news."

Henry came around the table in order to approach the old man and catch his upper arms in each of his hands to steady him. "What is it, John?"

"I can't imagine how it happened. The castle is in fine repair —" He broke off, gasping a bit for air.

Gareth was on his feet by now and came close as well. "What happened? Just say it."

"The steward, Sir Aubrey, was leaving the keep when one of the stones broke loose from the battlement and fell, striking him on the head. He lies dead on the ground in the inner ward."

3

Llelo

This was more like it. Llelo had listened to everything Prince Henry had said to his parents with something akin to disbelief. If Earl Robert had been murdered, then it was astounding to Llelo that Henry had allowed three weeks to pass with no more action than finding out if Bernard could swim and summoning Llelo's parents, regardless of William's objections.

In Llelo's—admittedly not vast—experience, very few Norman barons managed to die peacefully in their beds, and Earl Robert had undoubtedly accumulated a hundred enemies, King Stephen among them, any one of whom might have wanted to end his life quickly. Never mind that the man had been at death's door, if he thought someone had betrayed him, the traitor may have feared letting him live even a single hour longer.

But was that traitor William, Earl Robert's own son and heir? Llelo had never heard of William before a year ago, and he hadn't heard good things about him since. If William knew his father was about to disinherit him, or that his father had discovered William's plan to switch to King Stephen's party, Llelo could see William stepping in and hurrying nature along. On the other hand, Ranulf of Chester, Robert's son-in-law, was the devil incarnate. Why Earl Robert had given Ranulf his daughter was a question that would never be answered, but it implied to Llelo that Earl Robert put politics above all else. Perhaps he'd taught William to do the same.

Regardless, as investigators, they had a number of possibly insurmountable barriers to discovering the truth about Robert's death, chief among them the fact that they'd arrived late to the investigation. As a result, though they had three unexplained deaths, there were neither bodies nor crime scenes to examine and no witnesses, since the maid and the valet *were* the witnesses to Earl Robert's death, barring Prince Henry himself.

But now—now they had a new death, and they would be able to survey it within moments of it happening. They'd have a body, a scene, witnesses, and most importantly, a motive, since if Llelo had understood Prince Henry correctly, the two traitorous messages had been in Sir Aubrey's possession, and it had been his men who'd intercepted them. In other words, covering up wrongdoing was a genuine motive for murder, ripe for investigation, and was something his whole family knew how to handle.

Llelo knew his place—he was his father's advance man—so he strode purposefully after the aged messenger. Thus, he was the first to reach the inner ward where the steward had died, and he edged his way through the onlookers, telling people to keep back and clear the way for Gareth, Gwen, and Prince Henry. Initially, everyone was crowded very closely around the body, so it wasn't until the last two people gave way that Llelo could see where Sir Aubrey lay on the paving stones of the courtyard.

Instantly, Llelo's confidence evaporated as he gagged and put the back of his hand to his mouth, in very real danger of losing his breakfast on the ground. But he swallowed hard instead and turned all the way around, masking his discomfort by continuing to encourage the closest watchers to move farther from the scene of the crime.

Llelo's father wasn't fooled and put a hand on his shoulder. "If you must vomit, find a cleared space beyond the crowd. We don't want to mar the scene."

"I'm sorry." Llelo was embarrassed at his weakness and what undoubtedly was a greenish tinge to his face. "I'm managing." He'd seen dead bodies before, many times, but what had happened to Sir Aubrey's head had him swallowing down bile again, even though he was no longer looking at him. The man's skull had been caved in, the whole right side of his head sheared off by the weight of the stone that had fallen on him. Llelo had a genuine fear that he wouldn't be able to close his eyes tonight—or ever again—without seeing it.

"Truly you should feel no shame—and you're doing better than some." With a tip of his head, Gareth indicated Prince Henry, who'd come to a halt three feet from the body. He had his hand to his mouth too, and his face had gone past green to white.

Gwen had also taken one look at the body and turned away, as Llelo had done, to face the crowd. Henry was taller than she by several inches, but she effectively blocked his vision. She kept her hand on the back of Taran's head, to prevent him from seeing the body too, and was speaking quietly to the prince, words which Llelo wasn't close enough to hear.

Gareth's hand was still on Llelo's shoulder, and he shook him a little. "Clear out these spectators, will you?"

"Yes, Father." Llelo knew Gareth would never humiliate him, but he had an urgent need not to disappoint him either. It wasn't even that he knew for certain Gareth *would* be disappointed if he vomited. It would affect Llelo's image of himself. So, in as authoritative a voice as he could muster—and in his best French—Llelo said, "Move away! Move away! Go about your business!"

People actually obeyed, and then the closest people quickened their steps even more when Prince Henry bent over and vomited on the stones of the courtyard. Fortunately, Gwen managed to move discreetly away in time to avoid getting her boots splashed.

Then a man dressed in a deep red tunic and black cloak raced towards them, fighting the departing onlookers before bursting through a gap. Lunging forward, he caught the prince around the waist. "Henry!"

Henry threw out a hand, practically shoving the man away. "I'm fine, Roger! Leave me be."

Although there could be many Rogers in the castle, the man appeared a few years older than Llelo and was well dressed, indicating he might be a younger son of Earl Robert. From Gareth, who'd given everyone a lecture on the people they'd be meeting, Llelo knew that Roger FitzRobert was supposed to be a close companion of Henry. That also meant, since he was a younger son of a Norman magnate, he was destined for the Church.

Now Roger straightened and glared at Llelo and Gwen. "And who might you be?"

"Leave off, Roger," Prince Henry said in an irritated voice. Llelo knew enough of pride, however, to recognize that he was angry at himself rather than at Roger. "You know I sent for them, your spies at the gate would have told you they'd arrived, and they are here at this moment at my request."

Entirely calm, Gareth stepped to Llelo's side and spoke in an undertone in Welsh. "See what you can find up on that battlement, will you, son? We'll be following the prince's example in that it's better to ask forgiveness than permission."

"Yes, sir." Llelo suppressed a grin and headed at a fast but controlled walk towards the only entrance to the keep. Three feet wide, remarkably small given the size of the building, and able to admit only one man at a time, the keep's entrance had been designed as the last defense of the castle. If enemies breached both curtain walls, the defenders inside the keep could hold off any attack through this door indefinitely.

Llelo could appreciate Bristol's utter focus on security and attention to every detail, even if it meant many extra steps for everyone, depending on where in the castle a person intended to go. Llelo's countrymen had built very few stone castles, and those King Owain owned were small. Generally, he governed from his *llys*, or palaces, of which he had twenty from Aberffraw to Denbigh. These were far more comfortable places to live, many built over older Roman sites. While the outer walls were often stone, they were filled with comfortable wooden buildings. Most were large enough to be small villages in and of themselves.

Now that Llelo thought about it, in fact, though very different in practice, they were not dissimilar in concept from Bristol Castle. The castle and town occupied a narrow strip of higher ground between the rivers Avon and Frome. The latter had been partially diverted to form the moat, which protected the east side of the castle. The rest of the Frome flowed around the outside of the town walls, eventually meeting the River Avon to the west. Thus, castle and town were completely surrounded by water.

The castle as a whole ran from northwest to southeast and consisted of three wards: a far outer ward to the southeast, containing a church, domestic quarters, and a great gate, which was the primary entrance; a second outer ward behind the first, with a second large gate facing slightly northwest that allowed access to the town of Bristol; and an inner ward inside that second ward, which was protected by an inner wall with its own towers, battlements, and gate house. The square keep was inside this inner ward, and it was here, between the keep and the inner curtain wall, where the body of Sir Aubrey lay.

The space between the wall of the keep and the curtain wall was relatively narrow, perhaps only thirty yards wide, and contained no buildings. Important rooms like the treasury and chapel were in the keep, while the craft halls, laundry, stables, and blacksmith works were in one of the outer wards. As at Newcastle-under-Lyme, Llelo also understood that somewhere in the inner ward began a postern tunnel—one that he and Dai, if they had a moment, would very much like to explore.

Behind him, he heard his father say, "My lord, I am Gareth ap Rhys, and this is my wife, Gwen."

Llelo's smile grew broader as his father declined to embellish on his identity in any way. He didn't mention the number of deaths he'd investigated, that he was the captain of Prince Hywel's teulu, or that he had once saved Prince Henry's life. He said his name, as if that was enough. Unfortunately, Llelo was too far away by now to hear Roger's reply.

As Llelo approached the stairs, he couldn't help but glance up, fearing another stone might fall before he reached the safety of the porch. But he made it unharmed to the door at the top of the stairway. Once inside the building, he found himself in an anteroom to the great hall. They'd come through here when they'd first approached the prince an hour ago and had departed by this door when they'd learned of Sir Aubrey's death. This time, however, instead of walking straight ahead through the much larger double doors in front of him that would take him into the great hall, he took a right and headed towards the stairwell in the corner tower.

Llelo was determined to make up for his earlier misplaced confidence. Even if nobody else was aware of the way he'd scoffed at Henry's suspicions, longing for a real murder he could sink his teeth into, Llelo himself knew. He counted himself fortunate that he hadn't spoken any of his thoughts out loud to his parents. Arrogance was unbecoming in anyone, but much worse in a man who quested for the truth.

As he went up the tower steps two at a time, he told himself he wouldn't make that mistake again. His father trusted him—nothing could be clearer, given the tasks he'd set him just in the last few moments—and Llelo would do his level best to live up to Gareth's expectations.

The top of the tower was many stories higher than the wall-walk, so Llelo arrested his journey at a doorway halfway up, coming out of the stairwell into a room set up as a comfortable place for men on watch to rest when they weren't pacing along the wall-walk. A fireplace—not lit this morning—was set into one wall, and benches and tables took up the center of the room. Hooks, from which hung extra blankets and cloaks, had been hammered into the walls. Oddly, a dish containing what looked to be herbs sat in the middle of the table, smoking gently. Llelo leaned in to sniff at it and came away with the impression it was rosemary.

He would have asked why a dish of herbs was burning in the center of the table, but the guardroom was empty, so he had no one to question.

Before he could move to the doorway that would take him to the wall-walk from which the stone had fallen, footsteps pounded on the stairs and someone shouted from below, "Wait! Welshman, wait!"

The cry could be meant only for him, so he swung around. A man a few years older than he popped out of the same stairwell Llelo had just come up.

"The battlement is this way." The man strode past Llelo without introducing himself. His accent indicated he was Norman, though he looked Irish, with red hair, brighter than Henry's, and a face awash in freckles. In fact, he appeared to be a much younger version of Gareth's friend Conall, who served the King of Leinster, to the point that he could have been Conall's son.

Llelo had no reason not to follow this newcomer, who led him out onto what was effectively the roof of the keep. The man picked up the pace until they both were running along the wall-walk, which had been built around the inside of the keep's battlement. Even more than when he'd been down in the hall, the castle reminded Llelo of Newcastle-under-Lyme, which made sense as Earl Robert had built both.

They came to a halt, neither of them breathing hard, halfway along the walkway. While the messenger had called the fallen item a *stone*, it was more accurately the top half of a merlon, which was the characteristic tooth in the gap-toothed appearance of a castle battle-ment.

Llelo grasped a nearby merlon, which appeared to be solid, and peered gingerly through the adjacent crenel. It was only the top of the adjacent merlon that had fallen—one stone really, though a large one, perhaps two feet by a foot and half. But since one piece had come down, there was good reason to be concerned that the rest of the wall might come down too. Below him, a group of people, his father among them, stood around the body.

Llelo waved, catching the attention of Gwen, who stood a few feet away from the huddled men. Taran's little head was bobbing around. Some babies' heads still flopped to the side at this age, but Taran had been able to hold his head up almost from birth.

Llelo made a second shooing motion with his hand to indicate that his mother should take a few steps back, and called down to her in Welsh, "Can you move the body? It's still directly under the wall and more stones could come down at any moment!"

He feared that he was too high up—sixty feet or more—for his words to be heard clearly, but she nodded and spoke to the others. They each glanced up in turn to the battlement before nodding too and following Llelo's suggestion.

Gareth personally urged away a group of five well-dressed men, including Prince Henry and Roger, even going so far as to take the prince's elbow in order to move him out of danger. Then four guards arrived, carrying a stretcher between them. As Llelo watched, each man took a limb, hefted Aubrey's body onto the conveyance, and carried him into the middle of the courtyard, another twenty feet from the keep. That they didn't remove him from the area entirely told Llelo that his father felt he had more to see first. Several other men had acquired sawhorses from the craftworks and set up a barrier so nobody would walk where Aubrey had died.

Llelo's companion, who hadn't said anything beyond those first few words, was studying the damaged merlon. The stone had come off cleanly, with no jagged edges, and the man traced a finger along the break. "What say you ... accident or murder?"

Llelo blinked, surprised the man was speaking so forthrightly, but he answered in the same tone. "So you know of the prince's suspicions?"

The man barked a laugh. "Everyone knows of Prince Henry's suspicions. He will think it murder, and it's easy to see why, given all that has happened this past month. Sir Aubrey is dead! This is now the fourth death at Bristol Castle in as many weeks, the third since Earl Robert died."

Llelo bent to pick up a few chips and fragments of stone that had fallen to the walkway. The large stone had separated from the main wall at a seam, where mortar had been used to attach one stone to another. As he looked closer, he thought he could see chisel marks along the edge, but even if he was right, they signified nothing. The stone *had* been chiseled before it was put into place, in order to fashion it to the appropriate shape. He was not a mason, and thus was not trained to determine if the marks should be there or not. But he would show them to his father, and his father would find someone who could answer better.

He took a step back to examine the whole of the area. "The mortar is the same color here as between the rest of the stones, implying that the wall hasn't been repaired since it was built. Am I wrong about that? Has Bristol Castle ever been attacked?"

"No," the young man answered. "If the wall was mended, it wouldn't have been because it was breached. Not here inside the castle, anyway. Even King Stephen, when he brought an army to Bristol's doorstep nearly ten years ago now, took one look—and maybe a second—and went away unsatisfied, having determined that taking it would cost him too many resources and men. And even if he'd thought the cost worth the attempt, it still might have withstood him. We are impregnable." His tone was satisfied, but not overly so, more a confident assessment from a man who knew truth when he saw it.

Llelo was hardly one to argue, newcomer that he was and a Welshman to boot.

"What name do you go by?"

Llelo started, having lost the train of the man's French for a moment. He bowed, embarrassed that he hadn't pressed to exchange names sooner. In his country, such a lapse would have been a shocking offense. "I am Llelo ap Gareth. My father is the man Prince Henry sent for from Wales."

"You must be a bastard like me, for your mother is not old enough to have birthed you."

"I'm adopted."

The man grunted his acknowledgement of the difference. "My name is Hamelin, half-brother to Henry by his father, the Count of Anjou. I have never met a Welshman before."

Llelo tipped his head politely. "In Wales, it wouldn't matter if you were illegitimate. You would inherit from your father before Henry, since you are older than he is, or in some cases, your father's wealth and lands would be distributed equally among all his sons."

Hamelin stared at Llelo. "You tell me truly?"

Llelo grinned. "Prince Hywel, my liege lord, is a bastard but still heir to the throne of Gwynedd. In Wales, parentage is of no matter as long as the father acknowledges the son."

Hamelin made a *huh* sound under his breath. "If that were the case, I'm not sure my father would have acknowledged me. Besides, England would not be mine, since it comes to Henry through his mother." He paused and then said musingly, "I would inherit Anjou, however."

Llelo felt himself warming to the Frenchman. His calm assessment of his relationship with his father was without drama. Llelo's own birth father had been a hard man, and he could relate to a disapproving father. He was more glad than he could say that Gareth's way was different.

"Where were you when the stone fell on Sir Aubrey?"

"In the stables. I heard the screaming of the woman who found him. By the time I arrived in the bailey, a crowd had already gathered."

"Did you see anyone up here?"

"No." Hamelin shook his head regretfully.

Llelo looked around. "There were guards, surely. Someone has to have noticed something. I don't understand why nobody else is here now except for us."

"Well—" Hamelin's expression remained rueful, "Sir Aubrey is dead. He is the one who would have organized everyone."

"What about the captain of the guard?"

Hamelin frowned. "That I don't know. The castle's curtain wall is always manned, of course, and at least one of the towers above, keeping watch for an approaching army, but now that I think about it, these wall-walks are often empty."

Llelo allowed his surprise to show on his face. "I would have thought every battlement would be manned."

"This is a huge castle, with few threats against it, even with the war against King Stephen." Hamelin was matter-of-fact in his justification of what Llelo thought was genuine neglect—and the very opposite of what he'd been thinking earlier about Earl Robert's obsession with security. He didn't express the criticism, however, since Hamelin wasn't in charge, and it might only raise his hackles. Instead, Llelo craned his neck to look towards the top of the tower, raised some forty feet above where he stood. He couldn't make out a guard there, but the angle was bad, so he couldn't say there wasn't one. "We'll have to question everyone."

Hamelin pushed out his lips, in a move Llelo thought very French. "Sir Aubrey's death could have been an accident. It seems incredible that anyone would want to kill him."

"It's best not to make judgements with so little information." Llelo gestured to the gap in the wall. He'd almost grown used to it while he'd been talking to Hamelin, but it was as if the battlement was a grinning monster that had lost half a tooth, and it was impossible not to feel a sharp twist in his gut when he looked at it. "Accidental death or murder, you can trust my father to get to the bottom of it."

4

Llelo

amelin folded his arms across his chest, not in defiance but contemplatively, as he studied the oddly truncated merlon. "I have rarely heard anyone speak of his father the way you do of yours, with the exception of Earl William, who seemed to have a similar fondness for Earl Robert. You are truly a fortunate man. I can't wait to meet him."

"Llelo!"

As if on command, his father called his name. Llelo looked down through a nearby crenel, not one adjacent to the damaged merlon, to where his father stood on the ground. "Stay where you are. Your mother is coming—along with a mason who can tell us better what we're looking at."

Llelo nodded with satisfaction, pleased that things were moving along. If there was evidence to be found, this was the way to find it. While they waited for Gwen, Llelo directed Hamelin to pace along the wall opposite him, with the intent of searching for anything someone in a hurry might have dropped.

But when they reached the next tower and turned back, having found nothing, Hamelin sighed. "That was pointless."

"It wasn't, my lord," Llelo said. "We had to look, and now that we have, we can turn our attention elsewhere."

Hamelin eyed him. "You are a very strange man."

Llelo was inclined to take his words as a compliment. "How so?"

"How can you calmly direct me to look for a torn piece of a cloak or some other talisman that a culprit may have dropped, when a man lies dead practically beneath our feet?"

Llelo decided to take the question at face value, rather than balk at what was implied but unsaid: that he was uncaring. "Would lamenting help Sir Aubrey? Or explain why he is dead?"

"No, but—"

Llelo decided he'd been a little harsh and spoke more gently. "Truly, my parents believe, and I believe, that the best way to mourn a man is to discover the truth of how he died. I apologize if it seems insensitive, but you must remember that the first time I laid eyes on Sir Aubrey was just now. I didn't know him even to look at, and given how he died, I still don't."

Hamelin wrinkled his chin. "I suppose I didn't know him more than in passing either. It's just—" He peered over the battlement. The men below were finally preparing to move the body indoors.

Llelo didn't get a chance to respond or inquire further because Gwen appeared in the doorway of the far tower, the same one Llelo and Hamelin themselves had come up earlier. She was still holding Taran, who was awake but not yet restless in his sling, and once they were close, Llelo offered his finger for the baby to clutch in his little fist.

Then he introduced his mother to Hamelin, who swept out an arm and bowed gallantly. "My lady, it is my pleasure to meet you, though I regret that it is under such unfortunate circumstances." He gestured to the battlement. "Your son and I have examined the gap and pieces of mortar. We have found nothing else of interest. The killer didn't drop anything or leave a sign of his passage that we could find."

"Other than the fallen wall," Llelo pointed out, trying not to feel disgruntled that his report had been usurped by Hamelin.

Gwen canted her head. "If a person, rather than God, is responsible for these deaths, he has been invisible up until now. We can't expect him suddenly to become sloppy, though—" she paused as she thought, "—killing Sir Aubrey in broad daylight within an hour of our arrival serves only to focus our attention more acutely and confirm Prince Henry in his suspicions."

Hamelin took a step closer. "I know little of murder—well, nothing until today—but a man could have been so desperate to silence Sir Aubrey that he didn't care if it exposed him more than he has been up until now."

"You would have thought there would have been a more efficient—and surely a more certain—way to kill a man." Gwen pursed her lips, and then glanced at Llelo. "The last time someone dropped a body at our feet, it was to gain our attention."

"This certainly has done that," Llelo said, "but like Hamelin, I find it hard to believe that getting our attention was the goal."

"I know a little of what you speak, thanks to Prince Henry." Hamelin put his heels together. "I would like to offer you my services in whatever aspect of this investigation you think your husband can use me."

Gwen's eyes skated to Llelo for a single heartbeat and then back to Hamelin. "May I ask what you have in mind?"

"If I might be so bold as to assert the obvious, you are Welsh, and many of my brother's men and the men of Bristol might resent being questioned by you."

Llelo attempted to swallow down a snort and failed.

Hamelin nodded. "You acknowledge I speak the truth."

Before Llelo could muster an appropriate reply—something mature and adult regarding Prince Hywel's instruction not to assume anything—a burly man in gray-tinged clothing with hair to match trotted through the tower doorway. As the man drew closer, Llelo realized his hair was not so much prematurely gray as embedded with stone dust that might never come out, so he was nearer in age to forty than fifty.

"My lord," the man bowed before Hamelin and added in heavily-accented French, indicating he was Saxon and it wasn't his primary language, "the prince asked me to find you. I am Daniel Mason."

Hamelin gave him a sharp nod and gestured towards the damaged merlon. "As you can see, we need your assessment of this portion of the battlement."

The mason took a cloth and wiped at sweat on his brow. The cloth came away with gray dust. Gwen noticed too and said, "I apologize if we have called you away from your current project, but we really do need your expertise."

"I'm always building something, my lady. Today I was overseeing some repairs to St. Philips, the Benedictine monastery near the castle." Daniel made a deprecatory gesture. "I'm on loan to them from the Augustinians. We are nearing the end of our latest building phase there, and I had a moment to spare."

"Were you involved in building this castle too?" Gwen said.

"Yes, but only at the very end. I was an apprentice when it went up." He eyed the missing merlon. "I don't like the look of this." He put a hand to the mortar that remained. Then, as both Llelo and Hamelin had done, he crouched and ran some of the fallen mortar dust and stones through his fingers. Still crouched, he turned on the ball of his foot so he could look up at Hamelin. "What exactly are you asking?"

"Was this a deliberate breach or did the stone fall naturally?" Hamelin said.

"Is that all?" Daniel straightened and took a step back. "The stone didn't fall on its own." He pulled a hammer and chisel from the tool belt at his waist and put the chisel to the top of the wall that remained. Even Llelo, who knew nothing about stonework, could see that the mark was a perfect match to Daniel's chisel. "The one who did this was an amateur, borrowing tools." He gestured to the chopped-up mortar on top of the stone. "He made a mess of it."

Llelo couldn't on his own discern what the mason was talking about, and Hamelin, who'd been standing with an arm folded across his chest and a hand to his chin, laughed. "We'll take your word for it."

"So ... you're saying that the mortar was chiseled out, and then the stone was pushed onto Sir Aubrey as he walked across the ward?" Clutching Taran more tightly to her chest, Gwen peered through the adjacent crenel to the ground. "If that is the case, whoever did this had to have been lying in wait and known Sir Aubrey would be crossing the bailey at that moment. It would have worked only with absolutely perfect timing."

Llelo couldn't cope with how close to the edge Gwen was, even with the wall still waist-high, and caught her elbow. "Careful, Mother."

Gwen patted his hand. "We're fine, but I'll step back now." She looked at the mason. "How long would it have taken you to loosen the stone?"

"If I didn't care about the noise, no time at all, a matter of a quarter hour or less." He tipped his head. "If I wanted to be quiet about it, as someone would have had to be if he was breaking down the castle, it could have been a labor of several hours of repeated effort, perhaps not all at the same time either."

"Are you willing to say this to Prince Henry and Earl William?" Gwen said.

Daniel bent his head. "Yes, my lady."

Gwen thanked the man, who bowed and headed back down the stairs. Then she turned to Hamelin. "Please don't take offense, but I'd like to speak to my son for a moment in private." At Hamelin's nod of consent, she took Llelo's arm and drew him twenty feet down the wall-walk from the broken merlon. "What do you think? You met him first."

"Our Welshness is one of the reasons Henry summoned us, but I have no doubt that Hamelin is right. Until the residents of Bristol get used to us, if they ever do, we are going to have trouble interviewing them."

Gwen made a rueful face. "They are never going to get used to us, but—" she looked at him hard, "you must not respond to any insults or sign of contempt. No matter what anyone might do to provoke us, we must remain gracious. We rise above. Do you understand?"

Llelo wet his lips. "Yes."

Truthfully, Llelo was well used to English animosity towards his people. He'd experienced it daily after his father died, and he and Dai lived for a time in the monastery at Newcastle-under-Lyme where Gareth had found them. The English mocked the Welsh language, their customs, and even the food they ate.

Llelo had hated that disrespect as a boy, but as a man he could admit that he felt the same way about the English. They were farmers, whereas most Welsh made their living from herding sheep and cattle. Llelo had grown up with sheep, since his father had been a wool merchant, and he liked the way his family was constantly on the move. The English were set in their ways, it seemed, and few knew anything beyond a mile or two from the spot they'd been born. His new parents rarely stayed more than a month in any one place, traveling as they did with Prince Hywel. Llelo liked waking up every morning not knowing what that day would bring and felt sorry for anyone for whom every meal consisted of wheat and barley, and who never saw farther than the field of grain they cultivated.

"In the meantime, Hamelin could be useful," Gwen said. "He is Henry's half-brother."

"Does that mean we are more or less likely to trust him? He looks so much like Conall, I almost forget where he comes from."

Gwen laughed. "He does at that. You have to wonder if his mother was Irish." She gave her son a severe look. "Still, you need to remain vigilant."

"Of course. Never trust a Norman."

She shook her head. "I didn't mean that, and it would be wrong to treat them as they do us. I meant, rather, that we can't trust anyone but those in our immediate party. That's why Prince Henry asked us here in the first place—because we are outsiders and could have had nothing to do with any of these deaths. That said, I think we can give your new friend the benefit of the doubt in this. If he is a traitor to his brother, then better to keep him close."

"All right." Llelo took in a breath. "Four people are dead, and the killer could be anyone, even Hamelin, though what his motive might be I couldn't begin to guess."

"Fortunately, we are not in the business of guessing," Gwen said. "Would you be willing to question the soldiers on the wall-walks with Hamelin?"

"Yes." And then Llelo added a bit more vigorously, "The mason responded to him, not to us."

"If nothing else, Hamelin appears to have the ability to think on his feet. Out of everyone in the castle, he was the only one who came up here. You'll note that nobody else has, not even to gawk." Gwen met Llelo's eyes. "Why?"

Llelo looked disconcerted. "Because we're here? Because Hamelin is?"

"Where's the officious older man who is offended by our presence? Or the arrogant soldier who thinks he knows better than we do? We've met all kinds in our years of service to Prince Hywel, and I never would have expected to have been left to our own devices at the scene of any crime."

"What are you saying?"

She lifted her chin to point to a symbol scratched onto the stone to the right of the nearby tower doorway. "Do you know what that is?"

"I haven't seen it before, but I can guess that it has something to do with evil spirits. Like the wreaths in the hall, and the holly, and the rosemary burning in the tower room."

Gwen made a clicking sound with her tongue. "You noticed. Good. Before you came to us, Aber Castle was beset by a series of deaths, and the people responded similarly. We may find interviewing the residents of Bristol Castle is even more difficult than I already fear it will be."

"To speak of evil is to call it down upon us." Llelo's eyes went to Hamelin, who was leaning out a nearby crenel. Then he returned his gaze to his mother. "You can trust me to follow where this leads, no matter the end."

"I know we can." His mother put a hand on his arm. "You grow more assured by the day, and I am confident in your maturity and discretion, if either had ever been in doubt. Come see us afterwards, and we'll go over everything you learned. You never know what could later prove important, and we don't want to wait too long because it's easy to forget the little things."

Gwen departed with a nod at Hamelin, who pulled out of the crenel and looked at Llelo. "Is it agreed?"

Llelo nodded. "We would be grateful for your assistance."

"I've had my first thought, if I may be so bold as to say."

Llelo made a gesture. "Please."

Hamelin put up one finger. "Listen."

Llelo's eyes narrowed, but he stood silent as Hamelin had asked, looking east across the battlement. He could hear the flag flapping on the top of the tower, a few late-season crows were cawing, and he could just make out the sound of people talking below him. Somewhere a bell tolled, and over it all came the near constant *chink, chink, chink* of the castle blacksmith at work.

Hamelin was looking pleased with himself. "If the man timed it right, perhaps nobody would have thought anything of the sound of hammer and chisel."

"Well done," Llelo said, though he didn't know that it was his place to praise Hamelin, as if he were in charge.

But Hamelin grinned and asked, "Where do we start?"

Llelo tipped his head back to look up at the crenels of the nearest tower. "At the top, wouldn't you say?"

5

Gwen

By the time Gwen reached ground level again, everyone else had left the inner ward for the far outer ward, having moved the body to the laying-out room adjacent to the laundry. Not every castle was large enough to have a room dedicated to washing and preparing bodies for burial, but Gwen was always glad when one did, for it made the process of inspection and discovery easier.

But today, as she and Taran darkened the doorway, Gareth threw a sheet over the dead man.

"I saw him earlier," she said. "You don't have to hide him."

"No need for you or Taran to see him again," Gareth said. "For once, I can't say there is much to learn here. We know how this one died!"

"When I came down from the keep, the stone that killed him was still lying on the ground, so I had one of the guards put it in a box and bring it." She gestured to the guard to indicate he should enter the room. He, at least, appeared relieved that Sir Aubrey's body wasn't visible, and he set the wooden box inside the door, after which he departed with a nod.

"I'm being treated quite civilly," Gareth said, watching the guard go. "It seems you are too."

"I may have to reexamine my animosity to Saxons," Gwen said.

Gareth laughed. "Never that!" He paused. "Is the area still fenced off?"

"People are giving it a wide berth, as they should." And she told him what the mason had concluded and that she'd sent Llelo off with Prince Henry's brother to question the castle's guards.

"Llelo will be a difficult act to follow." Gareth rubbed Taran's cheek.

"Don't say that, Gareth. Each child is different, and none have to be like any other."

"Llelo feels it," Gareth said flatly. "He fears being usurped."

"He is our son," Gwen said in an equally flat tone.

"Hopefully someday he will truly believe it." Gareth's eyes turned to the door, tracking the progress of someone Gwen couldn't see from where she stood. He gestured with his chin towards the doorway. "Let's talk outside."

"Every time we give him a task you would have given to Evan, it helps," she said, following him through the doorway.

"I hope he discovers something from the guards." Gareth scowled. "The more I think about Sir Aubrey's death, the more it occurs to me that the man responsible had incredible aim. You could push that stone a hundred times at the same moment someone was walking underneath it and not hit the man even once."

"The priest would say it was Sir Aubrey's time, that God was calling him home."

"It could be he was unlucky." Gareth was still frowning. "What if … the intent wasn't to kill him?"

Gwen narrowed her eyes at her husband. "Then why?"

"To distract him or us? A stone falls off a battlement, and people are bound to come running. We did."

"We came because Sir Aubrey died."

"Then the question becomes, who would have come if it was only a stone? Sir Aubrey for certain—"

"If he hadn't already been walking underneath it."

Gareth bent his head in acknowledgement. "Many would have come running. Watchers who should be on the walls would be looking at the stone instead of attending to their assigned duties."

"I can testify to that," Gwen said. "We were alone on the wall-walk above the body."

Gareth's eyes widened in surprise. "Nobody came to observe or to question your presence?" He laughed under his breath. "The residents of Bristol are remarkably obedient."

"Or they don't want to know or think about these deaths," Gwen said. "I assume you noticed the signs against evil spirits? Llelo did."

"They're hard to miss, especially now that we know what to look for."

"You can't blame people for being fearful," Gwen said, "especially now with Sir Aubrey's death."

"Clearly the wards are not working." Gareth had always despised superstition.

By now, the two men Gareth had spied from inside the laying-out room were close enough to overhear, and Gareth and Gwen turned to them. The first man was tall, somewhat burly and middle-aged, with a neatly trimmed beard and piercing blue eyes. His garments were very fine—fit for a king, even—blue and brown with what could have been real gold trim at the edge of his tunic. He was accompanied by a smaller, sparer man, somewhat owl-eyed and round-shouldered, whom Gwen recognized as the understeward who'd written down their names.

Gareth made a welcoming gesture with one hand. "Gwen, this is Robert Fitzharding, a most trusted companion of both Earl Robert and William; and Charles de Cheyne, who was Sir Aubrey's second. He will be acting as the new steward of Bristol. He tells me his ancestors came with the Conqueror."

Charles bowed slightly at the waist. "It is my pleasure to serve you, Madam."

Gwen blinked. She really was starting to get annoyed by how nicely these English folk were treating her, with a respect she had not expected at all. As she'd said earlier, if this continued, she'd have to put aside long-standing grievances.

"I'd like to thank you for your quick action earlier," Fitzharding said to Gareth, continuing to be polite. "The wall has been weakened and could release more stones at any time. It was good that you called for the mason."

"I appreciate your acceptance of our presence," Gareth replied, being polite in return. "We have some experience with this sort of thing."

"Which is why Prince Henry sent for you." Fitzharding nodded. "Again, you have my thanks. It is my intention to maintain a well-ordered castle."

Gwen frowned. Gareth had just told her that Charles was the acting steward, but Fitzharding's words implied that he, not Charles, was going to be the new castellan. And yet, Charles just stood silently by without protesting. The charge of Bristol Castle was a huge responsibility and honor, and not one that Gwen would have thought any man would assume to have, even after a sudden death.

"How long had Sir Aubrey been the steward?" Gareth said.

"Many years," Fitzharding said.

Gwen hesitated, feeling the pause in the conversation. The conclusion to Fitzharding's sentence should have been along the lines of *I hope to do as good a job as he did.* But Fitzharding didn't say it.

She took in a breath, bracing herself for the first of many uncomfortable questions she would be asking over the next few days. She wasn't going to let Fitzharding off from their inquiries just because he was pompous and sure of himself. "You didn't approve of the job Sir Aubrey was doing?"

Fitzharding glanced at her. "Sir Aubrey was a good man and a fine manager for what he did and the time in which he lived, but there are new methods, new ways of doing things, that he was slow to accept." He gestured to the structure behind them. "Building a laying-out room was my idea, along with the laundry, which used to be in the basement of the keep!"

He made it sound as if the idea was horrifying, which, as someone who was intimately acquainted with her family's laundry, Gwen understood it could be. Basements had no air flow, so the clothes had to be lugged down the steps to be cleaned and then up again to be dried on the line outside. Because Bristol Castle was located next to a river, likely the laundry had been put in the basement because they'd dug a well underneath the keep, to allow its defenders to hold out virtually indefinitely. Because of it, nobody had to carry water for washing—but the location wasn't exactly convenient.

This new washroom, by contrast, was positioned against the curtain wall in a corner of the outer ward. The River Frome flowed past the castle, coming from the northeast. As the river had been diverted to form the moat, it had also been channelized to come into the castle here through a large clay pipe like the Romans used in their baths. Thus, the servants doing the washing never had to haul water, and there was always a fresh supply in the trough that ran right through the center of the room. The laundry drying lines were located just outside, and when the weather was unfavorable, as it often was, the laundry could be hung in the enormous thatched-roof shed, which was open to the air on all four sides and had been built for that purpose.

In turn, the waste water from the washhouse was diverted underneath the adjacent latrine block and then sent straight back into the moat, ultimately ending up in the River Avon. The arrangement was not unlike the bath at Aber, which diverted water from an adjacent river too, though this system was far more extensive because of the size of Bristol Castle. She would be sure to speak of it to Hywel, because the drainage systems at Gwynedd's palaces could always be improved.

"How old was Sir Aubrey?" Gareth said.

"Past sixty." Fitzharding was ten years younger. Gwen perceived him to have been chafing at the bit, seeing this role as the next step forward for him, and of the opinion that Sir Aubrey had been hanging on far too long.

"Did you have something specific you wanted from us?" Gareth said.

"I merely came to see that you had everything you needed." Fitzharding eyed the sheet-covered body through the open door behind them.

"So far, we do." Gareth gestured to Gwen. "My wife has just come from the keep where the mason examined the breach in the battlement."

Charles spoke for the first time since his introduction. "I conferred with him too. He claims that the stone was deliberately separated from the wall with hammer and chisel."

"I'm sorry if that's not what you wanted to hear," Gwen said.

Charles shook his head. "You misunderstand. What I want is of no importance. I'd much rather know the truth."

"So would I," Fitzharding said. "Since we are certain Sir Aubrey's death was no accident, we can pursue his killer with single-minded determination."

"Unlike the deaths of these others, perhaps?" Gwen asked, as innocently as she could.

Fitzharding looked at her—just a glance, but his gaze was piercing—and then away again. "It is not my place to accept or deny any assessment of how they died. I admit, however, with the sudden death of Sir Aubrey, their deaths look far more suspicious than they did an hour ago. It seems Prince Henry was right to send for you." He spoke the last words somewhat musingly. Then he lifted his chin to point to Dai, who was heading purposefully towards them, having entered the castle through the main gate closest to the priory. "It seems you are wanted." He bowed briefly. "We will take our leave. We have a castle full of people who must be seen to."

Charles set off immediately, but before Fitzharding could take more than two steps away from them, Gwen put out a hand to him. It was an opening she hadn't known she needed but wasn't going to pass up. "The wreaths and the holly—"

Fitzharding turned back, a grim set to his jaw. "I do not approve of people's superstitions, but even the priest felt it wrong to deny them the comfort these tokens could bring them." He snorted. "Small comfort now, with this other death." He set off after Charles, nodding at Dai as they passed each other.

"It seems you and Fitzharding are of the same mind," she said to her husband.

"Father! I was merely coming to see how things were going, and the gatekeeper told me what happened!" Dai came to a breathless halt in front of them, having slowed in his crossing of the outer ward only to be polite to Fitzharding. "I can't believe I missed everything again!"

"The man's death was gruesome," Gwen said. "Believe me, you haven't missed a thing."

Dai looked past them into the darkness of the room. "Is that he?"

Gareth tipped his head. "I will show you if you want to see."

To Gwen's surprise, Dai shook his head. "No. Not unless there's something to learn." At one time, Dai might have been ghoulishly curious, but he'd seen enough death by now—and almost died himself last summer—that it held less interest for him than it once did—and far less than the idea of adventure. Instead, he said, "Where's Llelo?"

"He's starting on the interviews." Gareth pulled at the door to the laying-out room to close it. All together, they set off across the outer ward. The sun had come out and was shining weakly down. "Your mother sent him to question the soldiers on the battlement."

"By himself?" That his brother was already involved in the investigation excited Dai's blood more than the possibility of seeing the body.

"He is with Hamelin, Prince Henry's half-brother." Gareth put a hand on Dai's shoulder, directing him towards the gatehouse between the two outer wards.

"Really?" Dai faltered, his expression disconcerted. "It's just as well, then, that I wasn't there, since my French isn't good enough for me to be of similar use."

"It will come," Gwen said bracingly.

Dai was incredibly bright, and he had made great strides in his education since Gareth and Gwen had adopted him. Unlike Llelo, however, who'd taken to his lessons with a will, Dai found it harder to focus on anything that didn't involve being outside, moving his whole body, or interacting with people. Studying French and Latin with a tutor was far too quiet.

"How's Tangwen?" Gwen said.

"Settling in. She was being fed when I left."

"And the Dragons?" Gareth asked.

"They're still here. Somewhere. Evan stayed behind to keep an eye on things at the priory." Dai smirked. "And Angharad." Dai had a thirteen-year-old's distaste for romance.

As if on command, as Dai finished speaking, the five Dragons each appeared separately from different directions. They'd been doing their job: keeping watch or inspecting the perimeter of the castle. None had raced to the scene of Sir Aubrey's death, and Gwen felt a moment of pride that they could be so well disciplined. They gathered near the gatehouse between the two outer wards, conferred briefly with Gruffydd, their captain, and then headed off again, though Gruffydd strode purposefully to intercept Gareth and Gwen.

When he reached them, he was frowning. "We're in the thick of it again, I hear." He ruffled Dai's hair. "I hope you're not tired."

"I'm not. Why?"

"I need you to run back to the priory and tell Evan what has transpired."

Dai's face took on an expression that indicated he was about to protest, but Gruffydd looked at him sternly. "We have a killer on the loose. He could have taken refuge in the town, but just think if he came to the priory, and Evan didn't know that another man was dead?"

The idea that the errand was necessary, rather than an excuse to send him away while the adults talked, had clearly not occurred to Dai, and his attitude immediately transformed into one of attention and obedience.

With a boy this age, Gwen was happy to leave his discipline to others. It hadn't been long ago that Gwalchmai had thought and behaved similarly to Dai, and Gwen well remembered the way he'd alternately contradicted and ignored everything she said, even at those times when he wasn't intending to be rude. Fortunately, now sixteen, Gwalchmai had come out of his malaise, having far more important things to worry about—like singing for King Owain Gwynedd—than doing the exact opposite of what his sister told him to do simply because it was she who said it.

In Llelo, that same insecurity inherent in the transition from boy to man was manifested in a desire to be perfect. Dai's response wasn't entirely opposite, but he had a willfully disobedient streak that nobody had quite managed to restrain yet. The key was to encourage in him the ability to manage it himself, and Gwen had hope that, given enough leeway and understanding, Dai would eventually find it.

So Dai went off too, leaving Gruffydd alone with Gareth and Gwen (and Taran, of course). "I ran into the steward just now. He mentioned that the prince would like to speak with you again as soon as possible."

Gwen glanced at her husband. "We just spoke to a man named Charles, the understeward, and Robert Fitzharding, who seems to be taking charge of the castle. Which steward is this?"

"I don't know anything about those men," Gruffydd said. "This was Roger, one of Earl Robert's sons."

"I met him earlier over Sir Aubrey's body," Gareth said. "Roger serves Henry specifically, as his personal seneschal."

"Like you will do for Prince Hywel," Gruffydd nodded his understanding, "as opposed to the steward of Aberystwyth, who stays where he is regardless of where Hywel goes."

Over the last few months, Hywel had come to realize that his vision of his own role in his father's kingdom needed to evolve. The first step had been to recruit the Dragons, which in retrospect had been one of Gareth's more brilliant ideas. The second was to promote Gareth from captain of his teulu to his *distain*, what the French called *seneschal*. At Christmastide, he would formally become Hywel's right-hand man, the position that Lord Taran held in King Owain's court.

In truth, Gareth had been playing that role for years. While Gwen knew her husband would be sorry to lose the camaraderie of Hywel's fighting men, having entered his thirties, he was ready for greater challenges. And Gwen herself wouldn't be sorry to see him spending less time thinking of war.

"Roger and Henry were educated together, though Roger himself is older than Henry," Gwen said. "Twenty or thereabouts. So many of these men are quite young to be charged with so much. Doesn't Henry have an older man in his household to advise him?"

"Not at this time. Earl Robert *was* the older man," Gareth said. "You recall Henry mentioning his soldiers being paid wages by King Stephen, so they could return to France after Henry's ill-conceived invasion of Kent?"

Gwen nodded, some of the details bubbling to the surface of her mind.

Gareth made a dismissive gesture. "Never mind if you don't. We were busy at the time. It happened just before we went to Shrewsbury, and Henry's arrival was the reason the sheriff had been called away by Stephen. Neither Henry's mother nor Earl Robert condoned his action. Stephen gave Henry the choice of returning to France with his men, his tail between his legs, or traveling to lands controlled by his mother's faction under safe conduct from Stephen."

"I remember now. He chose to remain in England."

"The caveat was that he was allowed only his household guards and a small number of supporters, Hamelin and Roger among them. The rest went home to France, presumably charged with explaining to Henry's father what he'd done."

That prompted a laugh from Gruffydd. "Undoubtedly Henry stayed away in hopes his father's wrath would have been spent by the time he returned. Bad enough to face his mother unshielded."

"And now Earl Robert is dead." Gwen sighed.

Gruffydd grunted. "A bad business. Is it your thought he was murdered?"

"It's too early to say," Gwen said.

"Still, one accident on top of the earl's death I could accept, but three?" Gareth shook his head. "Henry may not be right about his uncle, but how can I not think there's been murder done at Bristol?" He related to Gruffydd the little they knew, particularly the mason's conclusions.

Gruffydd put his heels together and gave Gareth a bow. "Consider me mortared to your side."

Gareth groaned at the jest. But while Gruffydd's response was playful, it was also very serious, and he didn't argue. Gwen herself patted Gruffydd on the arm. "Don't mind him. Prince Hywel knew what he was doing when he sent you here. None of us have any interest in risking our own lives, especially not in a Norman castle so far from home, over a cause which, no matter how grave, has nothing to do with us."

A tall, slender, thin-faced young man entered the outer ward from the inner gatehouse and stopped, looking around as if searching for someone. It was the aforementioned Roger. At the sight of him, both Gareth and Gruffydd lifted a hand. Roger immediately hastened towards them, followed by five men-at-arms. Gwen was starting to think that Gareth would be wise to wear a bell around his neck, to make the finding of him easier. This castle was so huge that it would be hard to know the whereabouts of any one person, especially if that person didn't want to be found.

Roger stopped in front of them while his five companions remained a respectful three paces away. "My cousin requests your presence in his chamber." He paused, his eyes on Gruffydd. "Of course, any of your Dragons would be welcome to join us."

Gruffydd bowed, but after Roger turned away and set off towards the keep, assuming they'd follow, he said in an undertone to Gareth, "Why would he want to see us?"

"You are renowned throughout England now, didn't you know?" Gareth laughed and clapped Gruffydd on the shoulder. "It is the Dragons who are Henry's heroes. Sad to say, I have been usurped."

6

Llelo

Gareth had discussed with Llelo the times he'd had to enter an English domain during the course of an investigation. He'd gone to Chester years ago and met the Norman Amaury, who turned out to be a villain at Newcastle-under-Lyme, where Gareth had rescued Dai and Llelo from the English friary. Gareth had worked with Saxons most recently in Shrewsbury, though Llelo hadn't been there that time. By traveling with his parents to Bristol, Llelo had expected to meet many Normans, but he was still surprised to find himself accompanied on the first day by a foreigner—who as it turned out wasn't even a Norman. Hamelin had been born in Anjou.

He was equally surprised by how accepting of it all he was, in large part because Hamelin was treating him with the respect he deserved as a man, but he was quite certain he didn't deserve as an investigator. Still, it seemed better to Llelo to brazen out whatever insecurities were voicing themselves in the back of his mind rather than tell Hamelin that he'd been on his own during an investigation exactly once before. Llelo had comported himself well at the time, but it wasn't as if he had a wealth of experience to draw upon today.

He had more than Hamelin, however, and perhaps that was all that was needed. Anyway, both men were gaining experience by the hour, and their first encounter with a soldier, whom they met coming out of one of the towers opposite the one Gwen had gone into, immediately showed the benefit of having Hamelin with him.

At their approach, the soldier halted and bowed his head, "My lord." He wasn't referring to Llelo.

"We have questions to ask you. What is your name?" Hamelin said in French. Now that he thought about it, Llelo realized he'd heard only French spoken since he'd arrived. It seemed to be a requirement for living at Bristol Castle, and Llelo was a little irritated that all his efforts this last year to improve his English might have been for nothing. The French, however, was proving to be very useful indeed.

The soldier replied in the same language, "Thomas, my lord. Please ask anything. It is my wish to serve." His eyes flicked questioningly to Llelo.

Hamelin saw the motion and responded to it. "This is Llelo, son of Gareth, who has traveled to Bristol at the behest of the prince, my brother. Llelo himself was meeting with Prince Henry when Sir Aubrey was struck down. You will answer every question he puts to you." Amazingly, and to Hamelin's credit, he didn't butcher the pronunciation of Llelo's name as badly as every other foreigner Llelo had ever encountered.

His Adam's apple bobbing, Thomas faced Llelo fully, implying with his wide-eyed questioning look that Llelo could ask him anything, and he would answer truthfully.

Llelo himself swallowed to see it, feeling the pressure now, but this was the task he'd been set, so he squared his shoulders and asked his first question. "Where were you when the stone fell on Sir Aubrey?"

"In the central guardroom, my lord." Thomas answered without hesitation and pointed across to the gatehouse that allowed access to the inner ward. "I was at the morning meeting."

"What was this *morning meeting* about? Who called it?"

"Our captain. We have it every morning."

"Wait a moment." Llelo couldn't quite believe what he was hearing. "Are you saying that the captain of the castle's garrison holds a meeting of the guards every day at exactly the same time Sir Aubrey died?"

"I suppose so, when you put it that way. When the tower bell at St. James's Priory tolls for Terce, it is echoed here at the inner gate, and we are to come to the guardroom. When Sir Aubrey died, the meeting was almost over."

Terce was the monks' mid-morning prayer. Bristol contained at least six monastic houses that Llelo knew of, plus several lay churches and the castle chapel in the far outer ward, so Llelo had heard bells tolling all morning. They'd sounded during his parents' conference with Prince Henry, but he'd thought nothing of it, since the sound of bells was a constant backdrop to life in any town. He'd experienced it first-hand at Newcastle-under-Lyme.

Hamelin's expression had also turned to one of dismay. "How many of your fellow guardsmen were there?"

"All of them, my lord." Thomas hesitated. "Well, all but the few needed to maintain the security of the main gates and the outer curtain wall."

Llelo bit his lip, giving himself time before speaking so he wouldn't come across as accusing. "So, if I am to understand correctly, when Sir Aubrey died, every man on duty who wasn't standing over one of the two main gatehouses was in the central guardroom?"

He didn't want to alienate Thomas, but he was having trouble encompassing what he'd just said. Llelo understood the need to meet with the men together every day. Every captain had to set out the daily duty roster, and it was much more efficient to call everyone together and speak to them at the same time. But at Denbigh, where Llelo had trained most recently, the new shift came on before the old shift was over, and that meant the meeting could take place while the current shift was still active. It meant the towers and walls were always manned.

For the security of Bristol Castle, Llelo couldn't imagine a worse scenario. He was shocked that any castle, never mind one in the middle of a war, would implement such a system—though in regards to his need to question everyone at Bristol, it essentially eliminated the majority of the garrison, since its members had been together in the same room when Sir Aubrey had died.

Despite Llelo's efforts, and even with French as Llelo's second language, the guard heard the criticism in his voice. Probably it would have been impossible for him to miss the horror on Hamelin's and Llelo's faces anyway. So now Thomas said, somewhat combatively, "Men remained on the outer walls! What do you take us for here?"

Fools was what Llelo was thinking, but of course he couldn't say it. Instead, he said, "How long did the meeting last?"

"A quarter of an hour, no more. It was just long enough for everyone to get their assignments for the day."

Llelo took in a breath, rearranging his expression so as not to rile the man further. This was not a good beginning, and he was sure his father wouldn't have allowed his emotions to show. "That your commander requires this of you is completely understandable, and certainly whatever arrangements are made for the rotation of duty at the castle is not within your purview." Llelo bent his head slightly, and at his understated apology, the soldier looked slightly mollified. "May I ask if you noticed anything unusual in the moments leading up to your departure for the meeting?"

Thomas pursed his lips. "No."

Llelo couldn't tell if the guard was being difficult on purpose, so he tried again. "Where was your post?"

Thomas tipped his head. "Right here."

Llelo and Hamelin had come to the right person. "Is this your usual posting?"

"Oh no. We rotate duty every day, and often every few hours so that no man becomes bored and complacent."

That sounded like good management, so perhaps the captain knew what he was doing—at least in this. "Do you remember who, if anyone, was about?"

Thomas didn't even have to think. "In the moments before the bell rang, I saw Earl Robert's widow, Lord Roger, Robert Fitzharding, John the ewerer, several kitchen helpers, and three servant girls carrying laundry to the washing room." He shrugged. "I don't see how that helps."

The castle was a busy place. Llelo had noticed that, as they'd been talking on the wall, at least twenty people had passed by the spot where Sir Aubrey had died—morbid curiosity, perhaps, or simply because it was on the way to wherever they were going.

"Was there anybody on the rampart of the keep?" Hamelin said.

Now Thomas shook his head regretfully, to all appearances having forgiven them both for their earlier criticism.

"Did you see Sir Aubrey?" Llelo said.

"He always came late for the meeting, and nobody expected him sooner."

Llelo tried very hard not to stare at Thomas, even as he was grateful for the unprompted bit of information. "Sir Aubrey was meant to attend the meeting?"

"Yes, of course. That's why he was crossing the courtyard, but as I said, he's always late. On purpose, I think, to give the captain a chance to settle us."

"Why did he attend at all?" Hamelin said.

"He was the steward," Thomas said, as if it were obvious.

Patience filled Hamelin's voice. "I understand that he was the steward, but I would have thought he had more pressing duties at that hour of the day."

The guard shook his head. "I don't know anything about that. Didn't he need to know what was going on with every aspect of the castle?"

"Of course," Llelo said, again attempting to be reassuring. "Did he usually speak to you?"

"Almost never. Mostly he poked in his head at the end and conferred with the captain after we left." Thomas made a motion with his head to imply he wanted to modify his earlier comment. "It was in some of our minds that he was checking up on the captain more than us." He stopped, pressing his lips tightly together as if he'd said too much and now regretted his frankness.

"Why would you think that?" Llelo said.

Thomas took in a deep breath through his nose. "I shouldn't say."

Few comments could have done more to pique Llelo's interest.

Hamelin too leaned in. "Now you have spoken of it, you have to tell us."

Thomas chewed on his lower lip, his eyes moving uncertainly from Hamelin to Llelo and back again.

Llelo spoke gently. "Sir Aubrey is dead. Whatever you have to say can't hurt him now."

"It isn't him it'll hurt."

Llelo canted his head. "Your captain?"

Thomas turned away for a moment. Llelo had no idea what he would do if the soldier actually walked off, but then he turned back. Bastard or not, Hamelin was a high-ranking lord and could not be snubbed, no matter how unwanted these questions. For a moment, Thomas glowered. "If you speak of this to anyone, it didn't come from me, my lords. Please."

"We promise." Hamelin nodded vigorously. Llelo decided it was too late to mention that he wasn't a lord himself.

"The captain went through a spell this past year where he didn't … wake early."

Llelo narrowed his eyes. "He was late for duty?"

"Some days he never came in at all." Thomas cleared his throat. "He would be well into his cups before the noon meal. But these past months he's been better!"

Llelo and Hamelin had the exact same response to the guard's confidences, which was to ease back and make something of a dismissive gesture. A soldier who drank his way through the day—and night—was nothing new. What was different was that he'd brought himself back from the brink of ruin.

"So the purpose of the meetings—and Sir Aubrey's attendance at them—was more for your captain's sake than yours?" Llelo said.

"We needed our orders, of course, but Earl Robert insisted the captain be given a chance to make amends, and he has done so. All the men respect him," Thomas concluded staunchly.

Earl Robert had been at the end of his life and had perhaps felt the need for forgiveness and absolution himself. Llelo was fifteen—not even a man yet by English standards—but he'd seen death. He'd also lived in a monastery. Men behaved differently when they knew they were about to be facing God himself in person.

"Can you tell us anything else about this morning—anything at all that might help us discover why Sir Aubrey died?"

The guard frowned and did appear to be trying to think. "No."

Llelo tipped his head. "Thank you for your cooperation. If you could direct us to where your captain might be at this hour, we will let you go about your duties."

"Of course, my lords." The guard's expression had cleared. Gone was his outrage and fear, replaced by straightforwardness, without obsequiousness or uncertainty. By Llelo's reckoning, Thomas should feel satisfied: he'd told the truth as he knew it, and nobody was going to punish him for it. "He should be in his office next to the guardroom in the gatehouse to the inner ward. As I said, that's where we meet each day."

Hamelin dismissed Thomas, and as they watched the guard pace along the wall-walk away from them, Hamelin said, "That puts vinegar in the beer, doesn't it?"

Llelo had never heard that expression before, and he despised the taste of beer—but he could imagine that vinegar would do nothing to improve it. "The entire guard of this castle was gathered in one place for a quarter of an hour, barring a few on the outer walls. This is something everyone in the castle had to know, isn't it?"

"I didn't." Hamelin grunted. "I suppose I've noticed on and off since we've been here that fewer guards patrolled the walls for a brief time every morning, but I didn't think anything of it. It has never mattered before."

"When he told us of it, my first thought was dismay, and my second was ridicule," Llelo said, "but as I look at the walls and the fortifications, I can see why the steward thought no harm could come from it. The purpose of the castle garrison is to guard the castle, not to watch the residents and inform on their misdeeds."

"This arrangement seems to have been in place for some time, and it has never been a problem until now," Hamelin said.

Llelo gave a snort. "That's always the difficulty with guard duty, though, isn't it? Days and weeks and months of nothing. Years even, but you must be ever vigilant because that *one time* it will make all the difference."

Hamelin eyed him. "You sound like you speak from experience."

"I have been on guard duty, yes."

"I wish I could talk to Earl Robert about this. I miss him," Hamelin said simply. "The world is a poorer place without him in it."

"I never really met him, but my parents solved a murder at Newcastle-under-Lyme when he was in residence—at his request—and he never struck me as one to be anything less than diligent or to accept anything less than complete attentiveness in his men."

"That was years ago." Hamelin started along the wall-walk to the tower they'd come up. "This past year he was much diminished, and he knew it. I haven't said as much to Henry, who is still in deep mourning, but it was no life Earl Robert was living. I think by the end he welcomed death."

Llelo hastened to come abreast, stunned and honored at the same time that Hamelin would trust him with these thoughts. "Who is the captain of the garrison?"

"Harold of Linfield."

Thomas had long since disappeared inside the tower, but now he reappeared on an adjacent wall-walk, where he stopped and spoke to another guard. From what Llelo could see, only two soldiers were on duty on the wall-walks of the keep at any one time. At the moment, the job belonged to Thomas and this second man. A third stood on the top of one of the towers, at the moment looking west towards the Severn Sea and Wales.

Llelo could also see a man patrolling the wall-walk of the wall that surrounded the keep and the inner ward, and he could just glimpse a second farther along. Logically, the bulk of the men on duty patrolled the outer curtain walls, since these would be the first line of defense of the castle. He assumed someone was guarding the postern gate as well, though he had yet to locate it. He hoped, too, that Harold had posted someone at the entrance to the tunnel.

"It is easy to become complacent," Hamelin said. "Bristol has never been attacked. Most of these men have no experience in war." He stopped abruptly to look at Llelo. "You have been a guard. Does that mean you have fought in battle?"

"Yes. Gwynedd was at odds with Chester until we took Mold last spring. I was on the front lines throughout." Llelo paused. "And then I was with Prince Hywel when he and his allies took Wiston from the Flemings.'"

"You know the Dragons?" Hamelin's expression lit, much as Prince Henry's had when he'd spoken of them earlier that morning.

Llelo found himself grinning. "Of course. They are my father's closest companions. You can meet them. They are here."

Hamelin instantly deflated. "They won't have any interest in me. I have never fought, not really. The few skirmishes last spring were with poorly-armed men and peasants. We should not have come when we did. My brother understood his folly almost immediately, but it was too late to turn back."

Llelo studied Hamelin's downturned head. In this, Henry reminded Llelo strongly of Dai, though thankfully Dai was merely a man-at-arms, and his impetuousness had never been on display for an entire country. "Prince Henry turned to Earl Robert for help, and he did not give it. Was that to teach him a lesson?"

As he asked the question, Llelo had a moment of fear that it was one question too many and that Hamelin would take offense, but his new friend answered seriously.

"I do not believe now that Earl Robert wanted to deny aid, but he had no choice since Henry's mother had already done so. He was ill, but he still welcomed us when we arrived. If you need to know more, that is a conversation you must have with the prince himself." Hamelin paused. "Or perhaps not."

Llelo gave a low laugh, knowing already that the prince had his own opinion about the circumstances of his debt to King Stephen. "Perhaps not."

They'd been talking freely, since they were alone in the stairwell, but one step from the stairway door, Llelo came to a dead halt. The foyer was full of people—he would have said unusually so. Hamelin butted up behind him, forcing Llelo to take another step, at which point everyone realized they were there. Many people had been talking animatedly up until that point, but as one their heads swiveled towards him and Hamelin. Silence descended on the room. Hamelin nudged Llelo in the back again, implying that Llelo himself should speak.

His mouth went dry, and all of a sudden he didn't have a single word of French in his head. His face coloring, he stepped quickly out of Hamelin's way instead, and Hamelin bent his head in acknowledgement of the attention they were receiving. "As you must know by now, Sir Aubrey is dead, killed by a stone falling from the battlement. If you can tell us anything pertaining to this matter, please come forward—if not now, then at your earliest opportunity." He stopped.

Llelo's heart raced as he realized that Hamelin didn't know what else to say to them—and how could he? That was Llelo's job. In a rush, before his brain could get in the way of his mouth, he added, "I am Llelo. It is my father, Sir Gareth, who has come at Prince Henry's request to address these matters. Our companions are known as the Dragons—" a murmur went around the room at his words, which, quite frankly, was why Llelo had said them, "—and any one of us would be pleased to hear whatever you have to say." He cleared his throat. "Thank you for your assistance."

Then, with Hamelin at his side, he strode for the door as quickly as he could.

7

Gwen

The five soldiers Roger had brought with him fell into formation around Gareth, Gwen, and Gruffydd, giving Gwen the feeling of being a prisoner, though she didn't believe that was the intent. Normans liked formality, and they had a tendency to stand on ceremony even though more might be accomplished with a jest and a *please*.

This time, however, when they passed into the keep, rather than taking them to the receiving room in which they'd met Prince Henry earlier that morning, Roger led them up the stairs in one of the towers—the same one Gwen had taken to get to the wall-walk—to an upstairs chamber located above the great hall. It was decorated like a noblewoman's solar, with soft cushions on the window seat, several wide chairs, a thick fur on the floor, and a blazing fire. Gwen was tempted to sit without being asked, if for no other reason than because Taran was heavy. Before she could, however, a middle-aged woman came through a far doorway—gliding rather than walking—and put a hand on the back of a comfortable chair nearest the fire.

"Wine, Roger."

"Yes, Mother." Roger moved with alacrity while the other men around Gwen shrank back slightly—the Norman men, that is. Gareth and Gruffydd had no inherent fear of her, though Gwen had a sudden thought that perhaps they should.

Mabel came serenely around the chair and accepted a goblet of wine from her son. Then, with a flick of her hand, she dismissed not only her own lady-in-waiting, who faded back through the doorway and closed the door, but the Norman guards who'd accompanied Gareth and Gwen. Before the man closest to Gwen turned away, he let out an audible sigh of relief, prompting a momentary laugh from Gwen, which she barely managed to swallow down. It would have been inappropriate, and the last thing she wanted was to get on the wrong side of Lady Mabel.

His expression solicitous, Roger returned to the table set against the wall to Gwen's right, and Gruffydd moved silently to put his back to the main door, as Llelo had done downstairs in Prince Henry's receiving room.

Gwen schooled her expression and studied Earl Robert's widow. By all accounts, and by Gwen's own assessment when she'd met him, Robert had been the kind of man who filled every room he entered. He was a strong leader—and a good man. The authority emanating from Mabel indicated that he'd also been a strong enough man to have a wife who intimidated everyone in her vicinity. Gwen had a passing thought that she'd love to know how Mabel and Empress Maud got along—and strongly suspected the answer was *not at all well*. That could be why Maud was mourning her brother alone at Devizes rather than with the widow here at Bristol.

Mabel was Gwen's height but very thin, as sometimes happened to women once their childbearing years were over. Even now, Mabel might not be entirely out of them, since she was somewhere in her forties. Earl Robert himself had been in the vicinity of fifty. Together they had more than a half-dozen living children, the eldest of whom, William, had now inherited his father's title. William was twenty-seven, having been born within a year of his father's marriage to Mabel, and was seven years older than Roger.

Gwen had noticed that sometimes when a couple had been married for many years, they started to resemble one another. Mabel was a much smaller person than her late husband had been, but they shared the same patrician nose, high forehead, and slate-gray hair, which in Mabel's case was pulled back in a bun on the top of her head. Inside her own quarters, she wore no veil or kerchief. Her dress was of the finest wool Gwen had ever seen. Gwen still hadn't changed out of her traveling clothes, and she felt drab and unfashionable by comparison. Probably, given her nursing mother's figure, she would have felt that way regardless of what she was wearing.

Having given his mother her wine, Roger poured a second goblet for Gwen, which she took with surprise and gratitude. Because of Taran's needs, she was constantly thirsty, and if Roger hadn't come to find her and Gareth, she would have made her way to the kitchen for refreshment.

As she took a sip, Roger retreated back to the table. "Mother, it is a pleasure to see you. I had thought it was Cousin Henry who would be here. That is what I told Sir Gareth."

"Henry had other duties to attend to, and I wanted to speak to our guests myself." Her look was severe.

Gwen was left with the impression that Roger had been deliberately deceived—for reasons Gwen couldn't yet decipher. Did Mabel fear that if she asked directly for Gwen and Gareth to come to her, they wouldn't have done so? The idea was ludicrous enough to be dismissed out of hand.

Mabel raised a finger to Gruffydd. "I would speak to Sir Gareth and Lady Gwen alone."

Gruffydd's eyes immediately went to Gareth, who conveyed his assent, and Gruffydd did as he was bid, though with obvious reluctance. "I will be outside if you need me," he muttered in Welsh under his breath before closing the door behind him.

While Roger had given Gwen a full goblet, Mabel hadn't granted Gwen, who still held Taran in his sling, permission to sit. It was incredibly rude of her. Gwen would have thought that a matron like Mabel, who saw herself as superior in every way to Gwen, would not want to appear ungracious. She could have offered Gwen a seat if only to appear like a queen to a lowly subject. Then again, perhaps in her eyes, Gwen's station was so far beneath hers that she didn't believe she was a person worthy of notice. That was the reason she'd looked daggers at her son when he'd given Gwen the wine.

She and Gareth were worthy enough of notice for Mabel to fix them with a beady gaze, however. "Henry believes my husband was murdered. I do not concur, and if it had been up to me, you would not be here now."

Taran, with the perfect timing of a baby, chose that moment to squawk. He flailed his arms, almost knocking Gwen's cup out of her hand, and arched his back, demanding to be let out of his blankets.

To Gwen's relief, even though Mabel had shown no concern for her up until now, the noblewoman's reaction was immediate. "Sit, my dear. You've traveled far, and my nephew should not have put this burden on you before you'd even had a chance to rest." While offering Gwen a place to sit, one woman to another, had been out of the question, one mother to another was apparently a different matter.

Gwen sat gratefully, putting the wine aside and pulling Taran out of his sling to hold him in her lap. Meanwhile, Mabel's attention shifted back to Gareth. "How could you have brought her so far?"

Gareth stood his ground, though he had his legs spread and his hands behind his back, as if fearing he was about to be buffeted by a high wind instead of merely Mabel's opinions. "Prince Henry indicated that his need for our presence was urgent, and circumstances were such that leaving Aberystwyth seemed a better idea than staying."

"Croup. I heard." Mabel canted her head, condescending to admit that Gareth might have a point.

Gareth bowed. "Please allow me to express my condolences for your loss."

Mabel didn't appear to know what to make of that. Either she was offended by his courtesy or surprised that such a pretty statement had come out of a Welshman's mouth. Instead of thanking him or making any reply, she took a long drink of wine, nearly draining the cup, and resettled herself in her chair. The back of the chair was to the fire so she faced Gareth, who remained standing somewhat awkwardly in front of her.

At which point Gwen realized that she had done Mabel a disservice. The Lady of Gloucester had been moved, not offended, by Gareth's condolences, and her fluster and bluster had been intended to give herself time to recover from strong emotion—something these Normans strived at all times to hide.

Finally, Mabel spoke again, though it was to address a new subject. "I hear you've already examined Aubrey's body."

"Yes, my lady, though my conclusions are of no great import. We know how he died."

"And the battlement?"

Gwen cleared her throat. "I've seen it, my lady. As did our son, who is even now speaking with the soldiers on duty at the time. The mason who examined the break does not believe it credible that the mortar failed in only that spot. He is of the opinion that someone deliberately chiseled out the stone."

"So this is murder." It wasn't a question.

"It appears so," Gareth said.

Mabel sniffed. "It seems you have made business for yourselves here after all."

That was so patently unfair, Gwen's breath caught in her throat.

Gareth struggled on. "With these other deaths—"

Mabel cut him off with a wave of her hand. "My husband's death aside, I do agree that we've been stricken by a series of unfortunate events. The common folk are near panic, and I myself have been at wit's end with them. The castle is in disarray, a condition I cannot abide. We've had enough death, murder, and betrayal with this infernal war without adding to it with unexpected losses like Aubrey's." She glared at Gareth, seemingly not having the heart to take Gwen to task with a baby in her arms. "I do not see the benefit in upsetting my people more than they already are. You must be more discreet! I can't imagine what my nephew was thinking inviting strangers to Bristol."

Gareth wet his lips. "I apologize for any unrest our presence and our questions may cause. But asking questions is the only way to uncover the truth. If there's a murderer loose in Bristol, it is only by making inquiries that we will catch him, hopefully before he strikes again."

"If." She sniffed again. "And can you guarantee that he won't strike again if you do ask your questions?"

Gareth was silent a moment. "No, madam. I cannot. Even now he might be plotting his next move."

Mabel shuddered and seemed about to speak, but Roger cleared his throat. "We can't send them away now, Mother."

"People might think I had something to hide, you mean?" Mabel was too ladylike to snort, but Gwen had the definite impression she wanted to.

Roger's next comment was more tentative. "It would also be ... unwise to overrule Henry. We can't have his authority undermined."

"You don't have to remind me of my place, Roger. William is the new earl, and while he didn't support Henry's accusations, it would have been impolitic to forbid Henry to pursue them." Mabel made a tsking sound under her breath. "And look where it has got us."

Mabel's comment implied that if Henry hadn't summoned Gareth and Gwen, Sir Aubrey would not be dead. It was a disconcerting thought, and Gwen was honest enough to acknowledge that it might even be true. But the thought, by definition, indicated that at least one of these other deaths was not an accident. Gwen didn't dare point out Mabel's flawed logic, but she wasn't going to cower before her either. "What can you tell us of these other deaths, my lady?"

"Nothing."

Gwen ground her teeth, striving for patience. Lady Mabel's response was one she might have expected from Dai or Gwalchmai, but not the dowager lady of Bristol Castle. Gwen was trying to make allowances for Mabel's grief, but she was already tired of being treated like a peasant or a serf—and Gwen herself would never treat anyone this way in the first place. "You must have known the maidservant who tended your husband. Who found her body?"

"I did."

Gwen resisted raising her eyebrows. That was a new bit of information nobody had bothered to tell them yet. "Can you describe the circumstances in which you found her?"

"I was passing by my late husband's room. I heard a noise coming from behind the door, which was partially open, and I found her lying on the floor, dying."

"Was there any blood or other indication that her death had involved another person?" Gwen said.

Mabel shook her head.

Gareth took a slight step forward. "Did you notice anything unusual about the room?"

"My husband wasn't in it." Mabel was back to obstructing, though her words were true as well.

"Did she vomit before she died?" Gareth said. "Was there foam around her mouth or petechiae around her eyes?"

Mabel paused a moment to consider before answering, and Gwen was glad to see she was taking the questions seriously for the first time. "Her lips were blue, I remember that. And she had a sunburned look to her cheeks, even though it was All Saints' Day, and we'd had little sun for weeks." She shrugged. "Neither our physician nor the herbalist could find an external cause of death. There's nothing further to say."

Gareth looked at Gwen. "That could be in keeping with a heart condition."

Gwen tipped her head noncommittally. "It's also a sign of poisoning from bitter almond—or perhaps a hundred other possibilities." The description did make her think of suffocation. She wished Saran were here, because she might have better insight, but she and Gwen's father had returned to Gwynedd. They hadn't even met Taran yet.

"Who was the herbalist you consulted?" Gwen asked.

"He is a monk at St. James's Priory, where I believe you are staying. You could speak to our physician, but he went off with William." Her chin stuck out. "Few men are more knowledgeable, and you would be wise to accept his judgement."

Gwen fought a skeptical smile. Lady Mabel's assessment sounded grossly optimistic, since most castle healers were good for pulling teeth and little else. Midwives generally knew something of herbs and their healing qualities, and most monastery herbalists had the basics in their stock. People like Saran, however, people for whom diagnosing and treatment were an art, were few and far between.

Gareth turned to Roger. "What about the valet?"

"He drowned."

"So everyone says," Gareth said, "but you have no body."

Roger sighed, as if impatient with the need to tell the story. "A boy walking along the bank saw him in the boat, and then when he passed by going the other way a quarter of an hour later, Bernard was gone, leaving his boots in the bottom of the boat. His hat was found washed up on the bank a short distance downstream." It was almost word for word what Prince Henry had told them.

Mabel's eyes were sad. "Bernard was fishing in honor of the earl, who loved it." She shook her head. "He'd had so little time to spare for it in recent years." She meant the earl, Gwen knew, not the valet.

"Where is the boat now?" Gareth said. "Is it available to be examined?"

Roger shrugged. "It is a boat. I can't see how there's anything to discover with it, but you may try. I will speak to—" He stopped. "I was about to say I would speak to Aubrey so he could arrange for it, but of course he's dead too." He took in a breath. "Someone will know what has become of it."

"Could Bernard swim?" Gwen asked, looking for confirmation of what Prince Henry had told them.

Mabel pressed her lips together, implying that she was impatient with the questions. "You should really let him be. He's probably in the sea by now." She swept out a hand and said, even more tartly, "Bernard was completely bereft upon my husband's death. It wouldn't be the first time grief overthrew a man's senses and caused him to take his own life."

Henry had denied the possibility of suicide, and this comment put Mabel again at odds with her nephew. It seemed Henry held multiple opinions that nobody else shared.

Then Mabel's voice softened. "It isn't the Christian way, but—" she paused again, and her stern appearance suddenly gave way, like the breaking of a wave upon the beach, and tears filled her voice, "—from the first, I wished I'd died too." She bent her head.

At Mabel's sudden tears, Roger looked utterly stricken. Gareth's feet were also frozen to the floor, but after a quick motion from Gwen, he hastened to her to take Taran, which allowed Gwen to move to Mabel's side. Gwen was uncertain about whether comforting Mabel was appropriate—or if her comfort would be rebuffed—but grief was grief, and even if every widow dealt with the loss of her husband in her own way, Mabel didn't have to be alone with hers.

So Gwen went down on one knee and placed her hand hesitantly on Mabel's shoulder. Mabel didn't dismiss her, and as she continued to weep, Roger brought Gwen a chair to put next to Mabel's. Throwing caution to the winds, Gwen sat and drew the older woman into her arms.

With that, the storm that had been building let loose, and the real tears came. With a flick of one hand behind Mabel's back, Gwen dismissed both men from the room, and they left with haste. It was customary to say that men feared a woman's tears more than battle, but in this case, it was true. Even though a part of Gwen herself feared this kind of grief, never again wanting to feel the way Mabel did, she didn't recoil from it. She'd lived it since she was ten years old when her mother died, and while she'd experienced loss in the interim, her grief had been renewed upon Rhun's death a year ago.

The longer Mabel's weeping continued, the more difficult Gwen found it to blink back her own tears that wanted to fall in sympathy. She struggled to swallow them down and simply act as a rock for Mabel, who was holding onto Gwen so tightly she'd caught the back of Gwen's cloak in her fists, giving Gwen no chance to draw away even had she a mind to.

"I loved him, you see," Mabel said, still holding on.

"I know."

8

Llelo

"You handled those people very well," Hamelin said, in what Llelo interpreted as a clear attempt to make him feel better.

"*You* handled them well. I completely froze."

"Still, you managed it in the end."

"I'm making it up as I go along, I assure you."

"You'd do better if you dressed the part." Hamelin put a hand on Llelo's arm to slow his progress across the inner ward. "Your French is good enough for an Englishman. Nobody need know you're Welsh."

Llelo took in a breath, surprised at the insult. But then, as he looked into Hamelin's face, he understood that Hamelin had spoken innocently and would be surprised to learn that Llelo was bothered by what he'd just said. That recognition slowed his reaction, and he took in another breath before speaking. He wanted Hamelin's cooperation and, truth be told, his companionship.

So instead of getting angry, he said simply, "I am not ashamed of who I am."

Hamelin's expression faltered. "I didn't mean—I didn't intend—"

"I know you didn't, but imagine you'd come to Gwynedd, and similar words had come from my mouth instead of yours?"

Hamelin grunted, and Llelo could tell he was genuinely thinking about what Llelo had suggested. He wasn't a bad person, just ignorant, which he proved a moment later when he bowed and said, "Please accept my apologies."

"There is much we don't understand about each other. Allowances must be made ... on both sides." Llelo started walking again.

Hamelin took some extra steps to come abreast, and they walked in silence for a few moments. Gradually, their breathing eased, and their postures became more companionable. Llelo decided it was up to him to change the subject, as a peace offering. "I would be surprised if any of those people in there come forward to tell us anything."

Hamelin had fallen into a long-legged saunter that Llelo couldn't help but admire. "Earl Robert was beloved. It may look as if nobody was open to your query, but inside, people are worried. You may be surprised at what comes from this."

"That's what murder does," Llelo said, and then at Hamelin's inquiring look added, "It exposes a community, divides it at times, and unites it at others. Nobody can know of a murder and remain impartial."

"I believe you." Hamelin looked at him sideways. "Is that your father speaking, or do you know this from your own experience?"

"Both. I started out at my father's side, of course—and my mother's—but I have investigated deaths myself. Once. Mostly I have watched and learned."

"From the best, I understand." Hamelin's expression turned thoughtful. "I admit to having been skeptical when my brother insisted that murder had been done. Even with three deaths at Bristol, it did not seem obvious to me. But now I feel like I must assume it." They'd come across the inner ward and arrived at the gatehouse.

"My lord says never to assume." Llelo came to a halt at Hamelin's side and looked up at the towers that confronted them. The stones of the inner curtain wall were thirty feet high, the battlements crenellated in the same fashion as the keep, and every gatehouse had a fair complement of portcullises and murder holes. "Let the facts speak for themselves, and you will never have to."

"Aren't you making an assumption that Sir Aubrey's death was murder, which is why we're investigating it?"

Their steps crunched on the gravel. To the right of the first portcullis was the entrance to the guardroom that Thomas had indicated. Llelo's stomach growled with hunger, and he was sorry it didn't look as if he was going to get to eat until the evening meal. He'd come a long way since the sight of Sir Aubrey's head a few hours ago had made him think he might never want to eat again.

"Yes, but even if the stone hadn't been chiseled out of position, it is equally an assumption that he was *not* murdered. In that case, better to err on the side of caution and investigate. If Sir Aubrey's death was an accident, we have lost nothing but time, but if it was intentional—" Llelo broke off as two guards turned to look at them. Their gaze was similar to that of the people in the foyer of the keep: disdainful and curious at the same time.

"Indeed." Hamelin elbowed him in the ribs to urge him forward.

As Hamelin and Llelo arrived on the threshold of the captain's office, Harold was striding around the center table, cursing under his breath. The door had been left open, giving Llelo and Hamelin a clear view of the captain's stiff posture and grim expression before they made themselves known. Beside him, Llelo felt Hamelin brace himself for the interview, and Llelo took a deep breath as well.

At the sight of the young men, however, Harold stopped pacing and turned to look at them. As usual, his first words were directed at Hamelin. "My lord, what brings you here in this grave hour?"

Hamelin gestured, again making sure that Llelo preceded him. If he kept it up, Llelo might start to believe he really respected him. On impulse Llelo stuck out his arm. "I am Llelo ap Gareth. My father is captain of the guard for Prince Hywel of Gwynedd."

To his credit, Harold didn't hesitate and grasped Llelo's forearm. "Harold Edgarson, at your service."

"You're Saxon?"

"Are you surprised to see one rise so high in Earl Robert's service? Out here, we're all English. Earl Robert rewarded those who were capable. I'm hoping his son will do the same."

"We have been charged with speaking to the guards about the circumstances surrounding Sir Aubrey's death," Llelo said.

Harold sighed. "If I'd been doing my job, Aubrey would still be alive, but as it is ..." He sat heavily in his chair.

Llelo stood awkwardly before him, disconcerted by the man's frankness. "May I ask you to elaborate?"

"He was only crossing that courtyard to check up on me."

"Because ..." Llelo left his question deliberately hanging.

"Because I was drinking too much. Although now I'm not, Aubrey wanted to be sure." He snorted. "Are you surprised I admit this openly? Some would tell me to keep my mouth shut, but I know the prince is asking questions, and I will answer them. In truth, I don't see what there is to investigate. Nobody could have stopped that stone from falling."

"While that is true, we must still inquire." Hamelin shot a look at Llelo, asking permission to say more. "Nobody reported that part of the stonework as weak?"

"Not to me—and evidently not to Sir Aubrey either."

"We'd like to ask each of your men in turn if they saw anyone on the wall-walk before the meeting," Llelo said, "or if any strangers entered the castle in the hours beforehand."

Harold narrowed his eyes at Llelo. "Other than you?"

It was a fair point, and Llelo raised his eyebrows to acknowledge it. "Other than us."

"Why does it matter?"

Llelo thought it was obvious, but he answered anyway, just to make everything as clear as possible. "In case someone made the stone fall." He left off the *of course*. It was on the tip of his tongue, but he managed to keep it back at the last moment.

Harold studied his face. "You think this was murder too? Bad enough to spread the rumor that Earl Robert was killed." Men like Harold were the foundation of any baron's retinue. He showed all deference to those in authority above him, but he had clear opinions, which most often he was forced to keep to himself. It was a wise lord who listened to such a man when he talked.

In this instance, however, Harold was Earl William's man, not Prince Henry's, and if he was as loyal to William as he'd been to Robert, the flash of disdain could have been for Prince Henry's suspicions—or equally for Henry himself.

Llelo pressed his lips together for a moment, debating how to respond. Harold was an established soldier akin to Evan. He wouldn't look on a fifteen-year-old boy as someone with any authority or wisdom. Still, it was Llelo's job to ask questions, and for that reason, he had to continue. It wouldn't do to go back to his father with his questions unasked. "It is not my place to believe or disbelieve. Prince Henry asked us to investigate, and that is what we are doing."

Harold's expression cleared, and he sat up straighter. "Quite right."

"May we speak to those on duty this morning?" Hamelin asked.

They were back to Harold's initial regrets. "Nobody was on any parapet but those above the main gatehouses. The meeting was for a quarter-hour only," he added, somewhat defensively.

"This meeting occurs every day at the same time?" Llelo asked, just to confirm what Thomas had told them.

"It does, and before you imply that no soldier should be such a creature of habit, this routine was condoned by both Earl Robert and Sir Aubrey. They agreed that the benefit of having every man aware of his tasks and coordinated with every other on duty was worth the slight chance of mischief." He grunted. "I will be sorry if it cost Sir Aubrey his life."

"The mason says the stone was deliberately loosened," Hamelin said. "It *was* murder."

Llelo's mouth dropped open. He hadn't remembered to tell Hamelin that important information like that should be held back if at all possible.

The color drained from Harold's face. "You tell me truly?"

"Yes." Llelo tried not to glare at Hamelin, but his shoulders had stiffened. "Though I can also say that if a killer is determined, he will find a way. The quarter of an hour was opportunity, nothing more. Sir Aubrey could just as likely have been set upon in a dark alley in the town, or in his chambers, or in some other circumstance."

Harold tapped the tips of his fingers on the table before him. "It is common knowledge that I pull most of the men off the battlements for our meeting. The fact that I do it every day—three times a day, in fact—is beside the point." He paused. "Or maybe that *is* the point."

Llelo knew he had to tread lightly, and he constructed his next question carefully in his head before he asked it. "Any good captain calls his men together daily to assign duties."

"Of course they do, or I wouldn't have done it!" Harold was on his feet again, back to pacing. He threw out a hand. "Excuses after the fact are worthless, I know, but if I had any defense, it is that we have done this for years, particularly since Earl Robert returned from his captivity. We have lost so many men." He shook his head. "These boys are young, untrained. They need guidance." He looked up. "In a way, I'm glad they were all here, so none can be blamed."

Llelo wanted to say that his father was not one to accuse a man without evidence, but he didn't think Harold was listening to him anymore.

"And, of course, we did it for Sir Aubrey."

Llelo blinked. "I'm sorry. Why would that be?" According to the guard—and by Harold's own surprising admission—they'd done it for Harold.

"He—" Harold stopped, his eyes flicking from Llelo to Hamelin and back again. "You don't know?"

Llelo spread his hands wide. "No."

"Sir Aubrey's wits weren't ... as sharp as they used to be. It was helpful to him to have the castle run on a strict schedule, unchanging, even."

Llelo rubbed his chin. "He was having trouble with his memory?"

"Yes." Harold looked relieved that Llelo had spoken straightforwardly, and with that business done, he turned to Hamelin. "I have doubled the watch and the guards around the prince. I have already spoken to Charles, and he will personally taste any dish that reaches the prince's table. Accidents or murders, we don't want any more."

Hamelin canted his head. "Thank you. I hadn't thought of it."

Harold gritted his teeth. "It is my place to think of it, though I would never have imagined such precautions necessary inside the castle."

Llelo would have thought it was precisely his job to imagine those very things, but instead of saying so, he cleared his throat, wanting to get back to Sir Aubrey. "Do you have any further thoughts about what happened today—or these other deaths, for that matter?"

Harold shook his head. "No, and none of the men in my charge do either. They're good lads, if young."

"How much interaction did they have with Sir Aubrey or the earl's servants?"

Harold's chin firmed. "I know the prince believes murder happened here, but Earl Robert died after being ill for most of this past year. His maid died because her heart gave out; and Bernard drowned."

"Have such a string of deaths ever happened before at Bristol?" Llelo asked.

Harold didn't like the question. He was on the edge of patience. "No." He flicked his fingers. "It is a run of bad luck, I do admit, but nothing that should cause such alarm in the prince. He has many other concerns that should have his attention, surely."

Llelo tried a different tack. "You are a soldier, sir, and responsible for many men. If several died within weeks of each other, even if all really were accidents, your men might grow concerned that God was punishing them or something wasn't right at Bristol. Wouldn't you see it as your duty to dispel their concerns?"

"Perhaps." Harold pressed his lips together. "The people *are* uneasy."

"That's all this is," Hamelin stepped in. "Bristol is a stronghold from which Prince Henry intends to retake England for his mother. If the people here are fearful, their uncertainties could spread to his other allies. Any rumor that his mother has given up her claim or that our advantages will no longer be pressed must be squelched immediately."

"That does make a certain amount of sense. It is well that the prince is thinking so far ahead." Harold's eyes turned thoughtful. "Very well—I will make inquiries among my men."

Llelo risked asking one more question. "Were any missing from duty today?"

"Yes." Harold was back to frowning, though this time not at Llelo. "The garrison is large, so I call out their names. We were missing only one this morning: George, whose grandfather died yesterday—not at the castle," he hastened to add. "He's been ailing and was almost eighty. He lived in the town with George's sister ..." His voice trailed off.

Llelo looked at him curiously. "Is there something else?"

"This past hour, I did a circuit of the walls, reassuring the men. Aelfric wasn't at his post, and nobody could tell me where he'd gone, though I know for certain he was here at the morning meeting."

If Aelfric had been at the meeting, he wasn't on the battlement tipping off the stone. But if Llelo had learned anything during his years as his father's apprentice, it was to record every detail and make sense of them later. "Please let me know if you find him, Sir Harold."

"He couldn't have had anything to do with Sir Aubrey's death," Harold protested.

Llelo looked directly at him. "But he could know something or someone who does—and for some reason may not want to tell us."

"Because he's protecting a villain?" Harold grimaced. "I admit he never has been the most reliable of my men."

A bell tolled above them in the gatehouse, echoing others more distant. Harold looked up at the sound. "I have my own duties to attend to." He put his heels together and bowed slightly at the waist in Hamelin's direction. "My lord." He departed.

"Means, motive, and opportunity," Hamelin said.

Llelo turned to him. "What was that?" He'd heard those words strung together before, though in Welsh and coming, if he remembered correctly, from Evan.

"It just occurred to me that a murderer needs each of these three things in order to kill someone. He has to have the ability to murder, a reason to do so, and a chance to commit a crime. In a way it's a blessing that we can eliminate all the guards, because that's a large number of people to question. It can't be Sir Harold either, whatever we think of his methods." Hamelin's expression turned thoughtful. "Who knew that Bristol Castle had so many undercurrents within it? How could I have been so unobservant? Why does nobody tell me these things?"

"The line between nobleman and servant is sharp and deep, but murder cuts across all groups and classes. I should warn you that it exposes secrets too. Look what we've discovered about both Harold and Aubrey that in the course of our normal lives we would have had no business knowing. And I assure you, what we've learned so far is only the beginning."

9

Gwen

Eventually Mabel's sobs lessened, at which point her lady-in-waiting returned, bringing another cup of wine. After some coaxing, Gwen convinced Mabel to drink it.

Like Mabel, this servant was in her middle forties, though unlike Mabel, her hair remained a rich brown, a match to her eyes which watched Gwen appraisingly. High-ranking noblewomen surrounded themselves with women of a slightly lower station. Often they were either unmarried maids or widows.

"I'm Eva," the woman said, meeting Gwen's gaze. "Can you help me get her to her chamber and bed?"

"Of course."

The weeping had made Mabel more human and softer, but not so much that she didn't raise her head to complain to Gwen again: "Your presence at Bristol is wholly unnecessary. I will speak to my nephew about it."

"As you wish, of course," Gwen said, mindful of what she'd said to Llelo earlier that morning about not rising to anyone's bait and hoping he was faring better than she. She looked at Eva over the top of Mabel's head and was heartened by Eva's apologetic and rueful expression.

"I am pleased to make your acquaintance, madam," Eva said.

But Mabel turned to look at Eva. "And where were you this morning when I needed you?"

"I was seeing to your breakfast, my lady."

Lady Mabel harrumphed. "Seeing to that Robert Fitzharding, I expect."

Eva's face flushed, prompting Gwen to look quickly down at her toes. Lady Mabel's comment had hit the center of the target.

Mabel's face was blotchy from crying, but she managed a sniff. "You are forgiven, and we will speak no more of it."

Once Mabel was settled in her bed, Eva moved with Gwen towards the doorway. "Thank you for your assistance. She needed a woman's shoulder to cry on, and for some reason, she refuses to show weakness in front of me."

Gwen canted her head, hoping for more, and Eva obliged. "My husband died two years ago. He was many years older than I, so it was not as surprising a death as Earl Robert's. Lady Mabel knows it was not a love match, so she believes I don't understand her loss. But nobody can reach my age without losing someone." She studied Gwen. "I see you have as well."

"My mother, at my brother's birth."

They were in the doorway, and Gwen could tell that Eva was ready for her to leave, but she hesitated, not wanting to lose the moment of intimacy. "Do you know anything about these deaths?"

Eva pressed her lips together for a moment before speaking. "Nothing that will help you. The maidservant and valet lived belowstairs, and we didn't mingle. Sir Aubrey was a fine man. I had hoped in time—" She broke off, shaking her head.

"You knew him well?"

"Of course. We often sat together in the hall of an evening, and for a while we were drawn together in mutual loss." At Gwen's questioning look, she added, "His wife died earlier this spring."

"You hoped to marry him?"

"Oh no! You misunderstand me."

Gwen bent her head. "My apologies."

At first, Gwen thought the problem was that it had been too bold a question, but then Eva said, "I know you didn't misunderstand my lady's barb about Robert. He and I are courting, but given the mourning throughout the castle, we felt that it was inappropriate to be seen together in public until several more months had passed. I was thinking of introducing Sir Aubrey to my sister."

Gwen smiled gently. "I apologize for prying." She met Eva's gaze and saw a flicker, deep down, of something more—an emotion that she quickly suppressed. Lady Mabel wasn't the only woman whose heart was troubled today. So Gwen took a chance and pressed Eva's hand for a moment. "I'm sorry also for your loss."

"Earl Robert was a great friend." Something eased a bit around Eva's eyes. "I must see to my lady."

"Of course." Gwen stepped back so Eva could shut the door to the chamber.

Alone in the corridor, she leaned back against the wall and closed her eyes. She was exhausted; it was well past noon, and she'd gone without her noonday meal on a day on which a man had died; and they had three other deaths to investigate. And still, she stayed where she was, doing none of the things she should, particularly rescuing Gareth from caring for Taran for too long. She tipped her head, listening for any wailing in the distance, no matter how faint, indicating he wanted to nurse again, and heard nothing. Maybe she still had a little time.

Mabel's room was located two floors above and on the opposite side of the keep from the great hall, which made it a quieter spot than almost any other room in the castle. Earl Robert's chambers now belonged to William, the new earl, but these were currently occupied by the prince. That fact may have contributed to William's decision to take himself elsewhere rather than witness his place usurped, even by the possible future King of England. William had to have resented his father's birth, bastard to old King Henry, knowing that, had things fallen differently, William himself would have been king instead of his cousin.

There was a difference, too, between the lot of a firstborn son, like Henry or William, and a son who had an inheritance thrust upon him, like Hywel. Rhun, Hywel's elder brother, had been a remarkable man and would have made a great King of Gwynedd, but a second son who never imagined he would rule, who labored in the shadow of his older brother, sometimes brought something special to the role. King Owain had been such a son. Gwen had never met William, but she suspected he was less like Roger, the only brother she'd met, and more like Prince Henry: an eldest son groomed to rule and taught to be protective of his rights and privileges.

That left Roger, the younger second son, in an uncertain position. It was he to whom Gwen wanted to speak, if she could find him. And then, as if on command, Charles came up the stairs. At the sight of Gwen, his face took on an expression of concern. "All is not well?"

"Lady Mabel has retired," Gwen said. "I was hoping you could point me to where I might find Lord Roger."

"In the chapel, my lady." He paused. "Might I be of assistance?"

"Not to me, thank you, but you might ask Eva if Lady Mabel needs anything."

Charles bent his head in a bow. "Of course." He hurried past her towards Lady Mabel's door.

For Gwen's part, as Charles had promised, she found Roger settled on a bench in the middle of the chapel. He was the only person present, and she made sure the leather sole of her shoe scraped loudly on the threshold as she entered.

He didn't turn around, but still said, "You may come in, Gwen."

Surprised and more than a little disconcerted that he recognized her without looking at her, she came forward to sit on a bench opposite him, though facing the altar and the stained glass rose window above it. "How did you know it was I?"

"Your footfalls are surprisingly heavy for such a small person, and I noted your passing with my mother earlier. Thank you, by the way, for caring for her."

Gwen was uncertain what the correct response should be beyond, "You're welcome."

"How may I help you?"

"These deaths—"

"Ah, yes. My cousin's suspicions have been confirmed, do you think?"

"That's what we are here to find out." Gwen wasn't sure what to make of Roger's droll tone. He was very young, younger than she was, but he spoke with the voice of a much older man. Normans grew up quickly, forced to do so by their education and training, even if convention dictated that manhood began at twenty-one. Admittedly, the rule was routinely overlooked or outright ignored, especially in those who were worthy of a man's responsibilities earlier.

Hamelin had given her a similar impression, though he didn't seem to be as quick-witted as Roger. In fact, now that she thought about it, Roger shared some of the same characteristics as Prince Rhys of Deheubarth, also a younger son. Though, on short acquaintance, Gwen liked Rhys much better. Roger was less sincere, with a far sharper tongue, to the point of being cunning or shrewd. If Hywel had been raised with less laughter, he might have become like this man.

"You don't believe he's right?" Gwen asked.

Roger gave her a withering look, the implication being that the very act of speaking to her at all was a gift, but that he wouldn't bestow it any longer if she continued to be so daft. "My cousin carries a great weight on his shoulders. Sometimes he is prone to … extravagances."

Gwen stared at him, shocked by this frank admission. Roger was the prince's steward and by rights should be the most loyal of his companions.

"Why do you think my cousin summoned you?"

Gwen thought back to the conversation with Henry. He claimed Earl Robert had spoken of Gareth often. And since Roger had been so rude to her, she decided she wasn't ready to answer directly. "You genuinely don't know?"

Instead of showing offense, Roger laughed. "Your skills as an investigator are renowned throughout Britain, and you saved my cousin's life three years ago. Yes, that is why. But I worry that there's another reason, which Henry has not confided in me. I cannot lose his confidence." He lifted his chin to point at Gwen. "What say you?"

Gwen forced herself not to swallow hard and decided again to be honest. "He called for us because we do not serve anyone here."

"Because you are Welsh? Surely not." Roger's scorn was plain.

"More than that, we stand outside any lord's purview."

Roger grunted, for once not arguing. "Henry is not blind to the way this war between his mother and Stephen has torn England apart. It has divided families, pitting father against son and brother against brother. It's been wasteful and bloody. Do you know how many unauthorized castles have been built in the last eight years?" He didn't pause for Gwen to respond but went on as if she had. "At least a hundred." Roger frowned. "You have confirmed my fears. Henry doesn't trust me. He doesn't trust anyone here."

Gwen again found herself in the strange position of comforting a member of this noble family. "Perhaps it is more that he wanted someone who wasn't beholden to him? He sees the value of independent intelligence."

"Few lords would agree." Roger was morose now.

Gwen didn't add that her own lord valued independent thought and rewarded those who spoke truth, despite risk of censure.

Heavy boots sounded in the corridor outside the chapel.

"Go." Roger made a quick motion with his hand, shooing Gwen towards a narrow staircase that led to a gallery above the chapel for the private worship of the lord or his lady when even the keep's chapel was too exposed, and a lord needed complete peace to pray.

Roger was used to being the authority and giving orders, and Gwen responded to him accordingly, without really thinking about it. Even though she was deeply offended—as well as fascinated and appalled—by his manner, she obeyed, hastening up the steps. Roger didn't want to be seen with her, that was for certain.

She reached the top step, to find herself in a little alcove that was hidden from the view of anyone below, and scurried forward to take a quick look down the adjacent passage. It led to an upstairs corridor.

Then she returned to the alcove, her ears perked and listening, and peered around the pillar. The chapel was lit only by the candles on the altar and whatever light was coming through the rose window, so it was dim at the back. She couldn't mistake the shape of Robert Fitzharding, however, when he strode into the room as if born to rule it.

Roger stood up to face Fitzharding, straightening his tunic with a jerk, and giving no indication that Gwen was still present ...

except for the flicking out of his right forefinger, just once. She wasn't sure if his intent was to order her to leave entirely or simply a warning to remain quiet. At this point, she wasn't going to leave, but she did shrink back, pressing herself to the wall of the corridor. She wasn't worried about being able to hear what they were about to say below her, since the acoustics in the chapel were excellent, and voices echoed. The Normans didn't have music in their souls like Welshmen did, but they did know how to construct a room for singing.

"You did the right thing to send for me," Fitzharding began.

"I hope it isn't too late, Robert. Henry respects you. He'll listen to you. You must go to him and stop this madness. My father must be rolling over in his grave."

"I have met the investigators. Welsh." If Fitzharding hadn't been in a chapel, Gwen had the sense he might have spat on the ground. "What could Henry be thinking?"

"They saved his life three years ago."

Fitzharding didn't respond out loud to that, and Gwen was tempted to peer around the corner. She imagined he was sneering, but without being able to watch his face and motions, she couldn't clearly tell what he was thinking, and she could be wrong. His French might be saying one thing and his face another.

"As it is," Roger said without giving Gwen further insight into what Fitzharding's actual response had been, "they appear well on their way to poking their noses into everybody's business. And now the woman, Gwen, has found favor with my mother."

Is that what she'd done? Gwen almost guffawed at the characterization. If that was favor, she would hate to see censure.

Fitzharding made a sound of disgust. "It is unconscionable that she would take advantage of a grieving widow."

"Advantage or not, she was just here, by all appearances prepared to ask *me* questions."

"Did you answer?"

"Of course not! I sent her away."

Gwen felt her eyes widen at this bit of subterfuge, because Roger had to know that she hadn't left. He had to. *Didn't he?*

"Good." The sound of someone—Fitzharding, she presumed—sitting heavily on one of the benches echoed in the chapel. "It would be a mistake to allow such people to act above their station."

Gwen would have loved to reveal herself, if only to wipe away the superior smirk that she just knew was on Fitzharding's face. Despite her best efforts to remain serene, he raised her hackles. But while he didn't like Welshmen, it didn't make him a murderer.

Now the heavy tread of a man's boots echoed on the floor, and Gwen risked a peek around the corner, thinking that someone new had come in, but it was only Roger, who'd started to pace. His head remained down, so he didn't see her, and Fitzharding's back was to the alcove.

"The problem, Robert, is that with Sir Aubrey's death, I'm beginning to have doubts. These accidents aren't looking so much like accidents anymore. What if someone did murder my father? What if Henry is right?"

"He isn't." Fitzharding had a deep voice. If he'd been a bard he might have been a bass. And then, more softly—"You really are worried, aren't you?"

Roger may have nodded, which Gwen couldn't see, since she'd withdrawn her head again, and then Fitzharding added, "If foul play is taking place in the castle, it should not be these outsiders who see to it. Henry should have appointed me and my men to oversee such an all-encompassing investigation. It makes no sense he brought in interlopers from Gwynedd. The Welsh should never be so encouraged."

If Gwen heard one more disparaging comment about her people she was going to hit something. Almost worse was how casual everyone was about it—as if the idea that all Welsh people were lazy, insubordinate, good-for-nothing cretins was a matter of common knowledge.

Of course, she didn't shriek, curse, or in any other way indicate her unhappiness. Instead, she clenched her hands into fists and thought of her counsel to Llelo.

"You are right, of course." Now Roger's voice was soothing. "But we tried to talk to him, and you know how he gets."

"He's as stubborn as his mother."

"We can try again, if you think it might help," Roger said.

Fitzharding grunted. "I fear it might do more harm than good."

"Perhaps the prince would be willing to have you work alongside this Gareth."

"I spoke to the man." Fitzharding sneered again. "His French is barely passable."

"I understood him fine." Roger's tone became heavy, his disapproval plain. In the course of a quarter of an hour, the young lord had been disdainful, welcoming, conspiratorial, dismissive, and now disapproving—and oddly, this time, not towards Gareth or Gwen.

Gwen had no idea what to make of someone so changeable. She had no idea what Roger's real thoughts were—or those of any of these Englishmen—but as she stayed in the shadows and tried not to breathe loudly, waiting for the men to leave, she grew more certain that Roger had wanted her to overhear his conversation with Fitzharding. And that meant she should believe everything—or nothing—either of them had said.

10

Gareth

"Don't Englishmen ever hold their children?" Gareth spoke in an undertone to Gruffydd after yet another woman had come up to him to coo at baby Taran. He and Gruffydd had settled themselves on a bench that put their backs to the outside of the inner curtain wall and allowed them to watch the gatehouse that guarded the way between the inner and outer wards to their right, and also the gate to the town to their left. He hoped that whenever Gwen finished with Lady Mabel, this might be one of the first places she'd pass in looking for him.

The location was also a good spot to observe some of the daily activity in the castle. People constantly moved in and out of both gates, which were left open, bustling from the craft halls to the keep, to the stables, into town, and back again. Though he'd felt a few drops of rain earlier, the sun had come out from behind the clouds, and he was almost too warm in his armor and cloak. He checked Taran's fingers and toes and found them warm too.

The child was particularly bright-eyed, his face surprisingly full of expression for one so young, and he held his head up as well as many babies several months older. His favorite position when Gareth held him was face down along Gareth's left arm, a pose that seemed to ease any tightness in the baby's belly. None of the women liked to see Gareth hold him that way, however, and each approached, hands out, and took Taran from him.

Gareth held his son often—much of the night sleeping with him on his chest when he wasn't nursing—so he didn't resent the women's fussing. Instead, he used it as an opportunity to question them about where they were when Sir Aubrey died. To a woman, they could tell him nothing. Like the first woman who'd stumbled on Aubrey's body, and whom Gareth had questioned at the scene, none had seen the stone fall. None had anything but praise for any of the people who'd died, particularly Sir Aubrey. If he'd had a wandering eye or hand, they didn't know—or weren't going to tell Gareth—about it. He tried to get a sense of Sir Aubrey's character, but the most anyone would say was that he was *stern but fair* and *always put the interests of Earl Robert first.*

Gareth could have guessed that, actually, seeing as how Aubrey had held his position at the castle for more than twenty years. It stood to reason and was the one bit of information he heard from them that he didn't think was either a half-truth or outright lie. All of the women also knew the maidservant who'd died on the floor of Earl Robert's room, and their words when they described her were equally full of platitudes.

She was lovely, that one, never an unkind word to say about anyone.

Busy, busy, busy, that's what she was. You could never get her to sit down for a moment.

"How was she with the earl?"

"Oh, he loved her. Always so helpful she was," one woman said.

"What about her husband?" he asked.

The same woman tsked through her teeth. "A good worker, wasn't he? And not an unkind bone in his body."

And so it went. None could give an explanation for why the maidservant had died, other than the sudden onset of illness, though all agreed that she hadn't been ill that day that they knew. As an assistant washerwoman reluctantly handed back the baby, having given them no new information, Gruffydd shook his head and said, "This is getting us nowhere."

"A negative answer is still an answer." Gareth eyed a young woman about his age coming towards them lugging a box, which turned out to be full of candle stubs. At the sight of Taran, she smiled and hitched the box higher on her hip so she could kiss the baby's head.

She didn't compliment the child on his handsomeness, however, nor try to take him from Gareth. Instead, she said under her breath, "I have something to tell you, but not here. I'll meet you in the church in the outer ward when the bell at St. James's Priory tolls for None." And then, with a nod, she walked off.

None was the mid-afternoon vigil kept by the monks at the priory. Gareth didn't think King Owain was any less devout than the next man, but his castles didn't keep time by the bells the way Bristol did, making him think that Earl Robert must have been very pious indeed. Admittedly, Gareth hadn't been to more than a handful of Norman castles, so maybe this was normal for them—and Bristol certainly had a huge number of churches. It could simply be they rang so often that the bells became the easiest way for the residents of town and castle to keep track of the day.

Gruffydd, however, was frowning. "Her words implied that she was concerned someone might see her speaking to us, but she had no fear in her otherwise."

Gareth's eyes went to the woman's back. Her hips swung suggestively, in a way that might have left Gwen grinding her teeth. The woman knew her own beauty—and was pleased to have men watching her.

Gruffydd nudged Gareth's elbow. "It isn't just us. Others watch too. I had thought, because of the angle, they were looking at us, but now I don't think so."

"Are *you* interested?" Gareth said.

Gruffydd scoffed. "In a Saxon girl? Hardly!"

Gareth grinned and looked away, up to the ramparts and towers above them. Then he frowned too because out of the corner of his eye, he'd caught a glimpse of someone ducking behind a merlon and a second man whisking around the corner of a building. "I'm not so sure you're right." He turned slightly and moved more into the shadow of the inner curtain wall. "If they're watching the woman, there would be no need to hide, would there?"

Gruffydd scratched the back of his head and casually turned this way and that, stretching. "I see them. Who is it, do you think, that doesn't trust us?"

"Could be individual curiosity." So far, Gareth hadn't felt any menace towards him and his family. And though the English disparaged his people at every turn, given that he and Gwen had Prince Henry's countenance, it should be obvious even to an English villain that if any of their party were harmed in any way, it would shine a beacon directly on the investigation. In the past, culprits who'd gone after him or Gwen in an attempt to silence them had ended up only exposing themselves.

So far, Gareth hadn't had the sense with these deaths that the man responsible was anxious to stick out his neck. The very fact that the deaths were made to look like accidents implied that the villain much preferred to watch and wait.

"I know what you're thinking," Gruffydd said.

"What's that?" Gareth's eyes traveled along the battlement, still trying to discern the faces of the men patrolling them.

"Why kill Sir Aubrey?"

"Why does one person ever kill another?" Gareth said, and then answered his own question, "Because he hopes to gain something from it, whether that be revenge, wealth, or freedom, from something or someone, or for something or someone. I was just telling myself that if he knew what was good for him, the murderer will be long gone by now—but if he has resorted to murder, likely he *hasn't* achieved his goal and is still here."

That was one reason Gruffydd was mortared to Gareth's side, of course, and why they were loitering in the ward waiting for Gwen to appear, so that she wasn't left on her own inside or outside the castle. Bad enough he had to leave her with Lady Mabel, who presumably wouldn't throw her in irons the moment Gareth's back was turned. So far, Gareth had been frustrated by the behavior of the people he'd encountered. He didn't trust any of them and was starting to regret bringing his family here.

He moved away from the wall a few steps to give himself a better view of the gate through which Gwen would come. It wouldn't make Gwen appear sooner, but it made him feel better that he would see her the moment she did. It was time his wife was back with him. If nothing else, Taran would grow restless soon. He was tethered to his mother by an invisible thread that Gareth didn't pretend to understand, but one he didn't have to understand to respect.

At two months old, Taran was still in the easily-portable stage of infancy, though it was also a time that required the constant attention of his mother. Fortunately, he was a good eater, and already his arms and legs revealed a strength and heft to them that boded well for the future. They had been thankful to avoid the croup, but Gareth had hope that had he sickened, Taran would have been healthy enough to survive it.

And before the baby could actually complain, Gwen herself appeared from underneath the gatehouse and arrived, breathless, in front of Gareth. He mutely held out Taran to her, and she took him into her arms. She kissed the baby's cheek and then snuggled him against her chest, breathing deeply.

"And all is right with the world," Gruffydd said, under his breath.

He wasn't wrong. Gareth had watched the reunion between mother and child a thousand times, and the relief for both was always unmistakable—until the child was old enough to think himself above it. That too passed, eventually. Even Dai, when he saw his mother these days, tended to wrap his arms around her waist at his initial greeting.

Gwen looked up from the baby. "People are talking to me. It's astounding!"

"Then you've had far more luck than I," Gareth said, somewhat morosely.

Gwen gestured with one hand. "It's your station, I think. I'm more of an outsider with no power and no hope of ever having any in this world. Maybe people feel they can be honest with me in a way they can't with anyone else, especially on such short acquaintance."

"Someone did just come forward," Gruffydd said, still from his position against the wall, and told her about the upcoming meeting with the woman in the church.

Gwen responded by telling them first about her meeting with Mabel and Eva, and then about the visit in the chapel with Roger and Robert Fitzharding.

"I wish these Normans would stop giving every child born the same name. There are altogether too many Roberts, Rogers, Henrys, and Williams to keep track of."

Gareth laughed. "Without a doubt they say the same thing about us."

Gruffydd snorted too. "That's why we have Rhys Goch, Rhys Fychan, and Rhys Fadog."

Gareth tipped his chin to indicate their son. "We named Taran for a man still living."

"There are no others though," she said, a bit defiantly.

"We may be here for a while," Gareth said. "It's too early to be complaining about Norman customs."

"It's hard not to, especially when they are so very difficult to comprehend." She shook her head. "Other than Eva's lover and possibly the next castle steward, who is this Fitzharding? He spoke formally at first with Roger, but they were familiar with each other too."

"His father was the King's Reeve in Bristol, and Robert has built on his inherited successes. A few years ago, he founded the Augustinian Abbey here in Bristol." Gareth pursed his lips. "As a Saxon, he's one of the few whose family retained their noble status after the Normans conquered England."

"He doesn't like that we're here." She paused. "He was friendly enough earlier over the body, when he was with Charles, but it was a two-faced deception. I don't know if it's because he doesn't want us investigating these deaths or if he just hates Welshmen."

"Or both," Gruffydd said.

"The fact that we're Welsh may only be an excuse," Gareth said. "It sounds like he thinks he should be the investigator instead. We are stepping on his toes and getting in the way of him finding favor with Prince Henry or Earl William."

"It seems to be the only thing anyone cares about," Gwen said.

"Men look to please Prince Hywel," Gareth said mildly.

"To some degree—and more now than when he was only the second son, but it isn't the same. We treat him with deference, but does anybody follow him blindly? We owe him our loyalty, but we expect the same loyalty in return. Even the lowest peasant knows he's under Hywel's protection, and we are all bound together by laws and family bonds. But here—" she adjusted Taran on her shoulder and patted his back, "The power the king wields has no check. The lords know it, and they know that if Prince Henry eventually becomes king, he will reward those who stood by him and punish those who doubted."

Gareth still had vivid memories of King Owain throwing *him* into a cell for a crime he didn't commit, merely because the king was in a temper, but he didn't speak of it. Gwen was right, in the main. These Normans had banned outright slavery, but Gareth had never seen more slavish behavior than in a Norman keep. The vast majority of the people of England were bound to the king with bonds that went only one way—up to the king.

Over the years, Gareth had come to understand the great power a lord in England wielded as compared to the power of a nobleman in Wales—meaning Gwen wasn't wrong. For a prince such as Henry—or an earl like William—their authority was all-encompassing. Once they achieved their maturity, their every wish could be granted, every desire sated, were they the type of person to demand it. The people they ruled had no recourse but to obey, for the English system of laws said the king *was* the law.

In addition, as farmers rather than herders, the people didn't move about like the Welsh did, so their dwellings, their churches, and their villages had a strange permanence to them. They were bound to one land and to one man. Even a young man such as Henry, who as of yet had accomplished very little except to be the son of a claimant to the English throne, was treated with a deference that was unknown even to the King of Gwynedd.

Gareth couldn't imagine any Welsh baron accepting the kind of capriciousness from their king that was normal in England and France. In Wales, the priests said every man was responsible for his own soul. In England, the king was responsible for all his subjects' souls. To excommunicate him put the entire country under interdict. What Welshman would stand for that? It was no wonder men like Robert Fitzharding resented an outsider like Gareth, who was his own man always, regardless of whom he served.

A shout came from directly above them, "Gareth!"

He turned to see Steffan gesturing from the wall-walk of the outer curtain wall.

"Something you should see." Then he indicated that they should look towards the gatehouse between the two outer wards.

All three of them groaned, worried about who might have died, but as they hastened towards where Steffan pointed, Cadoc came off the wall near the middle gatehouse to meet them, Aron in tow. "Did Steffan tell you?"

"Only that we should look," Gareth said.

"Probably best he didn't shout it from the top of the rampart. An ambassador from King Stephen has come." Cadoc pointed with his chin towards the far outer ward. "He's progressing towards the keep now."

"Anyone we know?" Gruffydd said.

Cadoc puffed out a breath. "Oh, I think so. It's Cadwaladr."

11

Gareth

It was the first time any of them had seen Cadwaladr since his men had killed Rhun—a year ago now almost to the day. The sight of him riding across the ward towards the keep as if he belonged—and surrounded by what appeared to be an honor guard—threatened to upend any hard-won equilibrium Gareth had managed to acquire in the intervening year. The fact that Cadwaladr had tried to murder Gareth himself was by now beside the point.

Gwen gripped his upper arm tightly. "I'm here. We are all here, and we're not going anywhere."

"Who are those men with him?" Gareth asked Cadoc through gritted teeth.

Nothing flustered Cadoc, and he answered with equanimity. "They belong to King Stephen."

"Why would King Stephen send Cadwaladr anywhere at his behest?" Those were the words he spoke, but it wasn't the real question going through Gareth's head, which was more of a wailing *why is he here?*

Or even, *I'm going to kill him. How many of you are with me?*

"Say the word, my lord, and I'll take him down." Cadoc fingered the point of one of his arrows, which he'd removed from his quiver without Gareth noticing.

For a moment, Gareth's breath caught in his throat, fearing Cadoc's sentence was in response to Gareth's own thoughts said out loud, but he hadn't, in fact, articulated what he was thinking. He hadn't needed to.

It was Aron, typically, who answered the question Gareth had asked aloud. "King Stephen sent Cadwaladr to Bristol to make use of him." He canted his head. "And to get rid of him."

Gareth turned to Aron, wanting to shout at him, or shake him, or punch him for speaking so calmly when Gareth was still so full of rage it was coloring his vision red. He may never have felt so angry in his life.

Aron stood his ground, and Gruffydd stepped between them. "This is not Aron's doing, Gareth. Take a step back."

His friends were holding their breaths, and Gwen still held his arm. The love in her face almost undid him more than the sight of Cadwaladr. Gareth's vision blurred, and instead of shouting or punching or strangling Cadwaladr with his bare hands, he took in a great, shuddering breath. "Forgive me, Aron."

Everyone eased off their ready stances.

Gareth had thought he'd see pity in their eyes as he apologized again, but Gruffydd said, speaking for everyone, "Cadwaladr is a rabid dog who should have been put down long ago. We all know it, and every one of us would help you do it, even though we ourselves might be imprisoned or killed for the offense. But you know our lord's mind. If anyone has the right to Cadwaladr's life, it is Hywel."

The thought of what Prince Hywel would be feeling were he here with them calmed Gareth further and made him intensely thankful that the prince remained at Aberystwyth. The sight of Cadwaladr had almost driven Gareth mad. Hywel might have more self-control, but he'd fought long and hard for internal sanity—if not peace—with his brother's death. Someday he would confront Cadwaladr again, but it didn't need to be today.

Gwen looked first at Gareth and then around at every man. "For now, if any of us were even to touch Cadwaladr, the consequences could be far worse than leaving him alive."

"I know." Gareth put a fist to his forehead, working on settling his breathing now that his mind had begun to work again. He'd never been this out of control before.

Immediately after Rhun's death, he'd had to be strong for Hywel. That was the image of himself he had in his head. And although during this past year the grief at Rhun's loss blindsided him every so often, though less and less as the months had passed, it had never been to the point of loss of control. It was his job to rein Hywel in—or Gruffydd—not the other way around.

One more breath and Gareth was able to ask Aron evenly, "You think Stephen has sent Cadwaladr to Bristol to use him, and yet at the same time to get rid of him? How can it be both?"

"Cadwaladr was a thorn in King Owain's side long before the war in Deheubarth and your service to him, Gareth. Even when Cadwaladr is on his best behavior, we all know what he's like."

"Boastful," Gruffydd said. "Always going on about his accomplishments, his rights, and his privileges."

"A liar and a traitor," Gwen said. "He will tell you one thing to your face and turn around the next day—the next hour—and do the exact opposite if it serves him better. Or even tell you that he will support a particular move and then, when you make that move, deny ever promising anything."

"King Stephen had to have noticed this by now," Aron said. "Earl Ranulf, before this latest betrayal, may even have told him of their dealings."

"But why entrust Cadwaladr with a message to Henry if he knows he's untrustworthy?" Gareth felt he ought to know the answer, but he supposed his mind still wasn't functioning properly.

Aron answered without judgement. "The king is a powerful man in the midst of a war, even if outright warfare is currently in abeyance. Taking Cadwaladr's side against Owain is utterly out of the question, because Owain is the only thing keeping the lords of the March from expanding their reach into Wales. Stephen can't countenance that when the whole of the March is held against the king, much of it in the hands of Alice's relations." Alice was Cadwaladr's Norman wife, and Ranulf of Chester was her uncle. "Stephen hasn't even made a move against Gilbert de Clare, despite the taking of Wiston Castle in the summer."

"He can't," Gareth said. "Earl Robert is dead, but William holds the southwest against him."

"Exactly," Aron said. "Stephen hasn't moved against Clare, who attacked one of his staunchest allies. Why would he pay any heed to Cadwaladr if it means going against King Owain, who has reached out to him and who keeps Ranulf in check on his western border?"

"Why not outright evict Cadwaladr from his court, then?" Gwen said.

"There's no advantage in that either, my lady," Aron said. "The war has split families right in half, so Cadwaladr's current position is hardly unique. King Owain never sent men in support of King Stephen, and I expect Stephen may, in fact, be hoping to eventually use Cadwaladr against Owain, once the war with Maud is over. But until then, he can't, because that would mean siding with a host of supporters of Maud."

As usual, Aron's analysis was dead on. Gareth hadn't before heard the problem so succinctly put.

Gruffydd was gazing in the direction Cadwaladr had gone, having entered the keep with his entourage. "It may even be that Cadwaladr's mission is a test of loyalty. If he defects to Gloucester, good riddance to a difficult problem. If he returns with news and reports of men, money, and weapon stocks, so much the better."

Gwen's eyes had followed Gruffydd's. "I'm confused, then, as to why Cadwaladr went to the king in the first place, when he has so many natural allies who oppose Stephen."

"It may be that he tried here first, Gwen, but Earl Robert threw him out." Aron drew in a breath. "I'm afraid I don't yet have the measure of Prince Henry."

"He wants to do good," Gwen said.

"He wants to be king," Gareth corrected gently. "Likely, he will have trouble being both."

Even while he cautioned his friends, Gareth's interactions with Henry had revealed to him a measure of careful thought in the young man that Gareth found daunting. King Stephen was just past fifty, born within a year or two of Earl Robert. He had a son, Eustace, who was a few years older than Henry. It was impossible to know at their respective ages exactly what kind of men either of these two noble sons might become, but reports indicated Eustace was brash and intemperate. In other words, he was spoiled in a way Henry was not.

If it came down to a battle for the crown of England between these two royal offspring, Gareth's silver would be on Prince Henry, not Eustace, for all that Eustace's father currently sat on that throne.

Gareth started walking toward the entrance to the keep, Gwen still with her hand tucked into his elbow. Taran was back in his sling, awake but starting to look sleepy, now that he was again attached to his mother. That would be the best thing for him this afternoon, given the upheaval among the adults in his life.

"Tell me you aren't going to antagonize Cadwaladr, Gareth," Gwen said. "You must stay calm."

"I am calm." Though just the thought of being calm threatened to overturn Gareth's tenuous hold on himself. "I know my duty."

The others had started after him, and Gruffydd came up on Gareth's other side, striding along beside him. "Does Prince Henry know the full story of Cadwaladr?"

"Nobody knows the full story but you few."

"And I suspect even I don't know it all. You have to tell the prince."

Gareth stopped abruptly. "How? How do you think that conversation is going to go?"

"You tell him the truth," Gruffydd insisted again. "Tell him what Cadwaladr did."

"Any time you speak ill of another man, you call into question your own integrity. It will look to the prince as if I'm excusing my own shortcomings by denigrating another."

"You told Prince Hywel about what happened in Ceredigion, and he listened," Gruffydd said.

"No, that wasn't me." Gareth shook his head. "He had his own informants in Cadwaladr's household. He already knew what had happened from others, and he sought me out. If Prince Henry doesn't know about Cadwaladr's misdeeds, I cannot be the one to tell him."

Llelo burst from the inner gatehouse tower, through which Cadwaladr and his men had just passed, spied his parents, and ran full tilt towards them. Fortunately it wasn't far and thus only mildly unseemly. "I just saw him." He arrived, breathless, skidding in the gravel. "He's here. Cadwaladr is here."

Gareth put a hand on his shoulder. "We know, son."

The young man, Hamelin, with whom Llelo had been sent to speak to the guards but whom Gareth hadn't actually met, hurried up just behind Llelo. "Who is this Cadwaladr that he engenders such dismay?"

Gareth knew his face was stony, but Llelo either didn't notice or was too excited not to answer without pretense. "He is a treacherous snake who can never be trusted. He murdered King Owain's eldest son."

Hamelin gaped at him. "Does Henry know?"

"We are going now to see why Cadwaladr is here," Gareth said, taking in the young man with a sweeping glance. "Lord Hamelin, yes?"

"The prince's half-brother." Hamelin put his heels together, in what Gareth was beginning to see as a very Norman way, and sketched a bow.

"Thank you for assisting my son, my lord," Gareth said, remembering to be polite. "I very much want to hear what you've discovered, but right now we have larger concerns."

He finally felt he had command of his emotions, and he turned to Gwen. "The meeting with the maidservant is soon. I was hoping that you and—" He took in the expressions of all the men facing him. None of them wanted to go with Gwen.

Gruffydd put up his hand. "It is better that I do not enter the hall, Gareth. If I didn't run Cadwaladr through, at the very least, by the time I was done with him, he would be left with a broken jaw." He bent his head slightly and spoke in an undertone. "You are not the only one who is angry."

Gareth gripped Gruffydd's shoulder reassuringly. "We all want to rip out his throat with our teeth, and none of us will do it."

His gaze went to each of the other men in turn. "I was out of line earlier. It will not happen again."

They all nodded.

With a quick squeeze, Gwen let go of Gareth's arm and headed off with Gruffydd. Before Gareth could talk himself out of his momentary composure, he set off again towards the entrance to the keep, his stride purposeful, and he felt the other men fan out behind him, like he was a boat and was pulling them along in his wake. Once up the steps and through the anteroom, he didn't break stride, continuing down the avenue created by the arrangement of the tables to the dais where Prince Henry had been enjoying a meal, but which he'd abandoned in order to greet Prince Cadwaladr.

Gareth came to a halt several paces away and to the left of Cadwaladr, such that his left knee just bumped the edge of a bench to the nearest table. They'd arrived in time to hear Cadwaladr conclude, "King Stephen expresses his regrets at the loss of his noble cousin." He bowed. "Please accept my condolences as well."

Prince Henry gestured to an empty seat at the high table, past Roger and Robert Fitzharding, who were to the prince's left. "Please join me for some refreshment." Then his eyes went to Gareth, and he canted his head. "Though, of course, if you'd rather dine with your countrymen, I would understand."

Gareth was drawing in a breath, without a single thought as to how to respond to Prince Henry's assumption—but knowing that he had to—when Cadwaladr turned to him, grasped his upper arms, one in each hand, and kissed his cheeks. "I can't tell you how pleased

I am to see you," he said in French. "I'd heard a rumor you were here. How goes it with my brother?"

Stunned by the effusiveness of Cadwaladr's greeting, Gareth could only stutter, "The-the king is well."

"It is my greatest regret that I was not able to mourn the loss of Rhun with him, but I knew the urgency of my mission to the court of King Stephen and didn't want to leave the task he'd set me undone."

This outright lie left Gareth—and all of his men—gasping. It seemed impossible to muster any response in the presence of Prince Henry that wouldn't show Gwynedd in a bad light, even as Gareth was desperate that the young prince not be seduced by Cadwaladr's charm. This was the first time that charm had ever been turned on Gareth himself, and he understood better why people succumbed to it.

"Why did King Stephen send you?" was all Gareth could manage.

Cadwaladr didn't look affronted by the question, perhaps because Gareth hadn't managed to put the emphasis where he meant it—on the *you* instead of the *why*. Regardless, it was clear that Cadwaladr was determined to maintain his current façade, regardless of Gareth's attitude. "King Stephen wants peace in Britain above all else. He considers me a valuable member of his court and knows that many of my relations have in recent months come over to Prince Henry's faction. He is hopeful that, through me, some kind of accord can eventually be reached."

That was, without a doubt, the most preposterous thing Cadwaladr had ever said, and his string of comments since he'd come into the hall were already at the outermost of absurd. But he delivered the words with such sincerity that Gareth again found himself struggling for an appropriate response.

Aron rescued him, speaking to Prince Henry, "My lord, thank you for your offer to sacrifice a meal with Prince Cadwaladr so he could eat with us, but the monks at the priory are expecting us. I'm sure Prince Cadwaladr would be more than happy to accept your hospitality." He bowed deeply.

Prince Henry gestured again to the empty seat at the high table. "Ease your journey at my table. I am grateful to my cousin for sending such a noble emissary at the hour of our greatest grief."

Gareth's relief was palpable. Like everything else that had passed for conversation in the last few moments, the prince's words were prettily said. Though Gareth had been briefly angry at Llelo for being so open with Hamelin, now he could not regret the bit of truth that had been spoken. It might even be that Henry himself had heard a little of what had transpired in Wales last year, in which case a small portion of Henry's words might be less than sincere. If Gareth knew anything about life in a Norman castle, he knew that all was not as it seemed—ever.

His suspicions were confirmed when Henry added, speaking to Cadwaladr, who was in the act of rounding the table to find his seat, "You must tell me how my uncle, the king, fares these days. I had heard that he too has not been well of late."

"I don't know who told you that, but it isn't true." Cadwaladr bowed regally before pulling out his chair and sitting. He had to lean forward to continue the conversation, and those between him and Prince Henry leaned back so as not to impede either prince's view. "His only regret is that he has not heard from you since he paid the wages of your men."

Henry had been trained to control his expression, so if Gareth hadn't been looking closely, he might have missed the slight pinching around Henry's eyes. His smile definitely grew stiffer, and though he still looked older than his fourteen years, it wasn't by much. King Stephen *had* paid the wages of Henry's men, and Gareth could well imagine that the line Cadwaladr had just delivered was the real message that King Stephen wanted to send. In other words, *You are in my debt, and you would be wise not to forget it!*

Perhaps to distract from the extreme awkwardness of the exchange with Cadwaladr, Henry focused again on Gareth. "Before you depart, did you have something to say to me, Sir Gareth?"

The last thing Gareth wanted to do was discuss the investigation in front of Cadwaladr with the entire high table looking down at him. He had no choice but to make some reply, however, so he bowed, feeling that giving Henry his full due as Maud's son was the wisest course of action under the circumstances. "I would not speak of it in open hall, my lord."

"Then you and I shall briefly retire." Henry tipped his head to indicate the side door. "The monks can wait for you for a little while."

Cadwaladr glared at Gareth for a heartbeat—the expression vanishing so quickly Gareth wouldn't have caught it if he hadn't been looking. Rather than churning Gareth's stomach again, however, Cadwaladr had settled it further. *That* was the Cadwaladr Gareth knew, and it was something of a relief to know that the treacherous version of the prince was still in there, and Gareth himself hadn't lost his mind.

Llelo and the Dragons resolved to stay behind in the hall. Given that Cadwaladr remained at the high table, Gareth didn't think he could have dragged any of them away, anyway, no matter how much they might have wanted to hear what he had to say to Henry. Only Hamelin came with him, and neither Gareth nor Henry questioned his presence.

As Gareth walked beside the young man, it came to him that the Norman habit of making noble bastards might have a method to it. It created an entire class of upstanding and capable noblemen who served their legitimate siblings and cousins. Because bastards could never inherit, they could be trusted like a legitimate brother never could.

This time Henry made no pretense of sitting in his regal chair but immediately began to pace in front of the fire. Hamelin took up Llelo's former position with his back to the door, standing silent sentry. Gareth wasn't quite sure what to do with himself. He couldn't sit unless Henry did, so he stood ten feet away, his hands behind his back and his legs spread, waiting.

As it turned out, Henry didn't actually want to talk about the investigation—or at least not yet. "There is more to this emissary, this Prince Cadwaladr, than I currently know, isn't there?"

Gareth spoke around a held breath. "I am not the man to talk of this, my lord."

Hamelin took a step forward. "Then I will. Cadwaladr is responsible for the death of Gwynedd's heir, Prince Rhun, a year ago."

His mouth dropping open, Henry stopped his pacing and looked from Hamelin to Gareth and back again. "You tell me truly?"

Gareth forced himself to give the prince a stiff nod.

"I'd heard that Prince Rhun had been killed, but not the circumstances," Prince Henry said. "As far as I knew, they were unclear. He was ambushed—"

Gareth's eyes went to Hamelin's face, but the young man didn't look at him. As far as Gareth knew, Hamelin had learned of Cadwaladr's treachery a quarter of an hour earlier—and yet he behaved as if he were aware of the full story.

Gareth didn't know why Hamelin was showing such fidelity to Gwynedd, but now that the truth had come out, Gareth wasn't going to hang him on the line to dry. "The day Rhun died, Cadwaladr was attempting to ambush and murder me, and he misjudged his target. Rhun was killed instead. In fairness, you should know from the start that I struggle to accord Cadwaladr any respect, deserved or otherwise. Our history goes back long before Cadwaladr's latest offense. He used to be my liege lord, in fact."

Henry put his folded hands on top of his head and lifted his chin to stare up at the ceiling. Then he gave a bark of laughter that echoed around the room before he dropped his hands and head. "I regret the loss of King Owain's son, but this explains the expression on your face when Cadwaladr embraced you." The young prince laughed openly. "Cadwaladr's brazenness is impressive. He lies with utter aplomb." Henry sounded admiring.

Gareth swallowed, unable to laugh but understanding why Henry might. The prince was more right than he knew, and Gareth chose his next words carefully. "You must not succumb to Cadwaladr's sweet words, my prince. I tell you truly, he is a snake in your castle. He may not lie with every word he speaks, but enough of them will be falsehoods that what is true and what is not will be wholly obscured."

"I will bear that in mind," Henry said dryly. "At least he will be housed here at the castle instead of the priory. I'm hoping you will find your accommodations at St. James's to your liking. It was my thought that, as Welshmen, you would feel more comfortable outside the castle walls. Like my mother does."

Knowing that Henry in no way meant to equate Empress Maud with Welshmen but that he merely meant to say that he understood the desire to be separate, Gareth said, "We appreciate your thoughtfulness, especially now. We have found throughout the day that more men than just Cadwaladr resent that you sent for outsiders, rather than looking to an Englishman for help."

Henry gave a low laugh. "Why does that not surprise me?" And though Gareth feared Henry still didn't fully understand what faced them, the prince was ready to move on. "What have you discovered about Aubrey's death?"

Gareth told him what he knew, without mentioning the maidservant, who would be meeting with Gwen. If her information turned out to be useful, he would add it to the pot. Then he gestured to Hamelin. "I have yet to hear what you and Llelo discovered."

While Hamelin told of his meeting with the guard and Captain Harold, Henry stared at the floor, his hands on his hips. "So I was right. Murder has been done. And the timing could not be worse."

"The timing of murder is always bad, but do you mean something more specific, my lord?" Gareth said.

Prince Henry looked up. "I have called a conference of allies to Bristol. It begins tomorrow, and with the weather threatening to take a turn for the worse, most everyone will arrive tonight."

Gareth swallowed, cataloging in his mind the identity of these allies. He thought he knew, but it was best to ask. "I was not aware of this meeting, my lord. Who comes?"

Prince Henry waved a hand. "Men from Deheubarth, Pembroke, Chester, and Hereford." He canted his head. "Hertford and Lincoln as well. Since you're here, it is my hope that you will represent Prince Hywel."

"Of course, my lord, but what about the investigation?"

"I'm sure your Dragons are fully up to the task," Henry said. "I need your acumen and experience at my table."

It was an odd pivot from this morning, when Henry had been desperate for answers about his uncle's death. But Gareth bowed and assented because he felt it was the only real option. Still, he wondered if he should be offended that Hywel hadn't been asked in the first place to send someone.

"Many of these barons are the family members Cadwaladr mentioned," Hamelin said. "Do you think King Stephen was aware of this meeting before he sent him?"

Where before in the hall, Henry had seemed very much fourteen, now his expression hardened, and his eyes looked much older. "If Stephen sent Cadwaladr to spy on me, then his timing couldn't have been better. The strength of our alliance will shake his throne to its foundation. And if Cadwaladr chooses to reconsider his allegiances?" He shrugged. "If he's a snake, there's no reason to think he can't turn around and bite Stephen's hand instead of mine."

12

Gwen

The church in the southern ward wasn't attached to a monastery, so the None bell didn't actually mark the Divine Office here, and no monks came to pray. Consequently, Gwen and Gruffydd were alone, sitting in companionable silence on a bench set against an inside wall of the church. Like the castle, the church was built in stone, with a large nave oriented roughly east to west. Nearby were several domestic buildings for the priest and the church's attendants. Taran had been fussing by the time they arrived, so he'd nursed again—at two months old he was growing quickly and eating nonstop—and had fallen asleep for the third time today.

"What do you think of all this?" Gwen asked Gruffydd, just as a by-the-way to pass the time while they waited for the maidservant, though she was genuinely interested in his opinion too.

"Whether or not the Earl of Gloucester was hurried to his death is a question I'm happy to leave to you and Gareth, but I'm certainly not surprised to find intrigue in a Norman castle."

"Not that we aren't prone to it too," Gwen said with a laugh. "The intrigue in a Welsh castle when Cadwaladr is present could rival any English court."

"Cadwaladr is here, so I imagine things have been much better at home."

"You forgot about Cristina."

Because Gruffydd couldn't argue with Gwen's assessment of King Owain's queen, he laughed instead, and then the chapel door opened and a woman glided in.

As she rose to her feet, Gwen said in Welsh to Gruffydd, "You didn't say that she was beautiful."

"Is she?" Gruffydd snorted under his breath. "I suppose." Putting aside his disdain, he held out his hand to the newcomer and switched to French. "Welcome. May I introduce Lady Gwen, wife to Gareth, to whom you spoke earlier."

Glad the woman couldn't possibly understand Welsh, Gwen smiled in greeting as well and hastened forward. "I was hoping you'd come."

Perhaps Gruffydd's eyes were failing him, because the woman was the very essence of beauty, with white skin, dark brows and eyes, and red lips. She'd pulled her hair back and caught it up in a wimple, though a few stray hairs told Gwen that the hair underneath was brown too, with just a touch of red, and her cheekbones were high enough to be the envy of any woman, noble, peasant, and everything in between.

"You can call me Edith." The woman took Gwen's hand. "Thank you for speaking to me." She glanced between Gruffydd and Gwen. "I am trusting you to be discreet."

"Nobody else knows of this meeting except Gareth," Gwen said. That wasn't quite true, but it was true enough for their purposes.

"If the prince asks—"

If the woman didn't want anyone who lived at Bristol to know she was speaking to Gwen, that was a secret Gwen was prepared to keep. So she answered Edith's question before she could completely voice it: "We will not tell him of this conversation if you do not wish it. We are in Bristol because Prince Henry asked for us to come, but he is not our liege lord. He has said outright that's *why* he asked us to come. He knows we will do what is right, regardless of who may object."

Edith still looked worried, so Gwen drew her to a different bench, this one farther into the nave and hidden from the front door by a pillar. Gruffydd moved to stand at the pillar, further blocking them from the view of anyone who might enter the church through the front door.

"Tell me what you have to tell me before anyone comes." She squeezed Edith's hand encouragingly.

Gwen was expecting more hesitation, but Edith now spoke without pretense, "The evening before he died, I heard Earl Robert arguing with his son. Earl Robert said that he was not his father." Her jaw was firm as she said it, showing no hesitation.

"Those were his exact words? *You are not my son?*"

"Yes."

"Do you know to which son he was speaking?"

Edith maintained a steady gaze on Gwen's face. "I wasn't sure at first. He kept his voice too low, but ... I think it was William." She shook her head. "I would never have said Earl William could have murdered his father, but it makes sense if—"

If Earl Robert was going to disown him. Gwen didn't speak the words out loud. Though Gareth had spoken of William to Prince Henry, generally it was best not to put words into any informant's mouth. Since Edith hadn't voiced her complete thoughts, Gwen didn't either. It was clearly the conclusion Gwen was supposed to draw, however.

While Gwen couldn't be happy that Cadwaladr had ridden to Bristol, she was glad now that it was she who'd come to hear Edith's story instead of Gareth. The woman's beauty was overwhelming, and it was difficult to read her face because every expression, every mannerism, was graceful and lovely. Gwen didn't think Gareth would have been swayed by it, but it might have made it hard for him to listen objectively to her story.

"Then what happened?"

"I don't know. I hid myself behind a curtain, and the son walked off in the other direction."

Gwen studied her through a few heartbeats. "Is there more?"

"More? Does there need to be more? William murdered his father in an attempt to keep him from speaking to anyone else. But then he discovered that Earl Robert *did* talk to other people: his maid, his valet, and his steward."

While the woman herself had an obvious intelligence and bearing that surprised Gwen coming from such a low servant, her hand, which Gwen still held, was coarse from labor, rough with callouses. Gwen would have thought she'd have risen higher, but then again, Edith was a Saxon in a Norman castle. It wasn't as bad as being Welsh, but opportunities for advancement must be few and far between. "Have you spoken of your suspicions to anyone else?"

"No." Edith pulled her hand away and stood abruptly. "And I won't. I'm in fear for my life, and I've decided to leave Bristol."

Gwen stood too. "Where will you go? We can protect—"

"No! I will go to my sister in Dorchester. I won't be back." And then, just like that, she set off for the door.

Gruffydd made to step in front of her, as if to bar her way, as surprised as Gwen by her sudden departure, but Gwen made a motion with her hand, telling him to let the servant go. She had come to them of her own free will, and Gwen didn't have any right to keep her. Edith brushed past Gruffydd on her way to the door and didn't look back.

Gwen watched her leave, waiting until the chapel door swung closed before speaking. "Did you hear all of that?"

"She thinks William killed his father?"

"She outright accused him of it."

Gruffydd tapped a finger to his lower lip. "You do realize that if William is not the earl's true son, that means in the first year of their marriage, Lady Mabel was unfaithful."

Gwen canted her head. "Such a threat to herself and her son as disownment would make Lady Mabel an equally likely candidate to do murder—and perhaps better placed for it than William."

"Earl Robert never struck me as one to be anything but practical. You would think if he suspected he wasn't William's father he would have made this accusation long ago."

"He might have just learned of it," Gwen said.

"Would he really have shamed his wife on his deathbed?" Gruffydd's expression was dubious. "I don't see that we can question either Mabel or William about this."

"I'm not even sure we can tell Prince Henry, at least not yet. And unfortunately, with these deaths, we have nobody left to question. Anyone who could deny or corroborate Edith's story is dead."

"That's convenient." Gruffydd made a skeptical sound. "William is due in Bristol by the evening meal. We can take the measure of him then and decide."

Gwen looked again to the door. "I don't like letting her go."

"Nor I, but did we have a choice?"

As Gwen started towards the exit, her thoughts were troubled. "Is it odd that we've heard so little favorable about William? Has it been different for you?"

Gruffydd scowled. "No."

"Can he really have inherited so little from his father? Llelo grows more like Gareth every day, and yet they share no blood."

"William has the burden of filling a powerful father's shoes. How many sons in that position are capable of it?" Gruffydd shook his head. "It's an impossible task. Just ask Prince Hywel."

Gwen conceded Gruffydd's point, but it was still an extreme measure to disown a son, even on one's deathbed—or especially on one's deathbed. It also hadn't escaped Gwen's notice that the loss of William would make Roger the heir. She didn't like Roger at all, and it made her think that William would have to be a terrible son indeed for the old earl to think Roger as his heir would be better, no matter his antecedents. Edith's story, if true, did rule out Roger as the killer, however, since it would have been in his best interest to keep his father alive and talking.

Gwen and Gruffydd left the chapel for the outer ward to find the wind had picked up considerably, whistling across the open space between them and the keep, which was visible above the curtain walls that separated them. The weather up until now had been atypical for November, far too warm for the season. Gwen supposed it was only a matter of time before it turned, and now that she thought about it, she'd been growing steadily colder as she'd been talking to Edith in the church.

She and Gruffydd pulled their hoods over their heads, and she fastened the toggles on her thick cloak. Taran slept on, well protected and warm. With quickening steps, they crossed the ward, passed through the various gatehouses, and reached the keep.

Two guards stood on duty in the porch. With a nod, one of them opened the door for Gwen. It was courteous behavior, and Gwen rewarded him with a smile, before sighing as she pushed back her hood.

They stood for a moment in the far back of the hall, so Gwen could survey the tables, looking for Gareth or the Dragons. It was

Llelo whom she sighted first, sitting with his back to the wall, with the other Dragons (barring Evan, who remained at the priory) around him. He saw her too and lifted a hand. She smiled to see him taking his duties seriously, as always. Gruffydd in the lead, they made their way around the margins of the room. Llelo's attention remained mostly on the high table, and when they reached him, he said, "You see Cadwaladr there, of course."

"He's hard to miss," Gruffydd said with a growl. But at the concerned looks Gwen and Llelo shot him, he gritted his teeth. "I am well in control. As the ancients say, *Reflect twice before striking once.* Our vengeance will be something he does not see coming."

Gwen herself had trouble looking at Cadwaladr at all. Like the men, every part of her wanted to throw herself across the room and throttle him. She'd felt that way about him *before* he'd tried to kill Gareth and murdered Rhun instead. The list of Cadwaladr's offenses was long and varied.

Llelo saw her watching and said, "He pretended he was happy to see Father."

Gwen swung around to look at her son. "How could he?"

"Cadwaladr seeks the prince's favor," Aron said, overhearing. "How else to get it when we are obviously here with Prince Henry's blessing?"

"I don't like it." Gruffydd's growl was back. "It is more two-faced than usual of him."

"There is no act of which Cadwaladr is incapable," Gwen said, "especially one which on the surface puts him in a good light."

"Father went to speak privately with the prince," Llelo said. "Cadwaladr—"

But he broke off as the outside door swung open, and someone new entered the hall. He was dressed entirely in black, and as he strode towards the dais, everyone in the hall rose to show respect as he passed. This had to be the new earl, William FitzRobert. At the sight of him, Gwen quickly revised yet again her perception of what was happening at Bristol Castle.

William was tall and broad-shouldered, with brown hair and a long nose, and in every way that Gwen could discern from here, making allowances for age and time, the spitting image of his father. There could be no question of his parentage. Instead, she began to review the conversation she'd just had with Edith.

Gruffydd saw the resemblance too, and before Gwen could say anything about what she was thinking, he stood and gestured to Steffan and Iago that they should stand too. "The maidservant might still be in the castle. We will seek her out and bring her back." He looked down at Gwen. "I know you promised Edith we would not talk to anyone about her accusation, but it's clear now that we have to."

Gwen shook her head, not at Gruffydd but at the circumstances. "What did she think—that we wouldn't notice what he looked like? Or better, that he wouldn't put in an appearance?"

"We Welsh are easily led astray. Everyone knows that." Gruffydd scoffed and stalked away, Steffan and Iago following.

"What is this? What's happening?" Llelo glanced at their companions' retreating backs and then looked at Gwen. Cadoc and Aron, the remaining Dragons, leaned closer to listen.

In a few words, speaking in Welsh so they wouldn't be understood by anyone else, Gwen related the conversation with Edith. All the while, she kept one eye on William. The respect accorded him in his own hall, Edith's and Prince Henry's doubts aside, was unmistakable, and he embraced Roger, who'd come around the high table to greet him.

Then William lifted a hand to his people, spoke audible thanks while requesting that they return to their seats, and then moved towards the far doorway.

Cadoc, who'd been sitting beside Llelo, snorted eloquently, and Aron beyond him said, "Not what I expected. In Gwynedd, I'd heard it said that the son was not the father."

Gwen coughed. "Do you think we've been lied to?"

Now Aron laughed wholeheartedly. "Unceasingly, I imagine."

13

Gareth

Gareth wanted to protest, to tell Henry that including Cadwaladr in any plan was a well-trodden path to disaster. All Henry had to do was ask Earl Ranulf. Gareth even opened his mouth to speak, but then he shut it again. Henry knew the truth now, and if he chose to ally with Cadwaladr, there was nothing Gareth could do about it. The result would be harm to him and everyone around him, one way or another, but that wasn't something Gareth could prevent. He wasn't an adviser, and he had no place here except at Henry's request. If the prince wanted to entertain Cadwaladr in his own domains, Gareth had no right to tell him that he couldn't. And he didn't want to become just another older adviser that Henry chose to ignore.

Hamelin had a look on his face that indicated he would love to argue too, but at a quick shake of Gareth's head, he subsided. Still, a calculating look appeared in Hamelin's eyes that told Gareth he'd made the right choice. Just because neither of them spoke up now didn't mean they never could again—Hamelin more so than Gareth.

And maybe, if Cadwaladr really did defect to the Angevin cause, it would be the best thing for Gwynedd. It was possible King Stephen had taken the measure of Cadwaladr and found him wanting—and King Stephen had far more power in England right now than Henry. Even if Gareth himself was immune to it, he acknowledged that Cadwaladr had the ability to charm. Better that he wasn't in London anymore to whisper in the king's ear and instead joined the side not currently on the throne.

So Gareth settled back on his heels and kept his mouth shut while the prince stared into the fire. At least this time Cadwaladr wasn't a suspect in their investigation, so Gareth need not speak to him, or of him, again. He wished he could avoid looking at him.

A rap came at the door, and it opened at the same time Henry said, "Enter."

A man slightly taller than Gareth and broader besides, though none of his extra weight looked to be fat, stood in the doorway. Gareth knew instantly that this was William. Like his father, he was the very essence of what a Norman lord should look like, down to his highly-polished black boots.

"William!" Henry strode forward, his hand out.

The Earl of Gloucester bowed, straightened, and clasped Henry's hand.

Henry held it for a heartbeat longer than necessary, looking earnestly up into his cousin's face. He spoke before William could, as if this was the continuation of a conversation they'd been having— which likely it was. "I know you don't agree with my suspicions, but you should know Sir Aubrey died today."

Gareth didn't know what to make of the display, since just this morning, Henry had accused his cousin of murdering Earl Robert. Since Henry couldn't have forgotten that fact, did Gareth need to see the accusation instead as that of a grieving child? Did Henry now regret having made it, especially since William had been absent from Bristol since his father's funeral and could have had no immediate hand in Aubrey's death?

"I heard, cousin." William pressed his lips together for a moment. "He will be missed."

"*Now* will you consider the possibility that we have cause for concern?"

William gazed down at Henry for a moment and then his eyes flicked to Gareth, who bowed his head and said, "My lord."

"You are Sir Gareth. Welcome to Bristol." William put out a hand as if he meant to shake Gareth's forearm. "My thanks for saving my cousin's life are belated, but know they are no less sincere for the delay."

Gareth was so surprised at this display of respect that he almost didn't put out his own hand in a timely manner. Fortunately, he managed it, and the two men grasped forearms. "Thank you. I am sorry for your own loss."

William sighed. "My father would have much preferred to die in battle. As it is, he is at peace, and that is all I wanted. He had a long struggle this year in a different kind of battle." He released Gareth and turned to Prince Henry. "Will you tell me what you know so far? I swear to you now that I am willing to listen."

Henry obliged—or rather, Gareth obliged—and he'd just finished relaying everything he knew so far when another knock came at the door, which opened to reveal Charles, the would-be castle steward. "My lords? We have more visitors. The Earls of Hertford and Pembroke have arrived."

Charles was speaking of the two Gilbert de Clares, referred to in this Norman castle exclusively as Pembroke and Hertford because otherwise their shared name was too confusing.

The corners of William's mouth turned down, however. "I didn't expect either until tomorrow."

"They tell me Earl Ranulf is close as well," Charles added.

Again, William's gaze fell on Gareth, who was standing with his hands behind his back, trying not to look like he was listening, though of course he was. "You fought with Pembroke's faction last summer. What say you? Can we take England back for my aunt?"

"England is not Wiston Castle, my lord. I will say that with so many high-ranking lords in residence, we are sitting on tinder that needs only a spark to light."

Gareth was thinking particularly of the uncomfortable moment he personally might have coming face-to-face with Ranulf. Gareth had last seen the Earl of Chester in his own hall, where the truth about Cadwaladr's latest machinations had come out. Since then, King Owain had taken Mold Castle, a fact Ranulf couldn't be happy about—and might make him more than a little displeased to see Gareth as Hywel's representative. Of course, Cadwaladr was here too, and the position he'd put Ranulf in was a far more awkward one than Gareth's.

"Unless it has already flamed." Henry tipped up his chin. "Stephen has few supporters left. We control most of the north and west of England. Soon it will be all."

That was not at all what Gareth had meant, and the next glance William sent Gareth showed that he knew it too. Neither man contradicted Henry, whose expression was again full of the glories of war, projecting a confidence that Gareth, for one, didn't think was deserved.

William cleared his throat. "It is you and your Dragons, Sir Gareth, who struck the first real blow to Stephen's power in a year. Our conference will begin tomorrow morning. May I count on your presence at the table?"

"I already asked him, cousin, and he has agreed," Henry said.

"Indeed, my lord." Gareth bent at the waist, deciding to continue hiding his uncertainties about this arrangement. "It would be helpful if my men who are continuing the investigation could retain the assistance of Hamelin, if he is willing. We *are* Welsh. I do not believe you will be surprised to hear we are not always welcome."

"Anyone who objects to your presence will answer to me," William said.

"Thank you, my lord." Gareth could well believe that what William demanded, he received. But Gareth knew in advance that he was unlikely to run to William for help. An informant forced to render information generally produced only that information he thought the questioner wanted to hear.

"Night is falling." William pulled in a deep breath through his nose. "Let's see about these barons, shall we, my prince?"

Henry went with William to the door, leaving Gareth with Hamelin, whose expression when he looked at Gareth was fervent. "Thank you, my lord."

Gareth raised his eyebrows. "You're welcome. But for what?"

"Your presence here has settled my brother—and it seems Earl William as well."

"We'll see how settled they feel when all this is over. Meanwhile, I'm not sure who has the more difficult task tomorrow. You must continue to search for our killer, and I must watch while Henry and William try to unite a host of barons, each of whom stands firmly in the center of his own world and despises any abrogation of his authority."

Hamelin stared at him for a second and then laughed outright. "Trust a Welshman to say out loud what we all think privately."

"Meanwhile, we will return to the priory and confer among ourselves. Will you come?"

Hamelin hesitated. "Am I welcome?"

"We will endeavor not to speak too much in Welsh."

Hamelin grinned. "I confess I am growing used to the cadence of it, though I understand not a single word."

* * * * *

Once back in the hall, Gareth tipped his head towards the main exit to indicate it was time to leave, and everyone was together by the time he reached the anteroom. Gruffydd was looking disgruntled, however, and Gareth asked him what was wrong.

"Not here," Gruffydd said shortly.

Fortunately, nobody troubled them about the spelling of their names as they left the castle, and thus they went unhindered to St. James's Priory. Evan, Angharad, and Dai were waiting for them, along with Tangwen, whom Gareth scooped up into his arms. It was a rare day when she saw so little of her parents.

The sun had set, and the monks were at prayer: Vespers, Gareth assumed, though it could have been Compline. The variation in sunlight in Britain created an oddity in the monks' rounds. In June, when the world experienced sixteen hours of daylight, the early morning prayers of Lauds and Prime blended together. In late November, with barely eight hours of daytime to work with, None, Vespers, and Compline could become blurred into one. Nobody wanted to waste candles unnecessarily by staying awake long after dark, and men who worked hard needed sleep.

They all filed into the dining room of the guesthouse, where lay monks were setting out their meal. They waited for them to finish before taking their seats, which gave Evan the opportunity to pull Gareth aside. "Why have you brought a Frenchman here?"

Others overheard and stopped what they were doing to hear Gareth's answer. So he lifted his chin and spoke so all could hear—though in Welsh, for their ears only. "Hamelin's presence isn't a whim on my part. We are treated with disdain in many parts of England and by most Englishmen, but not at Bristol today, or at least not by most. Prince Henry asked us to come, and Earl William shook my hand just now as one man to another. We will not barricade ourselves inside our Welshness. If we do that, we might as well go home."

Now he switched to French. "Hamelin has been invaluable so far in this investigation. In the past, we've had to keep some conclusions to ourselves, for fear of reprisals or misuse of our knowledge. But we are guests today, and when this investigation concludes, no matter how it concludes, we will go home. It is men like Hamelin who will live with the consequences."

Gareth didn't know that he'd answered Evan's question to his friend's satisfaction, but Evan subsided anyway. Gareth had a sinking feeling he'd merely shamed him into silence. He'd meant what he'd said, though. However much he despised the English at times, they were men like any others, capable of great deeds as well as heinous ones. Besides, he could hardly complain about their duplicity or arrogance when Cadwaladr, a Welshman from Gwynedd, was planted in their midst. His presence left no moral high ground upon which another Welshman could stand.

They ate together, trying to put the investigation aside until the servants and children were gone, speaking French to include Hamelin. Gareth didn't know if the priests would agree, but for a family such as theirs, dining together was nearly as sacred as attending mass. It brought their souls together. Though at times he and Gwen had corrupted their meals with talk of death, they actively chose not to do so today.

Once the trenchers and platters were cleared, Tangwen shooed off to bed, and Gwen tucked up near the fire nursing Taran,

Cadoc poked his head from the dining room into the adjacent sitting room of the guesthouse.

"We're alone." He pulled back inside, though he left the door slightly ajar, so they could hear if someone entered. "I'm uncomfortable with all of us in the same place. We could be ambushed here."

Iago responded immediately. "It has been bothering me too." He buffeted Steffan on the shoulder, silently asking him to stand up. "Isn't a general meeting the reason nobody saw the stone fall on Aubrey today?"

Steffan rose to his feet. "Iago and I will see to the perimeter. You can tell us what transpired later." They left, and nobody tried to stop them.

In French, Gareth said, "Let us begin." He looked around the table, taking in the faces turned towards him: the remaining Dragons; his sons; Gwen and Angharad; and Hamelin. Nine, plus Gareth himself. To have so many competent and capable people to rely upon—and whose heads could be put together over a problem—gave him hope that whatever was transpiring here was possible to uncover. "We have four deaths, three of which cannot be investigated in regular fashion because we have no bodies, no crime scene, and only guesswork even to say that any of them were murdered."

"All the more reason to lay out what we learned today, and what we think we know, and see what shape we can make of the puzzle," Gwen said.

They went around the table, each speaking in turn to tell their part in the investigation. Gwen and Gruffydd went last, prompting outrage from Hamelin. "That woman is absolutely lying."

"It does seem so," Gareth said, more mildly.

"We must send out a search party to bring her back," Hamelin said.

"Gruffydd went looking for Edith after Earl William arrived, but he couldn't find her," Gwen said.

"Nobody would have stopped her leaving," Gareth said, trying to make Gruffydd feel better about the failure.

"My initial thought was that she'd accused William as a distraction from the true culprit," Gruffydd said, "but it could also be that she knew of Prince Henry's distrust and sought to confirm it."

"Even without her, at a minimum, it gives us a new place to look for answers."

"For starters, it would be good to know what her relationship was to Sir Aubrey," Aron said.

"I never met the man, of course, and I haven't even been to the castle, but it sounds to me as if he had a hand in every little thing that went on," Evan said. "It was his right as steward, and I know we should keep speculation to a minimum, but I have to say that getting rid of him could have been more about what someone thought he knew than for his own sake. Earl Robert may have told him something that the killer thinks is incriminating."

"He also could have been silenced to stop him from speaking to you, Gareth," Angharad said.

"Angharad has a piece of it." Evan grasped his wife's hand. "But it might not be just us. We arrived today, but so did a host of lords from all over England and Wales. Perhaps the killer feared Aubrey's association with one of them."

Gwen pursed her lips. "In a way that makes more sense. Loosening a merlon to bring it down required effort, time, and opportunity. We were in the castle for less than an hour before it came down. That doesn't sound to me like enough time to chip it out without someone noticing."

"We did give warning we were coming," Llelo said.

On their journey from Aberystwyth, they'd first ridden east across the mountains before turning south, journeying through Abergavenny to Monmouth where there was a good ford across the Wye. Since they had safe passage across Norman-controlled territory, thanks to the letter from Prince Henry, Gareth had asked the lord there to send word to Bristol Castle in advance of their coming. A single rider could make much better time than their small party that included children.

Lips pursed all around the table as people considered what had been said so far. Gareth was pleased that his supposition had proved true yet again: putting his head together with his companions' was always better than him puzzling out answers on his own.

"Let's talk about what we know." Gareth put up one finger. "William is Earl Robert's son. I don't support starting with an assumption that he isn't."

"Agreed," Gruffydd said. "The fact that Edith is gone isn't suspicious at all." He rolled his eyes, intending to be *ffraeth*, what the English called *biting*.

"With that in mind," Angharad said, "why have we been left with the impression, even before we came to Bristol, that Earl William was less able than his father?"

Gareth looked at Hamelin. "Can you answer that?"

The young man's face colored. He'd been listening silently, perhaps struggling with everyone's heavily accented French. True to Gareth's word, they hadn't conducted their conference in Welsh, which obviously would have been easier for everyone but Hamelin.

"I-I don't know. I don't know what you've heard." As the bastard of the Count of Anjou, Hamelin had been forced to grow up quickly, and at seventeen he could pass for a man ten years older. For the first time, however, he looked Llelo's age—and uncertain.

"Take the story about Prince Henry's ignominious defeat and payment of wages by King Stephen, so he could send his men back to France," Gwen said. "For Earl Robert to abandon him was surprising. Whether or not Maud was of the opinion that her son should be taught a lesson, Henry appears to believe that William is the one responsible."

"He's not entirely wrong." Hamelin took in a slow breath and let it out. "This last year of his life, Earl Robert did not always have a clear mind." He gestured to Llelo. "But it wasn't just his memory. He ... made decisions that seemed out of character for him. William felt that he could not go against an order his father had decreed, even if he disagreed with it. Instead, he accepted responsibility for it, rather than let anyone outside of his immediate circle realize how his father was failing."

"Earl Robert wasn't so very old, was he?" Gwen asked in that gentle way of hers—not questioning Hamelin's assertion so much as asking for clarification. "What you describe is an old man's disease, far more likely in someone Sir Aubrey's age—about whom we've heard this too—rather than Earl Robert's."

"It appeared to be a result of his illness." Hamelin remained relaxed, not taking offense at being questioned. "If you've ever cared for someone who's failing, perhaps you've noticed their mind functions less well when they've had prolonged periods of difficulty breathing, or when they've not eaten for too long."

Gwen let out a breath. "This could explain Earl Robert's denial of William that Edith overheard—or says she overheard. He might not have been in his right mind."

"The issue with Henry was in the spring, though, and the earl didn't die until a few weeks ago." An expression of horror crossed Angharad's face. "That's a long time to be dying."

"He had a cruel bout of sickness in late winter, but shortly after our company arrived, he rallied." Hamelin canted his head. "Perhaps it was simply because we arrived, or maybe because we had such a beautiful spring. Regardless, he seemed better for months, regaining much of his former strength, but come autumn, he fell ill again. He fought it for weeks, but ultimately was forced to take to his bed, after which he lasted ten days, if that."

Gwen continued to study Hamelin with some concern. "What disease does that to a man?"

Hamelin shrugged. "Nobody ever gave it a name. You should ask the castle healer."

Gwen's lips pressed together in a tight line before she said what everyone else at the table was thinking. "I hate to say it, especially given our last investigation, but as we discussed this morning with Henry, what you describe could be the result of poison as easily as illness."

Dai groaned. "Don't remind me!"

"Good men are murdered to silence them," Evan ticked off the items on his fingers as Gareth had done earlier, "to get them out of the way, out of jealousy, or by mistake."

"Which brings us back to Sir Aubrey. Was he a good man? Could he have been killed by mistake? We don't know enough yet to say." Gareth scowled. "And that means our task for tomorrow is to dig."

14

Llelo

But it wasn't to be—or at least not in the way his father had envisioned the night before. Llelo and Gareth were up early as usual, and they stood together on the porch, watching fat flakes of snow fall from the sky. Four inches were already on the ground. They could make out the stables opposite, but it was through a veil of white. Llelo had a momentary thought that he should go back to bed. The investigation was urgent, particularly to Prince Henry, but they had long hours of work ahead of them. Tackling their tasks while deprived of sleep would do none of them any good.

"It won't last," Gareth said finally, with something like acceptance in his voice, "but we won't be searching upriver for that boat or the body either."

"I could still go—"

Gareth put out a hand to him. "We work through rain because if we didn't, we'd never work, but snow—" he shook his head. "Not a chance."

On the heels of that comment, the door to the dormitory burst open, and eight young novices came shouting and laughing into the courtyard. They scooped up the snow, smashing the flakes together to make snowballs to throw at one another. Their guardian, a monk no older than Gareth with a kindly face that was trying to look stern, followed, sputtering his protests at the cacophony. But even he laughed when a snowball splattered on his chest.

English or Welsh, snow made children of them all.

Gareth turned to Llelo with a smile. "It's just as well. Your mother and the children can rest after our long journey. Gwen won't like it, but she needs it. I am due at the castle for a day of conferencing with men I'd rather have nothing to do with." He rolled his eyes.

Llelo grinned. "Better you than me."

Gareth shook his forefinger at him. "One day this will be you, God willing." He paused. "So I gather you don't want to come with me?"

"Evan is a better choice for that, surely—" Llelo broke off, suddenly realizing what he wanted to do.

Gareth mock glared at him. "What are you thinking?"

"Everybody talks about these tunnels underneath the castle. Perhaps Dai and I can see what they're about."

Gareth guffawed. "Perhaps you can." Then he sobered. "Be careful. The tunnels under Aber are straightforward, but from what I understand, these here are not. If they're of any length at all, they will take you under the dry moat at the north entrance to the castle, and maybe under the river itself. While the ditch is dry today, that close to the river, any tunnel could flood at any time. As at Newcastle-under-Lyme, some might be more like catacombs."

"I will be careful, Father."

Gareth made a rueful face. "It isn't you I'm worried about."

"I will take care of Dai too."

Dai was already awake, seeing to the horses. He'd gone to bed right after their meeting the night before. They had three rooms in the guesthouse: one for the Dragons; a tiny cupboard for Evan and Angharad; and the largest room for Llelo's family and servants.

Instead of going to bed, Llelo had walked Hamelin most of the way back to the castle—not to protect him, but out of a sense of camaraderie. He wasn't blind to the fact that they both had been lonely children, and he recognized the tendency in himself not only to want to please people, but to try to make sure they were happy. That trait perhaps wasn't the most useful quality in an investigator of suspicious death, but in this instance, staying in tune with Hamelin might translate to good relations with his brother.

The future King of England.

It was strange to Llelo to know that he was rubbing shoulders with such powerful people. He'd come a long way from that friary at Newcastle-under-Lyme.

So, leaving their father to his own preparations, Llelo collected Dai from the stables and headed out of the priory. Enough carts had passed on the road before them that the snow was packed down, and they followed the tracks, trying not to lose their footing on uneven stones they couldn't see underneath the layer of white. They both wore waterproof leather boots, so neither was worried about cold feet, and Dai at times made a point to scuff his toes through the deepest parts of the accumulated snow.

"Why isn't the priory inside the city walls?" Dai asked as he stumped along beside Llelo. "You'd think the monks would want to be safe." The wall that surrounded the castle had been extended to include the town, but it started at the northeast corner of the castle and looped around inside the Frome, leaving St. James's Priory outside the city proper.

"Did you hear what the monk who greeted us said? Earl Robert himself founded the priory, but as Benedictines, they wanted quiet and independence."

Dai's shoulder's hunched. "That's what I want too. I like the bustle of a town, but I don't like being in enclosed spaces I can't get out of without passing an armed guard."

Llelo laughed. "You realize we're about to enter a tunnel beneath the castle, right? It's guarded on both ends—or should be."

"That's different."

They'd arrived at the castle, so Llelo didn't have a chance to mock his brother about how it really wasn't any different. And maybe he didn't need to tease him today—not until he was sure that Dai could handle the adventure upon which they were about to embark. They passed through the gatehouse with a wave to the guard, who nodded in recognition, and found Hamelin just inside the barbican, one shoulder propped against the wall, watching the snow fall.

He straightened as Dai and Llelo approached. "I was wondering when you'd show up."

"It's only just past dawn," Dai said, a little defensively.

Llelo put out a hand to his brother and said in Welsh, "Never mind Hamelin. He's jesting." Then in French he said to his new friend, "We thought we'd have a look in the tunnels."

Hamelin's expression turned curious. "Why?"

"Because they're tunnels," Dai said, as if it were obvious, which to him it was.

But Llelo chose to explain, even if it was a very much after-the-fact excuse to enter them: "Gruffydd went by the entrance yesterday when he was inquiring about Edith and was told she hadn't been there. He was also told she hadn't gone in or out of either main gate, and since she's missing, someone isn't telling the truth."

"So you think she left by the tunnels?" Hamelin looked dubious.

Llelo shrugged. "We won't know unless we take a look ourselves, not only at this end but at the other."

Hamelin's skepticism wavered. "The tunnel comes out in the middle of the town. If someone saw her—" He started walking towards the keep. "I suppose I ought to come with you, so you don't get lost. The entrance to the tunnel is in the basement of one of the keep's towers."

"I was hoping you would come." Llelo pulled from his coat one of the sketches of Edith that Gareth had drawn. "We'll show this around. Maybe it will jog someone's memory."

Hamelin's eyes widened when he saw the picture. "The whole time you were talking last night, I sat at the table not knowing who you were talking about. I didn't think anything of it because the castle is full of servants, and I don't know all their names." He pointed to the sketch. "Her name isn't Edith. It's Rose."

Llelo looked down at the sketch and back to Hamelin. "You're sure?"

"Oh, I'm sure."

Llelo found his eyes narrowing. "You know her?"

Hamelin scoffed. "Not the way you're thinking. She knew what she had and was aiming for a husband, not a romp in the hay. She is beautiful, though, isn't she? I would have to be older than Sir Aubrey and blind not to see it."

"Did you ever see her with anyone we might be able to question?" Dai asked.

Llelo grinned at his brother, impressed rather than resentful that he'd thought to ask that first.

Hamelin rolled his eyes exactly like Gareth had done an hour earlier. "She flirted with every man in the castle—or at least every man of a station higher than hers."

"Would one of those men Bernard, be the valet who died?" Llelo asked hopefully.

Hamelin pursed his lips. "No, oddly. Not him. But ... the captain of the guard, Harold, for certain. And—"

"Sir Aubrey?" Dai prompted.

"No. I was going to say Robert Fitzharding, though her interaction with him most recently was actually more of an argument."

They were still outside the keep, and Llelo stopped at the bottom of the steps, not wanting to carry on the conversation in the crowded hall. "How so?"

"Late one night a few days ago, I overheard them talking inside the laundry drying shed. I'd been drinking with some of the guards at the gate between the two outer wards and was returning from the latrine when I heard the sound of someone getting his face slapped. I went to investigate, but arrived just as Rose left the building, followed almost immediately by Fitzharding. They went off in different directions."

"When was this?"

Hamelin put his clasped hands to his lips as he thought. "Three or four days ago? Before you arrived. But, come to think on it, this was after you'd sent word you were a few days away."

"You have no problem consorting with the local men?" Llelo said. "And they with you?"

"We amuse each other at times." Hamelin snorted. "And recently the latrines in the castle have been unfit for use, even before Aubrey died. He was tearing his hair out about it. The ones in the outer ward are always fresh."

The three young men moved together up the stairs, perhaps a little more slowly than usual since the steps were slick with snow. A servant appeared to have swept them off not long ago, but the snow continued to fall thickly, making mockery of his work. Then they were through the door and into the anteroom. The main entrance to the keep faced northwest, in line with the gate that allowed entrance to the city. This time, instead of moving to the right, towards the tower Llelo and Hamelin had gone up yesterday, they went left, to the northwestern tower of the keep.

The stairs were positioned to the left of the entrance to the guardroom, circling around the inner wall of the tower. Hamelin went down the steps, arriving at the bottom in a second guardroom, something of a mirror to the one above, except this one contained no slits through which to shoot an arrow or crossbow bolt.

Two torches blazed from sconces on either side of the room, which was fifteen feet across and also contained a table, benches, and a brazier from which hot coals were doing a credible job of warming the room. An open trap door took up the center of the floor, revealing a four-foot square hole. Steps led down to an iron-barred door.

Two men lounged on separate benches placed against one wall, though both looked up as Hamelin entered the room and stood to see the prince's brother. "My lord, how may we be of service?" one of them said with a bow.

"We are going down the tunnel." Hamelin wasn't asking.

"Yes, my lord." The same guard plucked a ring with a single key on it from a nail on the wall and brought it to the trap door. "If you would follow me?" He led the way down the steps.

Hamelin went first, and Llelo was content to let him do so. He was starting to think maybe he was with Dai, and enclosed spaces with only one way out weren't really his favorite thing. Once down at the bottom of the flight of stairs, the guard unlocked the door and swung it open. Cool air bathed Llelo's face.

"You might want a torch, my lords, just in case!" Torch in hand, the second guard trotted down the steps and gave his torch to Llelo, who was closest.

Thus, because he had the light, it became his job to lead the way. With no desire to be seen a coward by Hamelin or these English guards, Llelo entered the tunnel first. Thankfully, the space turned out not to be as cramped as he'd feared, as the ceiling arched a good three or four feet above his head and the tunnel's width was at least that of a man. His torch wasn't the only light, either, since torches shone out from sconces placed on the wall every twenty feet.

Holding the torch in front of him, he made to march forward alone.

But he'd gone only a few paces when the first guard appeared beside him, holding an unlit torch in his hand, which he kept down at his side. "Perhaps I may be of further assistance?"

"We'd be grateful." Llelo wasn't one to dismiss guards or servants as beneath him. He hadn't always been a knight's son, having spent the first twelve years of his life as the son of a wool merchant. He hadn't really looked at the guard until now, however, not because he was inferior, but because Llelo had been just a bit nervous about this adventure. Now that the guard was beside him in the torchlight, he proved to be hardly older than Llelo himself, not yet twenty, with curly brown hair and brown eyes full of curiosity.

"What's your name?" Llelo asked, determined to follow through on his decision to be better about introductions.

"Bob," the man said.

"You're Saxon?" Llelo said, switching to English. 'Bob' was a Saxon nickname for 'Robert', one of the most common names in Christendom.

Bob thumped his chest with his free hand. "Born and bred right here in Bristol, my lord."

Llelo was getting so used to being called *my lord* he almost didn't even mark it. The tunnel had started to slope more steeply downward—on the map in Llelo's head, they were passing under the moat—and then rose again. At that point it split into two branches, one going off to the right and the other straight on.

Bob stopped at the crossroads and spoke in French, since Hamelin didn't speak English, "Is there some place in particular you wanted to go?"

Hamelin looked to the right, down a tunnel that was completely dark. "Where does that lead?"

"It dead ends at a cavern." Bob shrugged. "We sometimes use it for storage."

"And the other?" Llelo asked.

"It comes out near the market in the center of the town."

"Is it guarded too?" Dai said, speaking for the first time.

Llelo felt bad that he hadn't been paying attention to his brother. A close look at Dai's face revealed it to be paler than usual, maybe even a little green around the edges, like Llelo had been yesterday, though for a different reason.

"Of course." Bob glanced around at the three companions. "Two men guard it as well. It is a favorite posting."

"Why is that?" Hamelin asked.

Bob looked like he wished he could take back what he'd said, but he answered anyway. "Less supervision. Sometimes one of the tavern girls brings beer."

Llelo was about to suggest that they go straight to the town, for Dai's sake, if for no other reason, but Dai tipped his head towards the right-hand tunnel. "Let's see what's in here. If nobody goes inside but rarely, it would be a good place to hide something, wouldn't it? Maybe this is all about treasure!"

Thankfully, Dai had spoken the final phrase in Welsh, so neither Hamelin nor Bob understood. They'd been sworn to secrecy about the discovery of Empress Maud's lost treasure last summer. The last thing they wanted was to be responsible for word of its reappearance getting back to her son, and thus through him to Maud herself.

"Treasure? How could it be about treasure?" Llelo said in the same language.

Dai started walking. "Maybe Earl Robert's servants were stealing from the castle. Sir Aubrey found out about it, and he killed them, so he could have it for himself—no wait." Dai faltered. "He's dead too."

"It isn't a bad thought." Llelo was glad to distract his brother from how the tunnel was making him feel, and he didn't look so much like he was going to vomit now. "It's as good a motive for murder as any, as we well know—"

They'd reached the end of the passage and arrived at the entryway to the natural rock cavern Bob had mentioned. Llelo's torch was close to going out, but he held it higher, trying to eke from it the last of the light and illumine the walls more clearly. Bob hustled up and lit the torch he'd brought just before Llelo's torch plunged them into darkness.

This second torch flared, revealing a space twice the size of the tunnel behind them. It was filled with overturned barrels and empty crates. "See," the guard said. "There's nothing of interest."

Dai, being Dai, however, took nothing at face value, and wandered towards the back of the cavern where beer barrels had been congregated. Since empty ones would be exchanged for full ones at the castle dock, it was curious that any had ended up here, so Llelo asked the guard about them.

The guard shrugged. "If you look closely, you'll see that those are broken. The cellarer thought the wood and iron fittings might be useful later."

Dai had looked inside several in a desultory fashion. Llelo suspected he was looking for treasure, still disappointed that he had failed to participate in the events of last summer. But then he said, "Uh, Llelo? You'd better come over here."

He'd spoken in Welsh, so only Llelo understood. Thinking that his brother was feeling ill again, Llelo hastened to him to find him looking into a large barrel—nearly chest high on Dai—the lid he'd removed still in his hand. Along with Dai, who was definitely looking green again, Llelo found himself staring into the face of a dead man who'd been stuffed into the barrel. His head was, gruesomely, tipped back slightly, as if he'd arched his back in death.

His stomach dropping into his boots and swallowing down bile *again*, he waved Bob and Hamelin over. The newly lit torch illumined the man's face more clearly.

"Sweet Mary, no!" Bob's jaw was almost on the floor, and he stared, aghast.

"Do you know him?" Llelo asked.

"I've known him my whole life. He's one of the castle guards. His name is Aelfric."

15

Angharad

Being the only woman in a room full of men was rarely comfortable for Angharad, but it was also a position with which she was familiar. Castles always contained a disproportionate number of men. While menfolk went to war (or prepared for it), the countryside was full of women raising children much on their own. That Angharad herself was allowed to live with her husband was the consequence of being of a noble class, with Evan having been raised up from man-at-arms to knight. As a member of the Dragons, he had land and standing, which meant Angharad did too.

Still, sometimes she thought being married to a cattle or sheep herder would have been the best life: following the herds to the mountains in summer and the valleys in winter, with no possessions except what they could carry, but always together. Her people had lived that way for centuries, though she'd left that life behind many years ago upon her father's death and might therefore be looking at it with the eyes of a child.

Regarding this latest mission, Angharad's choice was between staying behind in Aberystwyth, either with Mari at the castle or on

Evan's new lands in Ceredigion, and coming to England with the Dragons.

She hadn't had to think about it for longer than a heartbeat.

But now, here she was in yet another abode filled entirely with men, though, since it was a monastery, the only swords belonged to her own company. From the relative warmth of the porch of the priory guesthouse, she waved to her husband where he stood under the eaves of the stable, Dai beside him. They were intent in conversation and neither saw her.

So she lifted her skirts and swished through the six inches of snow to Evan's side, though she instantly regretted leaving the warmth of the guesthouse common room where the monks had built a fire in the hearth, necessary today to keep the children warm. Angharad had breakfasted, somewhat chaotically, with Gwen and the children. The rest of the Dragons were long since away.

"I can see something has happened."

Yesterday had been taken up with settling in, while Evan had conferred with the abbot and seen to the security of the priory—made all the more urgent once Dai had brought the news of Sir Aubrey's death. While the priory did have a wall around it, it was too low to stop anyone who had serious intent to enter illicitly. It was to the castle that everyone looked for true safety.

And here Dai was, back again, his face drawn and white. Angharad might have waited for them to come to her, but she feared the news was worse than before—or about one of their own.

"Someone else has died." Evan took her arm and walked her deeper into the stables, out of the weather. Even so, a small cyclone of snow swirled around their feet. Yesterday had been a mostly sunny day, but almost always a northeast wind meant foul weather. Or fair, if you were a child and loved snow. The horses were giving off a degree of warmth that cut through some of the cold that was seeping into everything.

Then Dai related, as he must have just done to Evan, what he, Hamelin, and Llelo had discovered in the tunnel beneath the castle. Dai had trouble sitting still at the best of times, and finally Evan had to put a heavy hand on his shoulder to stop him from jiggling constantly up and down as he talked.

"The abbot was disturbed by Aubrey's death, but when I tell him of the murder of this man, Aelfric—" Evan shook his head.

"It's definitely murder?" Angharad asked.

"He was garroted," Dai said shortly.

"There's no denying now that we have a villain among us," Evan said.

"Does Gareth know?" Angharad glanced back to the guesthouse, thinking of Gwen. With this new development, she would want to go to the castle.

"Llelo tasked himself with finding him," Dai said.

"What can I do?"

"Nothing right now, not about this," Evan said. "The man is dead, and Gareth will deal with the body. I will confer again with the abbot, but he agreed yesterday to allow us to speak to the brothers here at the priory about the events that have transpired."

Dai appeared to be recovering from the shock of finding another dead man, and instead of jittering around, he'd started bouncing up and down on the balls of his feet. "It turns out the valet who died has a brother here."

Evan canted his head to the boy. "Off you go. If we're both in here, nobody is keeping an eye on the gate."

"Yes, sir!" And Dai was off like an arrow from a bow or a sheepdog corralling a loose lamb. In fact, the more she thought about it, the more she decided Dai resembled a half-grown puppy, with eager eyes and a grin that asked continually, *Can we go now? Can we go?*

Evan grinned down at Angharad. "He's thirteen but thinks he's twenty. It's best to give him real tasks because he can tell the difference."

"Have you spoken to this brother?"

"Not yet."

Angharad and Evan had been married for only a few months, and although Evan was no better than most men at expressing what he was feeling, she'd learned to read his face. At the moment, he looked sheepish himself, which was unusual for him to say the least. She'd found, in regards to what he was thinking and feeling, that if she went at him directly, she usually could get a truthful answer from him. While she didn't regret being married so soon after they'd met, Evan had been a bachelor a long time, and she had been past the age many noblewomen married. Both of them had been used to doing certain things in certain ways, and married life was a learning experience for both of them.

But they'd loved each other when they married, and they tried to be honest with each other at all times since then. So while she felt a little wary about what might be coming, she asked straightforwardly, "Why not?"

"*Cariad,* we're somewhat short-staffed. With Gareth at the beck and call of Prince Henry, and the rest of the Dragons at the castle, my task is to ensure the security of the priory and our family within it."

Angharad perked up. "So you should send me."

Evan wrinkled his nose. "I was hoping to keep you out of this. I'll do it myself when I have a moment."

Angharad put a hand on his arm. "You are one man, Evan. Let me help."

Evan still looked reluctant, but rather than becoming angry, Angharad studied him. And in the course of a few heartbeats, she realized that his hesitation was based on fear rather than the belief that she wasn't up to the task.

"You can't protect me or anyone else from all danger, not even were you to stand watch every moment of every day."

Evan narrowed his eyes at her. "I know that."

Angharad made her voice particularly gentle. "Do you?"

Evan kept his eyes on her face, and she looked back as openly as she could. Then he sighed. "I have never cared about anyone the way I care about you. I don't know how Gareth does it, bringing Gwen and his family on every investigation. I thought having you with me would be better than leaving you at our cottage, but with this new murder ..." He ground his teeth. "My distemper is worse than ever."

That was a new word for Angharad, but it accurately described what he'd been like these last few days. She rubbed his arm. "It is my understanding that if Gareth wants peace in his household, he is wise not to leave Gwen behind very often—like he did today, in fact—and to tell her everything."

Evan barked a laugh. "You are cut from the same cloth, is that it? I knew that, of course, when I married you." Ignoring the fact that they were currently in the stables of a priory with several stable boys mucking out the stalls at the far end of the building, he drew her into his arms and kissed her. No actual monk entered to interrupt them, but Angharad wasn't sure she would have cared if he had.

When Evan released her, he said, "Without a doubt, having you with me is better than not. And while my initial thought was that this brother—" he flashed a grin at the double meaning, "—isn't going anywhere, if you would like to be of service, I would be grateful if you'd question him. You obviously know what to do, and I trust you to do it."

Angharad's heart warmed at the compliment, but she pulled away slightly so she could look up into his face. "I will ask Gwen to come along as well. The two of us might do better than one. Do we have permission from the abbot?"

"Yes, of course. Didn't I just say so?"

"I meant *do I have permission because I'm a woman,*" Angharad said. "Monks admit they were born of women, but look askance at us otherwise."

"I told him something of our methods, and while I think he was taken aback by how thorough we needed to be, he knows that

Gareth has been charged with the investigation by Prince Henry himself. He wasn't going to say no. He was very clear that he and his brothers will do whatever they can to help us find the killer. It was Earl Robert who founded this priory, you know, and as such, the monks here support Empress Maud's claim to the throne."

"So who's the brother?"

"The herbalist, one Brother Edwin."

Angharad brightened. "I very much liked the herbalist in the monastery near Dinefwr. He was very knowledgeable. I don't know a great deal about herbs, but Gwen has been teaching me, and I've helped her write down some of what she knows in her book." She paused. "Gwen also mentioned that this herbalist was among those who were called to Earl Robert's bedside."

"All the more reason for the two of you to speak to him," Evan said, and then raised his voice further, "Dai, you can come in now."

Dai reappeared in the doorway, looking more like a sheepdog than ever. "I have been watching the gate, truly! But I can see it from over there." He pointed to a spot a few feet away to indicate where he'd been standing, out of sight but not out of earshot.

"Angharad and Gwen need an escort," Evan said. "The healer is the dead valet's brother."

"Yes, sir! I will keep them safe." Dai hesitated. "While they are speaking to the brother, I should inspect the area around the garden. I haven't been down there yet."

"Excellent idea." Evan grinned at Angharad behind Dai's back, since the young man had already set off. Angharad gave her husband a quick peck on the cheek before following Dai into the guesthouse to collect Gwen.

Before marrying Evan, Angharad had never traveled outside of Deheubarth, so she hadn't spent any time except in passing in religious houses other than St. Dyfi's, the monastery near Dinefwr Castle. She'd grown up in her father's house, and he'd been chief of their clan—first among equals, as the Normans might say. The family held the land jointly, and everyone worked it, farming small plots, fishing, and running sheep and cattle from sea to mountain and back again.

In southern Wales, her people had learned to coexist with Normans in a way the men of Gwynedd never had, and she'd grown somewhat used to their ways. If the Normans hadn't believed themselves to be superior to all others, they wouldn't have come to England eighty years ago to conquer it. But oddly, uniting Norman traits with Saxon ones had only made their arrogance more pronounced. Everybody knew there was nobody more stubborn, set in his ways, and sure of himself than a Saxon.

Rather than adapting to the land they'd conquered, the Saxons, and then the Normans in turn, had adapted the landscape to their own needs. Every plot of land from Pembroke to Hastings was now a plowed field. Because they valued bread above meat and milk, they rated farmers as better than herders, though why a man herding sheep and cattle could possibly be of less value than one growing grain and vegetables, Angharad couldn't say. No meal was complete without milk or meat, but a Saxon peasant could live for years entirely on porridge and thin gruel. Even their drink was made of grain instead of honey.

Here in the town of Bristol, the gardens couldn't be extensive, though the priory did own many acres of land outside the town. Most were planted in crops that fed the monks, and Angharad hadn't seen a single sheep since she'd arrived in Bristol. The herbalist, however, wouldn't be growing grain. He oversaw the cultivation of herbs and medicinals for the monastery table and infirmary, so his garden was conveniently located to the northeast of the main church buildings.

Having left Tangwen playing in the snow in her nanny's care, Gwen and Angharad followed their instincts and eventually fetched up in front of the herbalist's hut. Angharad loosened her cloak at the neck, looking forward to once again being inside. Even in the short walk from the guesthouse, the snow had accumulated on her shoulders and head, and she brushed at Gwen's cloak to rid her of her own layer of white. Taran was bundled warmly, and only once they were under the eaves did Gwen loosen the toggle at her chest too and let him peek out his head.

"Do you need me to stay with you while you talk to him?" Dai said. "I can quarter the area later."

"If we do, we'll call you," Gwen said.

"Then I'll just knock on the door for you." Dai was taking his duties very seriously. He knocked, but there was no immediate answer.

"Perhaps he's in the warming room," Angharad said. "You could hardly blame him for not staying out here on a day like this."

Gwen pointed to the thatched roof overhanging her head. "I smell smoke."

Once she started paying attention, Angharad could see as well as smell the wisps of smoke curling between the thatch and the thick beams that supported the roof. It would be warm in the hut, if a little smoky. It shouldn't be choking, however, since the smoke would eventually filter through the thatch, keeping at bay whatever bugs had survived the autumn and damping down sparks from the brazier before they could set the thatch alight. Smoke also helped to waterproof the roof, necessary on a day like today.

Dai, being Dai, did not give up, but put his ear to the door. "I hear someone moving around in there."

At the risk of being inelegant and possibly rude, Angharad put her own ear to the door. She frowned as she heard a pot rattle and what could have been a muffled curse. "You're right, Dai. Someone is definitely in there." She rapped more sharply on the door than Dai had done.

Finally, footfalls sounded on the other side of the door, heavy thuds, in fact, as if someone was out of temper and expressing anger by stomping on the floor. Angharad had time to take a single step back before the door was pulled sharply open, revealing a squat, balding man in a patched brown robe. "What is it?" he said in English.

There was no denying that Angharad felt taken aback. She'd expected in this heavily-Norman stronghold for the monk to be Norman and speak French, but then she reminded herself that the Norman conquerors made up a tiny fraction of the total population of England. All the monasteries in the country couldn't be populated only by younger Norman sons. If they were present, they were probably in the scriptorium, occupied with more lofty tasks, rather than getting their hands dirty in the garden.

That might also be the reason for the monk's combative attitude. Rather than responding to it, she accorded him a curtsey. "I am Lady Angharad and this is Lady Gwen. We were hoping we could speak to you about your brother."

Edwin glared at her. "My brother? I have many brothers, and it isn't my place to discuss any of them." He turned his back and returned to his table, where he'd been measuring seeds and apportioning them into dishes.

Angharad felt lucky he hadn't actually slammed the door in her face. She also hadn't considered the confusing use of the word *brother* before she'd spoken, despite the fact that Evan had noted it earlier, and she glanced questioningly at Gwen, who smiled and tipped her head as if to say, *Go on, now that you've started.* Angharad hastily stepped inside the hut and attempted to engage the healer again. "I apologize for not speaking more exactly. I'm not here for gossip. I meant that I have been tasked with questions about your late brother, Bernard."

The monk froze in the act of pouring seeds into a dish, such that a few spilled from the clay bottle and fell onto the table. He didn't reply, however, and after the moment of hesitation, he continued about his work as if Angharad hadn't spoken.

So she tried again, "I'm sorry if you think I misled you initially. My husband is among those investigating the deaths at the castle—"

"And he sent you here to talk to a grieving brother instead of facing that task himself?" Edwin sneered and turned away. "Typical Welshman."

Angharad found her temper rising, not only for her husband's sake, but for her people. "He is tasked not only with questioning the monks about these deaths at the castle, but with the safety of the priory, seeing as how yet another man has died, and his murderer remains free!"

Finally Edwin was interested enough to look at her. "Another murder?" He snorted. "I didn't know there'd been any."

Angharad ground her teeth at his obstreperousness. She knew her color was high, and she took in a breath to calm herself, glad only Gwen was here to witness her difficulties. And, because they were friends, Gwen gave a little cough and moved inside the hut too. She'd undone her cloak, so Taran's little head poked out, and he turned his face towards the brightness of the monk's lantern. Even a grumpy monk couldn't sneer at the boy's wondering eyes, and his expression softened, giving Gwen the opening she needed.

"Sir Aubrey, Earl Robert's steward, was killed yesterday by a falling piece of masonry, and another body has been discovered in the tunnel underneath the castle, that of a man named Aelfric."

Edwin snorted. "I didn't know the man. It has nothing to do with me."

Gwen made her voice even softer. "But you did know your own brother."

Edwin still didn't relent, so Angharad added, "Anything you can tell us about him would be helpful. The reason he died is as important to us as any of these other deaths."

"Bernard drowned. His death and these others are not related."

"Sir Aubrey's death was meant to look like an accident, but the mason assures us that the stone had been deliberately loosened. Your brother is said to have drowned by accident, but what if it was murder too?" Gwen said.

"Don't you want to know what really happened?" Despite Angharad's best efforts to control her voice, it rose in volume.

"He's dead. What does it matter?"

"Because others have died now too," Gwen said.

"Please, just speak to us of him," Angharad said. "Tell us who he was to you, and we'll leave you in peace."

Gwen took one more step closer. "We are here asking questions at the request of Prince Henry himself, and your abbot hoped you'd be cooperative."

Edwin's jaw was tight, he still looked mulish, and he appeared to be clenching his teeth around words he wasn't saying. For once, however, he didn't have a snide remark. It could even be that he'd goaded them not because he was angry at them specifically, but because it was his way of dealing with grief. Edwin wasn't wrong that many men avoided grief, and it was common to take refuge in anger rather than allowing themselves tears.

So Angharad tried one more time. "When did you last see your brother?"

"The day he died." Edwin's shoulders remained stiff, and he didn't look at her, but it seemed they'd finally worn him down. "He and I were not as close as some brothers, mind you, but we did make a point to see each other every Sunday, with my abbot's permission, in memory of our mother, who loved us both. Earl Robert died on the last day of October, which was a Friday. Bernard's wife died the next day, Saturday, and my brother died Sunday afternoon. He'd come for the funeral mass, and we'd breakfasted together afterwards."

"Did he seem different to you that day?"

Edwin's lip curled, and she blushed at such a foolish question. "Of course he seemed different! Though he'd served the earl for less than a year, in two days' time he'd lost his livelihood and his wife!"

Angharad wasn't proud of the way she'd goaded Edwin into a passionate answer, but she pounced on what he'd revealed as a result. "Why would he lose his livelihood? Hadn't he worked at the castle for some time before he became the earl's valet?"

Edwin snorted. It seemed to be his favorite thing to do. "He couldn't go back to being just a servant. He'd had status as the earl's valet, serving the most powerful man in England, barring the king. But Earl William wasn't going to keep him on."

"Do you know why not?"

Edwin gave her a look that implied she was dim. "He had his own man."

Angharad canted her head. "Did Earl William not like Bernard?"

"The new earl has his own ways." Edwin pressed his lips together for a moment. "When the old valet died and Earl Robert promoted Bernard, William was not pleased. He'd had his own man in mind then too."

"Which would be whom?"

"I wouldn't know."

"Did your brother express anything else to you—any hint of uncertainty about the way either the earl or his wife died?" Gwen asked.

Edwin shook his head, but then actually offered new information. "Earl Robert was ill for a long time. The wasting disease, you know. This past year, I spent many hours at his bedside seeking a cure for what ailed him, but nothing I tried worked. It would have been better in the end if his disease had killed him more quickly. I hated to see him suffer so." He turned away to pull down a jar from an upper shelf on the other side of the hut, and Angharad had the sense he was searching for control, rather than for a specific potion.

"I watched my grandmother die that way," Angharad said.

Gwen moved around the table and indicated one of the jars. "Is that poppy serum?"

"It is. I must replenish my stock. The earl needed a great deal of it by the end."

Angharad made sure not to look meaningfully at Gwen and made no mention of the fact that Prince Henry had called for Gareth and Gwen to come to Bristol precisely because he thought his uncle had been hurried to his death. It hadn't occurred to any of them that the reason might have been to ease his pain.

Edwin cleared his throat. "Some might find it odd that a healer would wish death to come sooner to those who suffer."

"No." Gwen shook her head. "Not at all. I have some understanding of herbs and healing, and my father's wife is well known for her knowledge. I've tended men after battle. It's almost harder to watch another in pain than to experience it oneself."

They'd come far enough that Edwin managed a rueful smile. "Earl Robert wouldn't take more than a few drops at any one time. He didn't like what it did to his mind, and I can't say I blame him, though I wished towards the end he would allow himself more relief than he did." Edwin was concentrating again on the herbs before him. "But God chooses the time, and we must abide by His decisions."

That didn't sound like Edwin had done anything more than help the earl with pain. They'd also strayed from a discussion of his brother, and Angharad thought she knew how to bring it back. "Did Bernard believe that?"

Edwin's head came up. "What did you say?"

Gwen put out a hand to Angharad, telling her that she'd take over for a moment. "Could your brother swim?"

Edwin's hands shook slightly, and a few more seeds spilled from the clay dish. "Yes. He and I learned together in the Avon."

"You said earlier that he drowned," Angharad said. "Do you really believe that?"

They'd been getting along better, but now anger suffused Edwin's face. "What are you implying?"

Angharad swallowed hard at Edwin's passion, but this time she'd made it rise on purpose, trying to get an unguarded answer from him. "Loved ones are often the last—"

He cut her off with a sharp response, "Bernard didn't kill himself."

Angharad put up both hands. "*I* didn't suggest it."

Now it was Gwen's turn again. "We have been thinking murder all along, Brother Edwin. Hadn't we made that clear? Who suggested suicide?"

Edwin glared from one woman to the other for few heartbeats, and then pinned his gaze on Gwen. "It's been said." He tipped his chin, indicating the world beyond the door. "Up at the castle, I know some considered it. The priest did as well, though Earl William persuaded him not to pursue the matter. However my brother died, he did not take his own life. He was grieving his wife and his lord, but still, he never would." He looked at Angharad. "So yes, he did believe that God chooses each man's time."

Gwen's face was full of pity. "Will you still not consider the possibility that someone wanted to harm him? Especially with more deaths before and since?"

The pause was even longer this time as Edwin stared down at the jar in his hand, as if surprised that he still held it. He looked at it for so long, Angharad didn't think he was going to answer at all, especially when he started to pick up the stray seeds one at a time to return them to the original dish. But she and Gwen stood there anyway, waiting, and finally he said, "I could believe it. But I have no reason to think anyone would want to harm my brother."

Then his head came up, and his face drained of all expression. "He was a good man."

16

Gareth

Another day, another body. Gareth's dismay at the sight of Aelfric's body could not be overstated. "Who was he, exactly?" he asked Harold. "You were his captain and oversaw his work."

Harold spread his hands wide. He'd expressed nothing more than a grunt at the sight of the body, which four men were now loading onto a stretcher so they could carry him to lie where Sir Aubrey's body had been until an hour ago. Aubrey's grave had been dug yesterday, and he'd been put in the ground this morning, despite the snow.

While the priest who administered to the castle community had, of course, prayed over him, Earl William also wanted a formal mass sung at St. Peter's Church (another church Earl Robert had founded, this one in the town just beyond the main gate on the northwest side of the castle) at a time when everyone in the castle could attend. That had been set for tomorrow afternoon. Perhaps poor Aelfric could be buried then too.

"He was a guard. Nobody of importance. Saxon, as I'm sure you can tell by the name. His sister lives in the town with her husband and children. That is all I knew of him."

"Would he have come down here as part of his duties?"

"No more than any other soldier—which is to say no, or not often. He wasn't posted here yesterday but on the outer curtain wall." Harold looked down at his feet. "I must admit, had he not been garroted, I would have wanted to believe he could have drunk too much, stumbled, and died down here alone in the dark." He lifted his head to look at Gareth. "I was not as helpful to your son as I could have been yesterday. I didn't want to believe."

"Aelfric's absence meant little at the time," Gareth said. "We see the past with clearer eyes."

Llelo's lips also twisted with regret. "I did mention the missing guard last night when we talked, but I didn't name him, and it was in passing."

Gareth held his tongue. It wasn't Llelo's fault for not emphasizing what turned out to be a vital piece of information. They couldn't have done anything about Aelfric's disappearance at the time, nor known that it, among all the bits of information they'd learned yesterday, was more important than any other.

"That his death is related to these others, however, cannot be denied." Gareth said.

"Can you tell how long Aelfric has been dead?" Harold asked.

"He is cold and stiff," Llelo said.

"While it's cold outside and cold down here," Gareth said, "which would affect how quickly the body cooled, the stiffness of the body tells me he died before midnight last night, and perhaps quite some time before."

"We must discover when someone last saw him." Llelo tipped his chin to indicate the path back to the castle. "Yesterday, I was told by one of your men, Thomas, that the men rotate around the castle over the course of their shift, so nobody becomes bored or accustomed too long to the same duty. But do the same men serve the same locations every day at a specific time?"

"It varies by the week and by the position. The shift in this guardhouse is four hours, after which a man moves elsewhere." Harold looked grim.

"We will need to speak to whomever was on duty yesterday from mid-morning on," Gareth said.

"Last night's guards will be asleep," Harold said, though he flushed after he spoke. "I realize that is not your concern. I will wake them and send to you all the men on duty around the time Aeflric left the castle." He turned to go.

"Wait—" Llelo pulled out one of Gareth's sketches of the woman they now knew to be Rose. "We're looking for her too."

Harold took the paper, glanced at it, and frowned.

"You know her?" Gareth said.

Harold snorted. "Of course I know her. What man at the castle does not?" It was a very similar response to what Hamelin's had been. Then his eyes narrowed. "I haven't seen her recently, however. She is missing?"

Gareth wasn't ready to betray all of Rose's confidences just yet. "We need to speak to her."

"Of course. Where will you be?"

"With the body," Gareth said.

* * * * *

The laying-out room wasn't where Gareth was supposed to be this morning, and while he couldn't quite be grateful that someone else had died, he hadn't been enjoying his time at the conference either. Talking over breakfast with great lords about their plan for the conquest of England was not his idea of a pleasurable way to spend his day. The conversation could easily have been about Wales—and probably had been at one time. Almost worse was the manner in which he was treated: with respect.

If he'd thought any of them was a murderer, he would have been highly suspicious indeed. As it was, he felt like a fool to have Norman lords praising him. He was good at his job, and he had been among those who took Wiston Castle, but it all seemed a bit excessive and ultimately false—which made him wonder if there wasn't something else someone wanted from him that he wasn't going to want to do.

He certainly didn't want to be examining another dead body, but they definitely had a killer on the loose, since Aelfric hadn't garroted himself. English or Welsh, murder was definitely Gareth's business.

"Do you know what was used to strangle him?" Llelo looked up from where he was examining Aelfric's belongings, which were few enough. He possessed the clothes on his back, an all-but-empty purse, and a satchel. The man had not been moving up in the world.

"A thin rope from behind." Gareth was bent to Aelfric's throat, which was bruised and broken, and he had a pair of metal tweezers in his hand. He turned to Llelo to show him the thin strand of rope he'd found in the wound.

Llelo picked up one of the candles and brought it closer so he could see better. "Hemp. That type of rope can be found anywhere."

Gareth canted his head. "My guess, it's from the laundry line next door."

Llelo's eyes widened. "I've been in there! I think you're right."

Gareth put the thin thread into a clay dish on a nearby table. "Not that it helps us identify the killer. Everyone in the castle had access to that rope."

"Can you tell anything about him from the way Aelfric was killed?"

"Being left-hand leaning would have been thoughtful of him, but I'm not able to determine that from the garrote. Perhaps if his throat had been sliced, we might see a deeper cut on one side or the other as the killer pulled the knife back, but even that might not be definitive."

"Never assume, I know." Llelo turned back to the satchel and began to lay out its contents. "Father—

At the surprise in his son's voice, Gareth looked over. It wasn't every fifteen-year-old who could assist the way Llelo did and, not for the first time, Gareth suppressed guilt that he was warping his son. "What is it?"

Llelo held a small mason's hammer in one hand and a chisel in the other. "These were in his satchel, at the very bottom wrapped in a pair of old socks. Could-could they have been planted on him to mislead us?" Llelo really was accustomed to deception for his mind to have gone immediately to that.

"Or, with some credibility, since he's dead, Aelfric really is the one who loosened the stone."

"He couldn't have killed Sir Aubrey, though. The captain said he was at the meeting, with other people, when Sir Aubrey died, unless ... Harold is lying?"

Gareth rubbed his chin. It was a quandary, but at the same time it was a thread, like the one he'd found in Aelfric's neck, and if they pulled on it, he was going to find something at the other end.

"Excuse me, my lord."

The voice wasn't one Gareth recognized, and he looked to the door. A man blocked the doorway—and the light—so his face wasn't immediately clear.

Gareth waved a hand. "Come in."

"If-if you could come out, sir, I would be grateful."

With a sweep of his arm, Gareth threw a sheet over the body. On his way to the door, he said to his son, "Lay everything out on the table, Llelo, so I can examine it. I'll take care of this."

"Yes, Father."

Gareth stepped outside the hut but halted immediately to stand under the eaves, not terribly surprised to find that the snow had turned to rain. In fact, he'd been hearing rain thudding on the roof for some time, but he'd been so focused on the dead man that the sound hadn't risen to the forefront of his mind. Outside of the stone walkways, the bailey was already turning into a muddy puddle. Two men huddled with him.

"The captain asked that we come," one of the men said. He was of medium height, with dark hair and eyes and a close-cropped beard like Normans often wore. The second man was blond with an even shorter beard, which it appeared he was trying (and failing) to grow. That wasn't uncommon in young men with his coloring. They were both younger than Gareth by at least a decade. "We saw Aelfric yesterday."

"When was this?"

"Near midday."

"He was on duty then, supposedly on the outer wall," Gareth said. "Did he say anything strange to you or mention what he was doing?"

"He said the captain had sent him on an errand to town." The dark-haired man was still speaking.

His companion nodded vigorously. "He didn't return."

The dark-haired man slapped his friend on the chest with the back of one hand. "Of course he didn't return. He was dead!"

"You didn't think to wonder why he didn't come back?" Gareth said.

Both men shrugged in unison. "We sent him on his way through the tunnel to town, but we didn't think anything of not seeing him again. Lots of times people walk the streets back, especially if it isn't raining," the blond man said.

"Did you know him well?"

The dark-haired man shrugged. "To speak to. Not to drink with except in passing."

The blond man's brows drew together. "He and I shared a few flagons just the other day at a tavern in town. He bought them."

His friend glared at him. "Where would he get the money for that? He's paid the same as we are."

The blond man shrugged again. "He didn't say, but it wasn't just me he bought for."

"Thank you," Gareth said. "If you think of anything else, please come find me."

"Yes, my lord." They both bowed.

Gareth watched them go. Then he called to Llelo. "Where's Hamelin?"

"He felt he needed to attend to Prince Henry before returning to us."

Gareth had been walking back to the keep from the latrine in the outer ward when he'd run into Llelo, who'd already sent Dai back to the priory. His son had told him of the body immediately, so Gareth hadn't returned to the conference nor disturbed it with the news of Aelfric's death. That was to have been Hamelin's job, and he'd been gone now for over an hour.

Gareth checked the sky, trying to determine the time of day. Then a bell tolled in the distance.

"Midday," Llelo said from inside the room.

Gareth gestured to the satchel. "Have you found anything else?"

"No, sir."

"Leave it for now, then. We have another task."

Llelo moved with alacrity, arriving nearly instantly in the doorway. "We do?"

"Did you ever walk to the end of the tunnel?"

"No, sir. We found the body first."

"Is that end guarded too?"

Llelo paused. "Yes."

"Good," Gareth said. "We have more questions to ask."

17

Llelo

"How many people did you say came through the tunnel yesterday afternoon?" Llelo was unable to keep the tone of surprise from his voice.

They were in a stone building built over the top of the tunnel entrance. Given that the town had guarded walls as well, for an enemy to reach the tunnel would have required significant effort—and couldn't have been done in numbers anyway. Llelo thought it was a major weak point in the castle's defenses, however, even if it made coming and going from the keep convenient at times. Then again, Aber had two tunnels, both also always guarded, and they'd proved useful in the past.

"At least a dozen," the old guard said. His name was Tom, and he was possibly four times Llelo's age. Whether or not Harold was lying about Aelfric's whereabouts, his assessment of the state of Bristol's garrison appeared to be accurate: they had a host of inexperienced young men and a handful of greybeards, and not much in between. If King Stephen realized this, he might be far more optimistic about the chances of an attack on Bristol succeeding—and far less concerned about the forces arrayed against him.

Then again, he could be in the same situation as Henry. Eight years into the war, both sides had lost far too many fighting men.

"How a dozen?" Gareth said.

"It's a gate like any other, the way is straight and well lit, even without one's own torch. If the weather is inclement, or we intend to store something in the castle, and it's easier to bring in this way, we allow it. Every man is known to us, however. We don't let just anyone pass."

"I want their names," Gareth said.

The man frowned, thinking. "One was Sir Harold, of course, checking that all was well."

"Wait—" Gareth put up a hand, asking the guard to pause while he brought out a paper and lead to write with. The pencil was a present from Abbot Rhys, with the lead wrapped in a thin skin to make it easier to hold and write with. The monks used them more for making lines in manuscripts than for actual writing, but it was perfect for Gareth's purposes, since he could carry it in his pocket and make notes. "What hour of the day was that?"

Tom looked at his companion, yet another man in his late teens, who said, "Around None, I think."

"That's right," Tom said. "The bell had just rung."

Llelo's brow furrowed. "The captain had left us by then, Father. He said he had duties to attend to."

"So he did." Gareth sighed. "Who else?"

"Several men coming off shift who live in the town." Tom turned to the table behind them. "You can read? Here." He turned back and showed a piece of paper to Gareth.

Llelo stepped closer to look. "It's a list of names."

"We keep track of everyone coming and going." Tom looked very proud, though almost immediately his smile faltered. "We did keep track, I mean. We've been told we don't have to anymore."

"Told by whom?" Llelo asked, remembering that nobody had written down his name when they'd left the castle last night or when he'd entered that morning, though it had seemed very important the day before.

"I don't know. The men we relieved only said that we didn't have to."

"Who wrote these?" Gareth said.

"I did." The younger man raised a finger. "I can write."

The list from yesterday had forty names on it, written in several different hands. Literacy seemed to be important at Bristol Castle. Then again, a man didn't need to know how to read to write out letters if someone knew how to spell his name. Llelo pointed to one, towards the end of the day: Rose.

Gareth turned the paper to show the young guard. "Do you remember her?"

The guard flushed. "Yes, my lord."

"Was she coming or going?"

"Going." He leaned forward. "That's the tick beside the name."

Now that the guard had pointed it out, roughly half the names had the mark—and half of those were on the list twice, since they'd returned this way as well.

"Why the different hands?" Llelo said.

"If someone can write, I have them do their own name. Sir Aubrey said that was best." If possible, the guard turned even redder. "Sometimes I don't spell so good. Better if they do it themselves."

Harold had clearly done his own, as had several others, including Charles, four names farther down. Llelo remembered the distinctive flourish he'd put at the end of each of their names when he'd written them down at the front gate. As at the front gate, and unlike Gareth with his pencil, the guards wrote in pen and ink on a standing desk.

"What happens to the lists?" Gareth said.

"We keep them here," Tom said. "Sir Aubrey would collect them every few days."

"Do you know what he did with them?" Llelo said.

"Kept 'em." Tom shrugged. It wasn't an uncommon reaction to writing from someone who couldn't read. The names were scratches to him, not necessarily foolish, but certainly useless.

Gareth held up the list. "May I keep this?"

Tom shrugged again. "Sir Aubrey's gone, isn't he? Nobody cares about them anymore."

Gareth thanked the two men and set off back through the tunnel. Llelo followed closely at his heels. "What now?"

"I have to return to the conference. It is most inconvenient."

"Surely the investigation is more important?"

Gareth stopped and fixed his son with a beady eye. "More important than keeping an eye on Cadwaladr? More important than being on hand when the barons of England make a decision to go to war again?"

Llelo was taken aback at his father's harsh tone. "No." He shook his head. "I can see that it isn't."

Gareth took in a breath and started walking again. "I'm sorry. I shouldn't have spoken thus to you."

"It's fine." Llelo hurried to catch up, the tension in his stomach easing at his father's apology.

"It isn't, but I appreciate you saying so. I'm not angry at you but at the circumstances in which we find ourselves." He took in another audible breath and let it out. "The investigation is continuing. It's just going to be you doing what needs to be done instead of me."

It was not only an apology but a vote of confidence. Llelo quickened his pace. "What do you want me to do?"

"Sir Aubrey obviously had a system in place with these lists. I'd like to go through his records, but I shouldn't without permission, and I don't know that I can corner Earl William before the banquet tonight. As it is, the day is waning, and we have too much to do. I'm also curious to know what your mother has been up to."

"She'll have discovered something."

Gareth shot him a smile. "We'd all be disappointed if she didn't. I will meet you at the priory once I'm let out of this conference. It'll probably be long past sunset by then. In the meantime, go to each guardpost, collect these lists, see what you can make of them, and we will confer tonight."

"Is there anything in particular I should be looking for?"

"I don't know." Gareth shrugged. "I accept that Aubrey's memory could have been failing him—or Earl Robert's—but my instincts tell me there's more to these lists than that."

They'd reached the door to the tower. The guard had heard them coming and already had it open. Before climbing the steps to the guardroom, Llelo paused, speaking slowly as he thought things out, "Robert Fitzharding believed Sir Aubrey to be set in his ways and uninterested in anything new."

His father was a few steps above him, and he stopped to look down. "Keeping lists like this is new to me. Aubrey had to have had a very good reason to require it. It takes an enormous amount of time and effort."

"Maybe Earl Robert, even on his deathbed, felt something was amiss at Bristol," Llelo said. "He was confined to his bed, so this was his way to gather information without relying entirely on someone else's recollections."

"Good. Good. I am thinking along the same lines. If there's more to these lists than meets the eye, I want to know what it is."

18

Gwen

The next morning, their third day at Bristol, Taran woke before dawn as usual, nursed for an hour, and then decided he was tired of lying down. Before he could start squawking and wake everybody else in the guesthouse, Gareth and Gwen got him, Tangwen, and themselves out the door into the garden. Everybody slept longer in the winter, and the monks didn't encourage early rising because it required the use of more candles. Breakfast would be served once the sun was fully up.

The day had dawned clear and warm again, as if the strange snowfall of the day before hadn't happened.

"We have a long day ahead of us." Gareth had been carrying Tangwen, and now he put her down so she could run along the path ahead of them. "Practically the whole of my yesterday was wasted in conference with those barons. I feel the threads of this investigation slipping away from me with every moment that passes."

"We do what we can, as always," Gwen said. "It's hardly your fault you were missing. Prince Henry asks too much."

"He believes himself a king. He can ask what he likes." Gareth shook his head. "I need time to really have a look at those lists of names Llelo collected, and we need to question the boatman and every servant in the castle."

"Not to mention Earl William himself," Gwen said.

"And then there's Roger. He's an odd one, isn't he?"

"He's a younger brother who's following a magnificent older brother, who himself is attempting to fill his father's too-big shoes. It could be a recipe for brotherly love, but it usually isn't."

"William is magnificent, eh?" Gareth said.

Gwen elbowed him in the ribs. "You know what I mean."

"I don't know that I do." He turned to look at her, mischief in his eyes. "He looks that wonderful to you?"

"Of course not. He's a Norman." Gwen reddened slightly and tried to backtrack a bit. "I'm just saying that he's the essence of what a firstborn son should be—and look like. He's a Norman version of Rhun, if you will. Roger is smaller and more intellectual. It's as if nature knew that one was born to lead, and the other was destined for the Church."

Gareth put his arm around her shoulders and pulled her close to kiss the top of her head and then Taran's. "I was teasing you."

After another turn around the garden, Tangwen swinging between them, they found Cadoc standing underneath the gatehouse, staring out at the road and the towers of the castle, which shone in the sunlight four hundred yards away. The morning mist was burning off the moat and rivers, even as the sun rose higher, and the sky grew lighter with the coming of the day.

"When I returned to Wales, I swore I'd never serve in England again," Cadoc said, surprising Gwen by revealing a bit of information about himself. "I wouldn't be here at all if Earl Robert were still alive."

Gwen found her eyes widening. "I'd forgotten about that. I'm sorry."

"Likely, if anyone knew who I really was and what I'd done, I'd be in the basement of the keep." Cadoc had worked for many years among the Normans as an assassin. Thus, his French was perfect, and Gwen had never met anyone who could blend in as well among the populace, though not usually when he wore his bow, which at the moment stuck up on his back behind his head, in its rest next to his quiver. He even had his cloak specially cut, so that it lay flat against his back even when he wore all his gear.

"Then it's a good thing nobody knows." Gareth clapped him on the shoulder. They were speaking in Welsh, so even if anybody else was up at this hour, they wouldn't understand their words. "Have you ever been to Bristol before? I never thought to ask."

"No. And I made sure that, whomever I worked for, I never had contact with the great lords directly. Whatever I did, and for whomever I did it, it's a long time ago now, and everyone involved is either dead or in France."

"Even so, maybe it would be a good idea to keep you out of the castle today," Gareth said.

"I will take on the task of speaking to the servants and maidservants," Gwen said. "You know I'd love to go over those lists with you, but—"

Gareth growled his dismay. "But you'd be of better use questioning the women in the castle. I know."

"My grandfather was a boatman," Cadoc said. "Give me Llelo and that Norman lad, and we will find out everything we can about the dead valet."

Gareth nodded his thanks. "I will take Gruffydd and Aron or Evan with me to Prince Henry's meeting."

"Aron. You don't want to separate Evan from Angharad." Cadoc smirked. "Send them to question the men in the castle. Most will be drawn to Evan as a fellow soldier and member of the Dragons, and they will be so bemused by Angharad's beauty they won't balk at answering the questions she puts to them." He paused and his expression turned somewhat musing. "I believe the two of them make quite a good team."

That left Steffan and Iago, the Dragons whom Gwen knew least well, to patrol the priory and castle.

"What about Dai?" Gwen asked her husband.

Gareth thought for a moment. "He's had enough excitement for the week with the discovery of Aelfric's body, don't you think?"

"He wouldn't want to be left out. That would shame him," Gwen said.

"You should keep him with Evan and Angharad," Cadoc said.

This was truly the longest conversation Gwen had ever had with the archer, and when she raised her eyebrows questioningly at him, he added, "As Llelo is apprenticing to Gareth, it makes sense for Dai to apprentice to Evan. Those boys are not the same, and their futures won't be the same. Dai is a Dragon at heart."

Gwen had never thought about her younger son that way, but Gareth said, "You may be right that it's a better fit for him."

"In light of the loss of Aelfric, what now do you make of these other deaths?" Gwen asked. If Cadoc wanted to talk, she had more to talk about.

Cadoc shrugged. "We came to Bristol because Prince Henry called, and the day we arrive there's another death? And then another? Hard to argue with him now, isn't it?"

Gwen's head came up. "You're not suggesting that *Henry* arranged for Aubrey's death—or, God forbid, Aelfric's—are you?"

"No! Not in the least!" Cadoc laughed. "I'm just saying that whoever killed Aelfric may have done so because we'd arrived."

"That's what Angharad said about Aubrey's death." Gwen signaled to Tangwen's nanny, who'd come out of the guesthouse, that she should see to Tangwen, who was digging a stick into the dirt between the stones of the courtyard. "Hard to imagine what either of these men could have said to us that he wouldn't have already told Earl William or Prince Henry. Even if this is about those intercepted messages, killing Sir Aubrey isn't going to prevent us from seeing them. Prince Henry, and who knows who else, already has."

"And what light does Aelfric's death shed on Earl Robert's?" As Llelo had done, Gareth gave Taran his finger to squeeze his little hand around.

Cadoc shook his head. "None at all, as far as I can tell."

* * * * *

"You don't have to do this, you know," Gareth said an hour later, as they gazed together up at Bristol's towers, having been bowed through the gatehouse with an almost disconcerting amount of respect.

Gruffydd and Aron had come with them too, along with Taran, of course. They'd breakfasted with Tangwen and then consigned her again to the care of her nanny. Tangwen was accepting of the lack of attention for now, but once life returned to normal, she would spend a few days clinging to Gwen and fearing her possible departure. Such was life with a two-year-old.

Dai, Angharad, and Evan had already gone off to question the castle's male population.

"I am anxious to find this murderer before he strikes again," Gareth added, "but that might be all the more reason for you not to involve yourself."

"I *am* involved. Better to work quickly, so as to neutralize him sooner." She canted her head. "I may dread doing this sometimes, but inactivity doesn't suit me either. A day like yesterday is nice every once in a while, but not all the time."

"Solving murders is definitely not a normal way to live."

"Nobody ever said our lives were going to be normal." She lifted her skirts and started up the steps to the keep.

"I confess I feel a bit out of my depth here, Gwen," Gareth said, following just behind her. "Five deaths now? And we don't have a single definitive suspect."

"I know that, and you know that, but the people here do not. We're trading on our reputation from Newcastle-under-Lyme—and yours from this summer—and we're going to exploit it shamelessly." Gwen smiled at the guard, who opened the door for them. "I honestly don't mind doing this. I just don't love Normans."

Gruffydd had come with them, and now he snorted under his breath. "Who does? And why would we?"

"They do seem to love themselves, though, don't they?" Aron said with his typical bite, though he made sure to speak, as they all had been, low and in Welsh.

Once inside the great hall, Gwen was surprised to find so few people in it. Bristol's hall was similar to dozens of other great halls Gwen had entered over the course of her life, and they were always the center of a castle's community. This one was arranged with many tables about which residents might mingle, drink, and talk. Rather than a central hearth, such as those found in Danish and many Welsh dwellings, a large fireplace, built in stone like the hall, filled a portion of one wall near the high table, so the higher-ranking diners could stay warm. Thankfully, despite the blaze, the hall wasn't filled with choking smoke, indicating Earl Robert, as in everything he'd done, had sought out the best architect and master mason, who knew what they were doing.

While Earl Robert had had a hand in the design of Newcastle-under-Lyme, the previous stronghold belonging to him that Gwen had been in, and had taken pains in its construction, Bristol Castle had been the seat from which he ruled his earldom and the pride of his personal kingdom. The rich tapestries, carved flourishes around the doorways, the great mantle in the hall, and the glass window panes all bore testimony to his care. Robert had never been profligate, and even had a reputation for austerity in his personal life, but if the man had spent money anywhere, it had been here.

All that was missing was a raised platform from which a bard might perform, even in a hall that was in mourning—or especially in such a hall. No Welsh castle or palace could be complete without it, but here, it had been forgotten. As Gwen's father had said more than once, usually accompanied by a shake of his head, *the Saxon soul has no music in it.*

With the steward dead—his funeral service would be held that evening at Compline in St. Peter's Church outside the castle grounds—things could have been in chaos. But they were not, in large part because of the efforts of Robert Fitzharding and the resolve of Lady Mabel, who, at the moment, stood near the dais. She was speaking pointedly to a much younger woman, almost a girl, who cowered before her.

Gwen would have stayed away, but she knew her job today, and it wasn't going to get done by hanging back. So she approached, warily at first until the lecture appeared over, and stopped within a few paces of the two women.

Both saw her coming, but it was the younger woman, whom Gwen had not met, who spoke first. She had something of a long face, and the way her brown hair was contained in braids indicated she was unmarried. She was also slightly older than Gwen had first thought, closer to twenty than fifteen. Her mouth and eyes had a pinched look to them, and she appeared to have been afflicted with terrible spots, though with time they had faded to pale scars. "You've returned. Why is it the Welsh are so intent on fostering mischief?"

Gwen blinked. Yesterday, she'd comforted Lady Mabel despite her bitter tongue and the barbs she'd sent in Gwen's direction. But Gwen had never met this girl. At the same time, it was not unusual for someone, who'd just been chastised, to cope with their humiliation by turning around and abusing another. It just wasn't very mature. Or kind.

But Gwen refused to rise to the bait, because that would only confirm their assessment of her and her people. She looked at Lady Mabel. "My lady, we now have five dead in less than a month and two in three days. I am here to speak to the servants of the castle, since three of the dead were numbered among them."

"We? How can you say *we*? It is our loss, not yours." The young woman's voice was biting and shrill.

Gwen couldn't ignore her, fearing, if nothing else, that her shrieking would unsettle Taran, who at the moment was happy and alert in his wrappings. With an inward sigh and a quick gritting of the teeth, she said, "We are all family in the eyes of God, are we not? Isn't the loss of every soul cause for grief in the body of Christendom?" She wasn't completely sure what she'd just said made sense, but it sounded pious, and something she'd heard a priest say more than once.

Lady Mabel stepped in. "You'll have to excuse Mabel. She has been much grieved by her father's death."

Gwen instantly reined in her ire, putting aside for a moment the identical names. "I'm so sorry for your loss. Who was your father?"

That was the wrong question to ask. The girl sniffed. "As if you don't know."

Gwen blinked. "I'm sorry, but I really do not." She looked from one woman to the other. They looked nothing alike, and Lady Mabel hadn't introduced the younger woman as her daughter, which would have been customary if that were the case—especially with the identical names.

"Earl Robert was Mabel's father." As Lady Mabel tsked her apparent disapproval, the younger Mabel turned away—literally turned to one side—so her back was to her foster mother.

Gwen lifted one hand in appeasement. "I understand." And she thought she did. The younger Mabel was Earl Robert's bastard, whom he'd named after his wife, perhaps in an attempt to make taking her in more palatable. Queen Susanna had accepted responsibility for King Madog's by-blow, Marared, and raised her as her own. The girl was engaged to Iorwerth, King Owain's eldest son by his first wife Gwladys. Gwen had met Marared, and she was lovely inside and out. What had happened in Bristol was clearly exactly the opposite.

Gwen swallowed, deciding it was in everyone's best interest to return to the reason she was here. "May I question your servants?"

The younger Mabel scoffed. "If there are any left."

Lady Mabel appeared to be within a hair's-breadth of rolling her eyes. Instead she said, somewhat conspiratorially to Gwen, "One of the servants, a laundry girl, was so traumatized by the events of the last month that she's taken herself off with no warning, and now half her fellows are threatening to do the same."

"It's your fault, you know." Child Mabel was examining her nails with a frown, still half-turned away and not looking at either Gwen or Lady Mabel.

"I'm sorry. How is that my fault?" Gwen bit the inside of her lip, inwardly cursing that she'd risen to the bait like a fish just waiting to be hooked.

Child Mabel sighed elaborately. "One of the other maids saw her speaking to your husband—and then apparently to you—yesterday. What did you say to her?"

"You're speaking of … Rose?"

"Of course I'm speaking of Rose!" Child Mabel said.

Lady Mabel was actually looking embarrassed, though why she didn't send her (daughter?) away, Gwen didn't know—unless she thought it would only make things worse. Gwen didn't need to have her time in the castle made even more difficult, so she renewed her attempt to be conciliatory. "I assure you, my lady, that Rose, who called herself Edith to us, came to Gareth and me all on her own. She said she had information that would convince us that Prince Henry's suspicions were correct and that your father genuinely was murdered."

Child Mabel sneered. "And did she?"

"I'm sorry, but it's too soon to say. She had nothing to tell us that was enough to pin a conclusion on. After we talked, she said she was going to leave Bristol. Truly, I tried to stop her and had nothing to do with her decision."

Child Mabel harrumphed and stuck her nose even higher in the air, though her shoulders weren't as tight as before, and when she spoke next, her words contained less vinegar. "Everybody is upset by this new death, coming hard on the heels of the others. You have to forgive our short tempers."

"Of course, my lady." Gwen gave a little curtsey.

Lady Mabel tipped her head to her daughter. "I will leave the two of you alone to sort out the servants." She turned on her heel and departed.

Gwen gaped after Lady Mabel, shocked and disturbed to be left alone with her hostile namesake, but Child Mabel looked morosely up at Gwen. "Your baby is very sweet. And you can call me Mabs. Everyone else does."

Gwen's heart softened, now seeing Mabs less as an enemy than one of the wounded. In a different world, with a different mother, Mabs could have been a much-cossetted member of the household. But she hadn't been raised in Wales or in a Welsh court, where being illegitimate and female to boot would have mattered far less, if at all. Though Earl Robert himself was a bastard, claimed her as his own, and brought her into his household, Mabs was unloved by the woman who was supposed to raise her.

"I'm sure you have a finger on everything that happens at Bristol Castle, upstairs and down. I would be genuinely grateful for your help today." Gwen was careful to keep the pity out of her face. Mabs would have lived with pity her whole life, when it wasn't outright hostility or disdain, and knew it in all its many colors.

This time, it was Mabs who blinked. Those inferior to her would have to treat her with courtesy, but Gwen's words had been sincere, a sentiment she may not often have heard. "Perhaps I can help, at that. I can tell you straight away that Rose was in love with my father's valet, even though he was married already, with a child on the way."

Gwen knew she had been right to rein in her animosity, because the information that Jenet was pregnant was brand new, and Gwen hadn't had to do anything to attain it. "We are speaking of Jenet, the maid who died on your father's floor, who was married to Bernard, your father's valet?"

"Yes, of course." Mabs looked taken aback. "He would have had only one wife. Do men in Wales have more than one?"

Gwen smiled. "No. One is the usual number."

Mabs nodded, as if Gwen had confirmed a rumor she'd heard but hadn't dared believe.

"Did Jenet have any particular friends?"

"I couldn't say. She would have been seeing the midwife, of course, especially since it is my understanding that the pregnancy had not been going well. Her feet and ankles were badly swollen, and she hadn't attended my father for several days because of it."

All of this was news to Gwen. Gareth had questioned a dozen women yesterday while waiting for her to return from Lady Mabel's room, and none of them had mentioned pregnancy, difficult or otherwise.

"Is there a castle midwife?"

Mabs looked surprised at Gwen's ignorance. "Of course. Even with the two midwives in town, she's run off her feet." The young woman shook her head. "Between here and town, there's a baby born every day."

"Might I speak to her?"

"A baby was born last night. Perhaps we ought to start with someone else." Mabs reeled off ten names too quickly for Gwen to catch even one.

"Thank you. I will need to speak to each of them in turn."

Though Mabs had been suddenly and genuinely helpful, she rolled her eyes at the request. But Gwen knew how investigations worked. It was the routine questions that led to what at first seemed to be routine answers—or maybe no answers at all—that ultimately could change the course of the investigation.

She didn't outwardly show her annoyance, however, and despite their rocky beginning, Gwen even began to wonder, had circumstances been different, if she might have enjoyed Mabs's company.

They began with Dena, a prim woman with thick red hair she'd probably only managed to contain by smoothing it with an entire bottle of oil.

"How well did you know Jenet?" Gwen said.

"Not well at all. She kept to herself." Dena's eyes skated to Mabs as she spoke. Mabs nodded, and all of a sudden, Gwen was uncertain again, because she didn't know if Mabs was nodding encouragingly or telling Dena that the answer she'd given was the correct one.

"What about her husband, Bernard? Did you know him?"

"We didn't mix," Dena said.

"What can you tell me about Rose?"

A brief expression of distaste crossed Dena's face, though her words belied her apparent thoughts. "I can tell you nothing. We worked in different areas of the castle. Her place was in the laundry, you see."

"Did you know that she was interested in Bernard?"

Dena's eyes widened. "Was she?"

"Did you like Bernard?"

Dena folded her hands primly. "It is not my place to like or dislike. He was an upstairs servant. His station was well beyond mine."

"It is my understanding that he was in charge of the earl's wardrobe, the tailors, and the laundries." Gwen tried to keep her expression neutral. She knew Bernard's station already, of course, but while the conversation about Jenet had involved straightforward denial, which sounded either genuine or so well-rehearsed Dena believed it herself, this denial of knowledge of Bernard was far more elaborate for no reason that Gwen could discern.

"He was."

"So he must have known Rose too."

"I'm sorry. I couldn't say. I didn't know either of them well." Dena gave an elaborate shrug before curtseying to Mabs. "May I be dismissed, my lady? I have many duties this morning."

And so it went. Everyone denied knowing Rose well because of her station or because she kept to herself—with no mention of her outstanding beauty. When discussing Jenet, the women were much more sympathetic to her plight and death, but she came across as a shy mouse. Finally, after the fourth interview, Gwen turned to Mabs. "Was Bernard handsome?"

The way Mabs colored told Gwen she'd finally understood an important piece of the puzzle. "I suppose."

"I suppose ... or *yes, he was very handsome.*"

Mabs didn't like to be pressed, and she stuck her nose a bit in the air, but she did finally admit, "He was very handsome."

"Charming too, I imagine."

"I couldn't say. I hardly ever spoke to him."

Gwen swallowed down a grumbling reply. *I couldn't say* seemed to be the standard response any time anyone didn't want to answer a question.

"What about Rose? Did you think her beautiful?"

Now Mabs looked positively mutinous.

"I thought she was," Gwen prompted. "The men I asked about it agreed."

"They would."

"So she was beautiful." Gwen paused a moment to give Mabs a chance to disagree. The woman's lip was sticking out so far a bird could have landed on it. Gwen had to constantly remind herself that Mabs was only a few years younger than she, a grown woman. She certainly didn't behave like it.

"Could there have been a relationship between Rose and Bernard, both beautiful people?" Gwen was grasping at straws, but she would ask anything at this point to elicit a genuine response.

"Oh no! It wasn't like that at all. He would never be unfaithful!" Mabs spoke without thought, and she immediately withdrew into herself, once she realized how unguarded she'd been.

Gwen merely gazed at the woman, who flushed for a moment before continuing somewhat more soberly, "He was generous, always laughing, which I think is why my father liked him so much. He was never above taking the time to speak to anyone who crossed his path."

It was exactly the kind of honesty Gwen was looking for. "Including you?"

Mabs gave a stiff nod, and then consented to answer more fully, "We all liked him very much." She paused. "He was the only one in the castle who, when he looked at me, liked what he saw."

"Why will nobody else speak of him so forthrightly?"

Mabs laughed. "You're an outsider and Welsh in the bargain! Why would they?"

"To discover who killed him?"

"He drowned, by accident or suicide, what does it matter? He's dead." Mabs looked genuinely sad. "The light had gone out of the world for him."

"Do you mean because of his wife's death? Or your father's?"

"No, no. Because of his child's." Mabs was grieving again. "He was faithful to his wife, but he didn't love her at all."

19

Evan

The big ewerer, John, bobbed his head in greeting. Evan was Welsh, but he was dressed as a knight, belted with a sword at his waist. Even a Saxon could tell that he and Angharad were worthy of respect. "Och, man. That lad, Bernard, could charm the wax off a beetle and make him think it was his idea to give it away."

Evan had never heard that expression before, but the ewerer—the man responsible for all the hot water in the castle so the nobles could wash, and also for the laundry—appeared to be a force of nature in and of himself. Evan and Angharad had started their day by interviewing him because he had been crossing the great hall, having emptied a bucket of warm water into the washing basins near the high table.

"Why do you say that?" Angharad said.

John tipped his head towards the door to the keep. "Walk with me. I must refill my bucket." He took long strides across the floor, and they hustled to catch up. Dai kept pace a respectful distance away, since he saw his role today as guard rather than investigator himself. "The water in the basins throughout the castle must always be warm."

"That's quite a responsibility," Angharad said in total seriousness.

John nodded gravely. "Lady Mabel insists on clean hands for all of us, high and low alike. Nobody wants dirty handprints on the sheets or mud in the food."

Evan could only agree with that policy, and he was grateful that John seemed willing to talk to them without discord. Earlier, Angharad had wanted to go to Gwen's defense in her conversation with Lady Mabel, but Evan had held her back.

Angharad had subsided, even though she hadn't wanted to. "Passionate answers are the truest answers, I know."

"Most of the time," Evan said, though his mind had immediately concocted a scenario where a culprit fooled them by feigning anger or tears to mislead them. "Anger and disdain are legitimate responses to questioning, even if they are unpleasant, and Gwen wouldn't thank you for interfering."

As they headed out of the keep, Angharad had to take two steps to keep up with every one of John's. "So you liked him?"

"Bernard? Of course I liked him. Everybody liked him. It was impossible not to, even as you suspected those dice he insisted on using were weighted."

Evan took in a breath. "He gambled?"

The ewerer waved his hand in the air. "Earl Robert—and Earl William in turn—forbade gambling for coins or possessions. The man caught gambling finds himself in the stocks for a day. We gambled for bragging rights and occasionally whose turn it was to fetch another flagon." His face fell. "I was up three hundred pennies." He looked down at Evan and Angharad. "Bernard really wasn't very good at it."

Three hundred pennies, if the gambling had been for real, would have been a fortune. The ewerer's sorrow at his friend's death appeared genuine, however, and had nothing to do with what may or may not have been owed, in life or imagination.

"Do you know of anyone who would have wished harm to him?" Angharad said.

"No one. I can't think it." But then the man stopped his relentless forward movement, chewing on his lower lip.

"There is someone?" Angharad pounced on the moment of hesitation. "Who?"

"I don't know of anyone specifically," John hastened to say, "though I have to admit Bernard did have a way with women. If anyone wanted to murder him it would have been his wife, but she died before he did." Then he tipped his head in a way that again qualified his answer. "Or a cuckolded husband."

"He was unfaithful?" Evan said.

John's eyes flicked to Angharad and back to Evan. With a little snort under her breath, Angharad moved away towards Dai, both suddenly greatly interested in those coming in and out of the gatehouse.

Once she was out of earshot, Evan raised his eyebrows.

John sighed. "In a word, yes."

"He had many women?"

"Bernard had every woman he could, and given how happy he made them, few could resist him." John put up a hand. "He didn't seek out maidens, mind you. He liked married women. Less need to worry about the aftermath." Again the tipping of the head. "Though if he was murdered for it, he may have greatly underestimated the wrath of a husband who found his wife no longer his sole possession."

"What about the young woman with Lady Mabel in the hall?"

"Mabs?" John half laughed, half gasped his surprise. "Not in this lifetime."

"What about Rose, the laundress?"

The ewerer's expression turned thoughtful. "I don't know for certain. She wasn't married, it's true, so I wouldn't normally have said she'd caught his eye, but—"

Evan tried not to lean forward and press the man. "But?"

"She is beautiful." Then he shook his head forcefully. Evan had seen few men—especially Saxon men who tended towards stoic—reveal themselves so clearly by motioning with their head. "If I had to guess, I'd say she was already taken—and by someone even Bernard would not want to cross."

"Who might that be?" More head waggling ensued, encouraging Evan to guess. "Earl William? Sir Aubrey?"

John laughed outright. "No! I was thinking of Robert Fitzharding."

"He can be intimidating, I suppose. He is a Saxon, of course, so disadvantaged here as a result."

"Is he? That may have been true by birth, but in practice?" John shook his head. "Fitzharding is a worthy man, and he knows it. Bernard would have been beneath him, and not only did Bernard know it, he would not take a woman from a man of higher rank." John pressed his lips together.

"There's more?"

"I'm probably wrong about them. At least, I haven't seen them together recently."

"Rose has gone away, anyway," Evan said.

"Has she? When?"

"The day before yesterday."

John made a sound at the back of his throat that sounded like a *huh*.

"Why do you think they were lovers?" Evan said.

"Because Fitzharding was trusted by Sir Aubrey and Earl William, he was a frequent visitor to the castle and had a room in one of the towers. Rose would bring fresh linens to his bedchamber, passing me after I'd filled his basin. She would stay longer than necessary."

That was definitive enough for Evan, but entirely beside the point. Rose was a mystery woman, but it was Jenet who was dead.

"Did you ever see Rose with Jenet?"

John shook his head. "Jenet was a quiet little thing. I have no idea why Bernard married her. Maybe he felt sorry for her. Maybe—" He closed his mouth over whatever words he thought better of expressing.

"Yes?"

John shrugged. "It may be that the child she died with was not their first loss. If he made her pregnant, he did have enough honor to marry her. That was before I knew him, and before they were elevated to Earl Robert's chamber."

"So they had no other children?"

"No."

Angharad wandered back. "Who else should we speak to about Bernard?"

"Anyone. You'll see. Just ask."

Evan thanked him, but as he turned away, he saw that the big man's eyes were thoughtful.

* * * * *

John's description of Bernard, at least according to the men in the castle, proved to be wholly accurate. He had many friends, made both before and after he became Earl Robert's valet.

"It is my understanding he began serving Earl Robert only recently," Evan said to the butler, the next man with whom they chose to speak. In charge of the drink at the castle, he had an army of brewers, dispensers, distillers, and servers under him.

Before answering, the butler handed Angharad a cup of beer. She smiled sweetly as she took a sip, though Evan knew she hated the taste. Evan himself had spent enough time on the border between England and Wales to no longer despise beer—or perhaps it was merely that he was older and his sense of taste had dulled over the years.

To keep on his wife's good side, he took the cup Angharad offered to share with him, as if he didn't know that her goal was to avoid drinking it.

"He worked his way up through the castle. Earl Robert himself picked him out. When the earl's illness caused him particular pain, Bernard could make him laugh. And he could sing like a Welshman." He put out a hand. "No offense meant."

"None taken," Evan said.

"A worthy enough reason to elevate a man," Angharad said. "Did some resent his advancement?"

"Only those with jealous souls. The earl was dying. We all knew it. Who could resent bringing a little light and joy to his last days?" He shrugged. "In the end Earl Robert lived months longer than we thought he would."

"Bernard sounds like a good man," Angharad said.

The butler's eyes narrowed. "Good? Amusing, certainly. But I wouldn't say good. He had a wandering eye, and though he laughed a great deal and was proficient with the ladies, I'm not sure his joy always rose to his eyes." He paused. "I know he was in debt too."

Evan felt a chill between his shoulder blades. "To whom?"

The butler tried to cover his frankness with a laugh. He waved his hand dismissively. "Don't mind me. It is unlucky to speak ill of the dead. Now that I think about it, I'm sure I'm wrong about that and shouldn't have said anything."

Evan wanted to say that it was too late, but Angharad reached out a soft hand and put it on the butler's arm. "His wife died, and then he died, and now Sir Aubrey and Aelfric are dead too. If you can point us in any direction that might lead to an explanation of who and why, please tell us. More lives may depend on it."

The butler stared at her, as if it had just occurred to him why they had been asking him all these questions. "I never thought—" He stopped and took in a breath. "Bernard used to go into town. Earl Robert wasn't one to skimp on the beer, but we kept the stronger stuff for feast days. If a man wanted more, he could go to a tavern, and Bernard was known to do that. Mostly we assumed it was for female companionship, but one day I was looking over a shipment that had come upriver by boat, and I saw him arguing with someone near the dock." He put up a hand. "Don't ask me who. I don't know. It was raining, and the man wore a hat pulled down low."

This was the first time anyone had mentioned the possibility of a stranger, though with murder it was the safest answer and one that many minds went to.

"This was at the castle dock?"

"No, at the town port. Bernard would never have met with someone unsavory inside the castle."

Evan's eyes narrowed. "Why would that be?"

"Because of the lists. You know about the lists?"

Evan and Angharad nodded. They'd gone over the lists themselves last night with Gareth and Llelo. The names numbered in the hundreds and were so many, it seemed nonsensical to keep them. But Gareth was convinced Sir Aubrey wouldn't have gone to such effort without good reason.

"You should ask the steward. He—" The butler broke off, his face turning ashen since, of course, the steward had been Sir Aubrey, and he was dead. "Ask Charles, then. He knows all about it."

20

Cadoc

Cadoc had agreed to become a member of the Dragons because, for a man to whom killing had been a profession, serving Hywel as a member of an elite squad sounded, by comparison, fun. Killing was what he knew best.

In fact, it was all he knew.

Since he was seven years old and his uncle had put his first cut-down-to-size bow into his hand and told him to draw it, he'd felt an affinity for the weapon that was akin to a man who could track a deer or one who could read the weather. Cadoc's father had been a drunkard, and all Cadoc had known up until that time was hunger and the back of his father's hand.

To hold a bow and shoot it, even at seven, had been like touching God. From the very first, he'd felt the hair on his neck rise at a breath of wind, evaluating its speed and direction. As he'd grown, he'd been able to see tiny differences in terrain from a distance, like no one he'd met before or since. Almost immediately, his uncle had realized what he had. Even before Cadoc could shoot an arrow a hundred yards, he was accompanying his uncle to war as his eyes, to tell him where to shoot, how high or low to aim above what he wanted to hit, and the distance to his target.

Admittedly, there'd been a ten-year period during Cadoc's twenties and thirties where he'd lost himself to the bow and to drink and had no life outside of either. Later, after he'd drunk away his payment, he occasionally had second thoughts, but it was never enough to change his course in life. When a man had the ability to kill other men the way Cadoc did, and when he allowed himself to be used for that purpose by other men—not always the most honorable of men either—it created dark patches on the soul. Dark patches that could never be returned to the light.

Cadoc had killed for Rhys, who himself spied for Geoffrey of Anjou. And yet, knowing that a man of Rhys's mettle was on his side had changed Cadoc. Under Rhys's command, he'd begun to wonder if he might have a chance in the world of the living. It had made him recognize the way he'd been used in the past and despise the idea of being used in the present.

He knew himself well enough by then, however, to acknowledge that most of the time he couldn't honestly say what was right and what was wrong. The Bible said *thou shalt not kill*, but war was the single greatest occupation of kings and lords. How was it that a king could be chosen by God and yet spend his reign ordering the death of hundreds of men, whose own king or lord was also divinely ordained?

These questions were too thorny for Cadoc, and he hadn't the temperament to turn priest and abbot like Rhys. But he recognized grace and integrity in other men, even if he retained none for himself. Over time, Cadoc had come to acknowledge that he needed men like Rhys in his life. He could trust that they wouldn't ask him to aim an arrow at someone who didn't deserve to be shot. Thus, if his bow was to be put to use for its intended purpose, he'd resolved only to do so at the command of a man like Rhys. Once Rhys had left Geoffrey's service, and thus stopped providing work for Cadoc, he'd discovered that it was a type of man that was few and far between.

Prince Hywel was not, in fact, such a man.

But Gareth was.

And if Gareth, whom Cadoc knew to have left more than one lord's service because of that lord's lack of honor, could serve Hywel, then who was Cadoc to argue or choose a different path? He already knew he had no soul, but Gareth's glowed around him like a halo.

The only man to whom he'd ever hinted any of this was Abbot Rhys. While the former spy had not told him what to do or which path to tread, his blessing had been clear enough. And somewhere along the way, despite Cadoc's best efforts to live his life apart and behave as if he was self-sufficient, he'd found himself in the center of a large family. And one that he loved.

Over the years, Cadoc had learned to fear emotion, convinced that feeling anything at all for anyone would harm his ability to kill. Instead, he'd been surprised to find that his new emotions sharpened his attention. It was his job to protect his friends, to watch over them, like he'd done at Wiston Castle.

He slept much better these days too.

Even so, he was a little surprised at himself for volunteering to assist in the investigation in the way he had, and particularly that he'd suggested the addition of the two young men who walked behind him. But he'd told Gareth the truth when he'd said that he knew boats. And almost despite himself, he was growing interested in Llelo's development. While Cadoc had spoken his true opinion when he'd suggested that Dai was a born Dragon—a soldier-spy—Llelo had too much of Gareth in him to take to it easily. His mind was sharp, however, which when investigating criminals was a good counterbalance to his mile-wide streak of honesty. Too many Gareths in the world might make life a great deal less colorful, but Wales could afford at least one more.

"So you're the Welshman, are you?"

Cadoc had inquired at the priory gatehouse as to where and from whom the valet would have acquired his boat and had been told that the boatman, Edgar, was the man to speak to.

"One of them," Cadoc said mildly, also in English. He didn't introduce the two young men, which was a calculated strategy. He feared that the presence of Prince Henry's brother might in this instance silence talk instead of encouraging it. Edgar was his own man, but simple, and not under the authority of the castle in the same way as a guard.

They were standing on the edge of the River Frome, adjacent to a wooden dock, one of many jutting into the river. Pilings that supported the dock had been driven deep into the riverbed. In his forty years of existence, Cadoc had traveled from the tip of Anglesey to Italy (the latter in the service of Geoffrey of Anjou). Many of the trading cities on the Continent were larger and more sophisticated than any town in England—certainly than in Wales—but he found that he liked the smaller, more rough-and-tumble, free-wheeling nature of Bristol better. If nothing else, it was more honest. The Venetians prettied up their politics and social interactions with politeness and polish— right before they crept up behind you and stabbed you in the back.

The castle dominated the town, and all trade was taxed for the Earl of Gloucester, but from what Cadoc could see, he kept a light hand on the reins. Though the rumors of William's character were not favorable towards him, Cadoc was more impressed with the man in person and thought he might be as capable as his father. One indication of Bristol's success, in establishing itself as a trading center of importance, was the construction of a Templar stronghold south of the castle on the other side of the River Avon, on land granted to them by Earl Robert.

"Where's the boat?" Llelo said, apparently wanting to hurry the conversation along and impatient with Edgar's apparent prejudice against the Welsh.

"Just there." Edgar indicated the third boat in the row, tied amongst a dozen others.

Cadoc left Edgar to crouch above the boat, studying its shape and sturdiness. It was an English boat, like every other one at the dock, and nothing out of the ordinary. Welsh fishing coracles were round, in appearance something like a basket, in which the fisherman stood rather than sat to row. This craft was made with wooden strakes shaped around a frame of ribs and risings. It had a pointed bow and stern, a center seat, and rowlocks for the oars.

Cadoc asked Edgar over his shoulder, "Why was he fishing in the Frome instead of the Avon?"

"The Avon is busier. He and Earl Robert had a favorite spot, up past the weirs and sluice gates."

Cadoc allowed himself a low laugh, which he couldn't seem to help every time anyone said the word Avon. *Afon* meant 'river' in Welsh, so those early Saxons, perhaps thinking to keep the Welsh original name for the river, had dubbed one of the largest, most significant rivers in England *River River*. He could imagine the Welshmen those long-ago Saxons had displaced similarly laughing at their conquerors' expense and never mentioning the mistake they'd made. Cadoc didn't either.

Edgar didn't seem to notice Cadoc's amusement and added, "He was last seen rowing up the Frome towards one of the fishing holes."

"Who saw him?" Cadoc hated asking obvious questions, but Edgar wasn't imparting information quickly. Maybe he was wrong not to sic Hamelin on him. Except Hamelin likely spoke no English.

"Two boys. My sister's lads. They saw him get into the boat with his fishing net."

"Did you think to wonder why he was fishing that day?" Llelo said. "It was the afternoon of the earl's funeral, and Bernard's wife had died the day before."

Edgar shrugged. "Each man grieves in his own way. The earl himself liked to fish every once in a while. Bernard would go with him."

Cadoc's eyes surveyed the river. From the sluice gate upstream that diverted the Frome around the castle, the course of the river quickly left the bounds of the town and headed northeast. "Where was his body found?"

Edgar blinked. "It hasn't been."

Cadoc knew that, of course, but he wanted to know if Edgar did. "Perhaps you could explain to me again why you think he drowned?"

"The boat was discovered after it floated back downstream. Bernard's boots and fishing gear were found in the bottom. Even a fish! But no Bernard." Edgar nodded sagely. "I've seen this happen before. The body ends up on the bottom of the river and is caught there. The bones are found months later."

Cadoc knew from talking to Gareth—thankfully not from his own experience—that if a man drowned, his body did sink to the bottom, but eventually would bloat and rise to the surface again. Enough time had passed that this should have happened to Bernard. What Cadoc didn't say was what he'd been thinking all along, being suspicious and cynical by nature: Bernard had faked his own death. He'd seen it before, in the father of Prince Hywel's wife, no less. There was no reason to think an earl's valet couldn't do the same.

The question before him was if it would be a waste of time to pursue that line of thought. If it was true, Bernard should be long gone by now, living in a different town under a different name. It would be good to know, however, why Bernard had done it.

Cadoc tipped his head to indicate a path he could see that followed the bank upstream. "The boys and I will walk a ways. Thank you for your time."

"Oh—" Edgar put out a hand. "One more thing." He hesitated. "Maybe it's nothing."

"So many have died that everything is important," Llelo said. "Please, whatever it is, just tell us."

"Maybe a week before he died, I saw Bernard arguing with another man, one of the traders in town who deals in wine. Italian." Edgar sniffed, indicating a typical English disdain for foreigners, no matter how good their product.

"Do you know what the argument was about?" Cadoc said.

"Only Bernard's side. The other man's accent was thick, and he spoke low. But he was threatening Bernard. Bernard said, *I'll pay. I need more time.*" Edgar scowled. "I know what that sounds like to me, but when I asked him, Bernard shrugged it off and said I'd misheard."

"Was anyone else close by?" Cadoc said.

"None closer than me, and that was by accident. I was in the shadows, seeking to relieve myself in the river."

Cadoc thanked Edgar, and Llelo did too, somewhat more profusely, which Cadoc thought was fine. The more everyone here realized they were genuinely interested in solving the mystery of these deaths, the more likely they would be to come forward. In truth, they were coming at the investigation backwards. They needed to find the person who could talk them through these events from beginning to end. Now that Gareth was distracted by Cadwaladr's arrival and

Prince Henry's conference, it was up to the rest of them to discover the truth.

Hamelin had already started down the trail that followed the river, but he said as Cadoc and Llelo caught up, "You were right not to introduce me."

"I didn't mean to offend," Cadoc said mildly, "but he wasn't a guard to be intimidated. He's the king of his own castle and knows it."

"Merchants are a different breed," Hamelin admitted, "these Saxon ones in particular. I never know what to make of them."

As they walked, Llelo related to Hamelin (who didn't, in fact, speak English) the gist of the conversation with Edgar. The houses petered out after fifty yards, and they found themselves walking through farmland, with stone walls to demarcate individual fields. Cadoc saw sheep for the first time and a few goats. There might have been cattle too, farther on, but trees blocked his view.

Part of the flow of the Frome had been rerouted around the eastern side of the castle, but upstream from the sluice gate remained unchanged, and it wound sinuously through the relatively flat English countryside. Hamelin made to cut across a field rather than follow the river exactly, but when neither Llelo nor Cadoc followed him, he turned back. "Why not?"

"We are looking for a body," Llelo said, his long legs eating up the yards, "and I may have found one."

"In the river?" Hamelin's head swung back to look upstream to where Llelo was pointing a hundred feet ahead. "After three weeks?"

"You came along thinking it was a lark and that we weren't going to find anything, didn't you?" Llelo's steps quickened, and he outpaced the other two men.

Hamelin was appalled. "You can't be serious! This is your third body in three days!"

Cadoc was interested to see that in those three days, the young men's relationship had advanced enough that they would speak to each other so openly. It wasn't a prince's brother to a knight's son, if it ever had been, but one man to another. Equals.

Soon Hamelin caught up enough to make out the shape Llelo had seen, lodged against the bank. "It's a woman!" He took one look and immediately turned away to vomit in the bushes.

Llelo crouched on the bank, his elbows resting on his thighs and his hands dangling between his knees.

Cadoc eyed Hamelin's back for a moment and then put a hand on Llelo's shoulder. "Is there anything we need to determine before we get her out of there?" He was deliberately asking for advice, to focus Llelo's mind and to distract him from the horror of what they'd found. The young man had shadowed his father for long enough that he knew the basics of investigating—more than Cadoc, in truth. And it was Llelo who'd found her.

Although Llelo appeared just short of puking himself, he managed a quick shake of his head. "We should never assume, but it's unlikely this is where she went in." He paused. "My father would know more, but I think we should just pull her out."

"I agree." Cadoc glanced to where Hamelin's gray face was peering at them from around a tree. He hadn't soiled his shoes, which was something. But Cadoc didn't ask him to help, instead turning resolutely back to the river and steeling himself for the cold water.

Llelo was there ahead of him, however, sliding down the bank and into the shallows. The body appeared to be stuck on a submerged branch, and Llelo put a hand on it for balance.

The body was turned face down, the dead woman's dark hair swimming around her head, so as they tugged and heaved her away from the branch, they were spared having to look into her face. But once she was out of the water and onto the river bank, they lay her down facing the sky.

Hamelin's skin was very white. "She's been garroted, just like Aelfric."

Puffing with the effort of heaving the body out of the water and as soaking wet as the dead woman, Llelo didn't join Hamelin in losing his breakfast, but he bent over, his hands on his knees, and spat on the ground. At the sight of her face, even Cadoc, who was no innocent, turned away. The mist on the river was long gone, and the November sun shone weakly down on the macabre scene.

Llelo had pulled off his cloak before he entered the water, and now he grabbed it from where he'd draped it over a nearby bush and covered the body with it.

Hamelin cleared his throat. "What can I do?"

Cadoc lifted his chin, impressed that the young man's voice barely shook. "Get help." He tipped his head to point downriver. "No need to run."

But Hamelin was already hastening away.

Cadoc turned to Llelo. "You all right over there?"

"Well enough." Llelo spoke with more equanimity than Cadoc was currently feeling. "I'm certainly doing better than Rose."

21

Gareth

When Gareth had come to Bristol, it had been to investigate the suspicious death of Earl Robert—and while for most people that would have been an uncomfortable proposition, it was within the range of normal for Gareth. If he'd known, however, that not only would he be participating in a council of war, but sitting across from Cadwaladr at the same time, likely he would have seriously reconsidered his decision to come.

But then he would have come anyway. He knew himself well enough by now to recognize that he did his duty, regardless of the personal consequences to himself. Besides, Prince Hywel had been searching for Cadwaladr for a year—and now Gareth had found him. Knowing was better than not knowing, even if it would sharpen Hywel's anxiety about what mischief Cadwaladr could be getting up to. While Gareth hadn't yet determined the true purpose behind Cadwaladr's visit to Bristol, and though he would have loved to pin any one of these deaths on him, it did seem that Cadwaladr had truly arrived after Sir Aubrey was dead. He couldn't blame him this time.

"You're the expert, Gareth," Aron said in an undertone. "How do we kill him and get away with it?"

Gareth didn't look at the younger man, but kept his gaze steady on Cadwaladr, who was talking animatedly with Hertford, his brother-in-law. The other Gilbert de Clare, the Earl of Pembroke and the first Gilbert's uncle, was here too, speaking intently with Humphrey de Bohun and Maurice FitzGerald. Pembroke had not brought his son, Richard, whom Gareth had met six months before, during the endeavor against the Flemings, and had quite liked. Nor was Cadell, the King of Deheubarth, or Rhys, his youngest brother, present. Instead it was seventeen-year-old Maredudd, whom Gareth had not met before, who had arrived late last night to represent Deheubarth.

In fact, half of the lords who'd come to Bristol had benefited from the taking of Wiston last summer and its aftermath, including the discovery of Empress Maud's treasure. That none of them had mentioned its existence to Henry was a relief, since Gareth wouldn't have wanted to explain his silence either.

At that moment, as if reading Gareth's thoughts, Pembroke turned to look at him. Gareth gazed steadily back, and after a few easy breaths, Pembroke lifted his chin in acknowledgement. Gareth was not blind to the fact that one reason he was being treated so well by these Marcher lords was because they were worried about what he knew and what he might say to the prince.

Gareth could not be bribed or bought. They didn't like it, but there was nothing they could do about that either. It gave Gareth power that a few years ago might have made him uncomfortable, but now he accepted—not as his due, but as something he could work with.

"Believe me, I've been considering our options," Gareth said. "Any attempt on Cadwaladr's life would be instantly put at our doorstep, however. You know that."

"Do we care?"

Gareth heaved a sigh. He'd asked this question and answered it a dozen times in the last year—and the last day—even as he'd entertained himself with visions of Cadwaladr's demise, each death more gruesome than the last. "Prince Hywel would care. King Owain would care. We do not have free license to kill, no matter how guilty the man." He paused. "It is not who we are."

"Not who you are, maybe," Aron muttered under his breath, but he didn't argue anymore.

Gareth felt the need to add, "Furthermore, we must treat him with respect."

"I was afraid you were going to say that."

Gareth wasn't happy about having to say it, but he well remembered Hywel's words to him about biding their time. Which meant that Gareth had to play along, to smile when he wanted to punch Cadwaladr in his teeth while gutting him with a dull knife. Gwen had once wished for Cadwaladr the long decline of dying unloved and alone, but it was a wasted curse. Cadwaladr was his own best companion and loved only himself.

Yesterday the council had met for nearly the entire day, hashing out the state of England from north of York to the tip of Cornwall and everywhere in between. While the lords here were haughty, arrogant, and often rivals, in Henry's presence they were allies. They were trying to come up with a way to take the throne from Stephen, and they were united in their desire to do so. Thus, while the atmosphere had been intense, it hadn't been because the men here were at odds.

Henry's receiving room had been transformed from when Gareth had first met the prince in it. Two tables had been placed side by side so they abutted each other along their length, making a rectangle. Six men could sit along each side with two each on the ends, and sixteen seats were more than were needed. Having spent yesterday in their company, Gareth would have been happier to have been left out today, or at least to have found himself at a place other than at the main table, but Maredudd, the only other Welshman, fetched up beside him, and somehow Gareth found himself guided to a spot just left of center. "My brother Rhys sends his greetings."

Gareth looked at Maredudd sharply. "Your brother knew I was here?"

"We did."

That did *not* give Gareth a good feeling, but he didn't have time to pursue the topic because Prince Henry took a seat in the exact center of one long side, making him the focal point of the meeting. William was the new Earl of Gloucester, but it was Henry who was calling this conference, and the more Gareth saw of him, the clearer it was to him that he was claiming the dead earl's mantle for himself.

Unlike what sometimes happened in Welsh councils, the next-highest-ranking baron, Pembroke, did not sit opposite the prince. The chair of honor was to the king's right. Gareth was a little embarrassed to watch Pembroke and Ranulf fight Cadwaladr for the seat. When Ranulf finally did manage to sit, Cadwaladr's nose went up, and a smile appeared on his face. He moved down several seats to the end of the table. Pembroke retired to the seat opposite Prince Henry, next to Gareth.

That brief exchange was all Gareth needed. After two days of unfailing grace, Cadwaladr had allowed his true personality to show for just a moment, before covering it again with a small smile and polite words. Gareth had never known a man as false-hearted as Cadwaladr, but his behavior had been spectacular mumming, even for him.

Cadwaladr had been included in yesterday's council too. Gareth had thought William and Henry were mad to invite him to join them, but as he'd sat between his various relations, kin through Cadwaladr's wife, Alice, Gareth realized that everyone was taking for granted that he was with them, and it could even be that Cadwaladr had gone to Stephen as a spy in the king's court—on his own initiative or at the request of one of these Marcher lords.

At the thought, a frisson of unease put up the hairs on Gareth's neck. If Cadwaladr spied for Maud, it was no wonder his return here had been triumphant. Gareth hadn't given King Stephen's men a thought since they'd arrived, but he realized he hadn't seen them recently.

Again it was Aron, standing behind Gareth's chair at his left shoulder, who bent down to whisper in his ear and put words to his thoughts. "Did you see that? How long do you think he can keep this up?"

"By all indications, he'll manage as long as he needs to."

"The question is *why* does he need to?"

"I may have just figured it out."

"Welcome again, all of you." From his chair placed at the end of the table opposite Cadwaladr, William rose to his feet. Unlike Cadwaladr, he'd given way to Ranulf without protest—and seemingly by his own choice. "Yesterday was spent outlining our current situation. Today, we will put the pieces together and devise a plan, without which the war cannot continue." He lifted his chin and spoke a little louder. "We must ensure that King Stephen understands the stark truth: despite my father's death, nothing has changed."

Prince Henry sat quietly through William's introduction, but at a bow from the earl, ceding the floor, he lifted a hand. "My mother is the rightful Queen of England. We all know it. I believe even Stephen knows it. I believe it is still possible to make him see it."

Strangely, it was Cadwaladr who spoke first. "Why should he?" At the startlement in the faces of the men near him, he laughed and carried on, "As you well know, I ask this not as a supporter of Stephen, but as someone who wants to see the Empress succeed. But I must ask ... on what grounds does hope rest? Stephen was crowned twelve years ago. What's to prevent the war from lasting twelve more?"

Gareth wanted to despise Cadwaladr for his speech, but he agreed with nearly every word—and he felt a sense of grim satisfaction that his new evaluation of Cadwaladr's role appeared to be exactly right.

Prince Henry spoke into the silence that followed. "The answer, my friends, is *me*. Twelve years ago, I was an infant. I am fourteen now, and while I acknowledge that my uncle carried England on his back for many years, and I cannot replace him, I am my mother's son. I am the rightful heir to the throne of England. This fight is not only one we *can* win, but it is one we *will* win. I will not be denied. King Stephen has to know that the war has only just begun."

These were fighting words, righteously spoken. The blazing expression on Henry's face belied its youthful softness. What's more, in that moment, Gareth believed him, believed he could win back the throne—and by the looks on the faces of the men who surrounded him, the rest of the men in the room did too.

It was another reminder of the way Normans wielded power. This was a fourteen-year-old. If he'd been born a Welshman, he would have been construed a man, but he was still far from his maturity by Norman lights. And yet, everyone in the room sat completely silent as he spoke, they nodded at his certainty, and they girded their loins for what the next few years would bring. They were ready to follow him to the throne if he could achieve it.

These barons had come to the conference because Prince Henry had rank, even though his mother was uncrowned and—unless the conference produced a meaningful plan—had no hope of being crowned. He had no official status at all, even in Bristol. This was William's castle. But unearned or not, Henry ruled here because the people in the room believed he did.

As Gareth listened to these great lords put forth their pledges of men and arms and construct the next phase of the war, he felt a growing respect for Prince Henry—along with a cold fear in his belly of what would happen if the boy really did achieve his aim. King Stephen hadn't turned his attention to Wales, not just because he was occupied with keeping his crown, but because he was inconstant, unwilling to sustain any campaign for long. He wasn't interested in taking the necessary steps to conquer each little kingdom of Wales in order to claim the whole as his own. For now, he had been content to let his lords of the March rule their small portions as they saw fit.

While crowning Henry might be good for England, especially if he was able to provide a steady hand after all these years of war, from the glimmer in Henry's eyes and the forcefulness of his personality, the day the crown was placed on his head could be a very bad day for Wales. All these lords were men of the March. If they continued their present course, and if Henry did win the throne eventually, they would want to be repaid for their loyalty.

Most likely in Welsh land and blood.

22

Llelo

While they waited for Hamelin to return with a cart, Llelo walked up and down the riverbank, looking for the place the woman had gone in. With the snow and rain of yesterday, he found nothing definitive, not even footprints, but as had been the case on the battlement after Sir Aubrey died, he felt better for having looked.

Finally, he came to stand beside Cadoc, who was gazing into the slow-moving river, one arm folded across his chest and a fist to his lips. Rose remained on the bank behind him, covered by Llelo's cloak. He himself was soaked from neck to toe, and while cloaks were expensive, there was no way he was putting on that cloak ever again. He had it in his head that he would leave it in the alms house as a gift for the poor, who would never know to what use it had been put. He was glad he hadn't been wearing his armor and padding. Not only would he now weigh twice as much, but he would have had to spend this evening polishing each link, so it wouldn't rust.

"Don't ever get used to it, Llelo," Cadoc said. "That's when you know your soul has gone to a dark place."

"My parents are used to it." Llelo shivered and wrapped his arms around himself, wishing he'd asked Hamelin to bring him back a blanket, though it was taking so long he might well be dry by then.

"Are they?" Cadoc turned slightly to look at him.

"Aren't they?"

"Why do you think they take each death so seriously? Why do they go to bed late and rise early?" Cadoc answered his own questions. "Because each death goes right to the heart of them, and they cannot let it go until they discover the truth. It's because they still have souls that they continue to care."

Llelo blinked back a sudden wetness in his eyes. He could have blamed it on the bright sunshine reflecting off the water, but he knew it was really his own misery and the aching in his heart. "How do they do it?" He didn't bother to keep the pain out of his voice. Cadoc had read him perfectly.

"They almost quit, you know. After Shrewsbury."

Llelo looked up quickly. "I didn't know that."

"They worried they were harming their family."

"If they didn't lead these investigations, who would? Nobody would ever find the truth!"

"Exactly." Cadoc grunted. "And now you understand."

Responsibility and duty were ideas Llelo did understand. Last summer his father had asked him if he wanted to be formally apprenticed, and at the time Llelo had eagerly agreed. But over the past few days, he was seeing more clearly the fine line his parents walked. From the outside, to investigate murder a man needed a strong stomach and a hard heart. Cadoc was telling him that to do it right, the first was a necessity but not the second, which would harm both him and his quest for the truth.

He shivered again.

"Are you regretting your decision?"

Despite his newfound realization, Llelo's response was instant. "No."

Cadoc seemed to snort and said under his breath, "Like father, like son."

There were few things he could have said that would have done more to stiffen Llelo's resolve, if not his heart.

Eventually, Hamelin returned with the boatmen, three soldiers, and a half-dozen workers, all overseen by Charles, the under-steward.

"You brought an army," Llelo said to Hamelin in an undertone.

Hamelin shrugged. "I had no choice. I had to give your father fair warning, though he told me not to tell anyone else who this was until he could see her himself. He's waiting for us in the laying-out room."

While Charles hovered around giving unnecessary instructions, the men lifted the body into the back of the cart, and once it was there, Llelo covered it further with a hemp tarp Edgar had brought. With Hamelin's words, Llelo realized that none of the newcomers knew it was Rose. Underneath the cloak, one body was much like another. He imagined they all thought they'd found Bernard.

Once they returned to the castle, the same four men maneuvered the dead woman onto a table next to Aelfric, who lay ready for his burial, and Hamelin set off immediately with a few muttered words about finding his brother. Charles hesitated in the doorway for another heartbeat, his expression questioning, but Gareth told him he wasn't needed, and he left too.

"It's bad, I gather?" Gareth was waiting for everyone else to leave before pulling back the coverings.

"She wasn't in the water long, but it was long enough," Llelo said.

Before their arrival, Gareth had lit six candles and a lantern, which hung on a hook from the ceiling, and had set the sage in its little dish to smoldering. This wasn't to ward off evil spirits, though Llelo saw one of the guards cross himself as he passed it, but to cover the smell of the dead, which actually wasn't as bad as it could have been. The woman had possibly been killed the day they'd arrived—two full days ago—but the water appeared to have leached out the worst of the smell, even as it had attacked her tissues.

Another saving grace was the lateness of the year, which meant the water in the Frome was relatively cold. Llelo knew from his father that sometimes a person's face could be eaten off by fish and other creatures. That had not happened either.

Cadoc tipped his head to Llelo. "Your son needs a new cloak."

Gareth put a hand on Llelo's shoulder and squeezed. Llelo fought the return of the tears from beside the river. He didn't fight them as hard this time, and to his surprise, they subsided just as quickly. Meanwhile, his father dropped his cloak to the ground, revealing Rose's body, and Llelo forced himself not to look away. *Yes, it's as bad as I remember.*

Hamelin pulled up just outside the doorway, breathing a bit more quickly than usual. "You should know Roger is coming—" He moved so they could see through the door to the young lord approaching, accompanied by Fitzharding and also Prince Cadwaladr, of all people.

Gareth barked a cynical laugh. "Really?" Then he bent to pick up Llelo's cloak once again and throw it over the body. "We do not want Cadwaladr and me in an enclosed space together." Thus, before the oncoming lords could reach the doorway, the three of them filed out of the room.

But Cadwaladr, Roger, and Fitzharding had already halted a hundred feet away, and the latter two appeared to be arguing.

"I will see the body!" Roger said.

"Son—" Fitzharding put out a hand as if to grab Roger's arm, though he stopped just short of doing so.

"I am not your son!" His face white to his hairline, Roger spun on his heel and stomped towards the laying-out room.

Fitzharding, daunted as one might expect, fell back a pace, leaving Cadwaladr to walk beside Roger.

Roger, however, cleared his throat and said in a calmer tone, directed not at Fitzharding but at Gareth, who filled the doorway of the laying-out room, "Let's get this over with before I decide whether or not to trouble my brother with it."

Nobody mentioned that Hamelin had already gone to do so, nor the thundercloud over Gareth's head, which was so obvious to Llelo he was surprised it hadn't started raining. Roger didn't seem to notice, and once he was within closer conversational distance, he tipped his chin in that haughty manner of his. "Quite frankly, you should not have brought him here. He was a suicide. He cannot be buried in consecrated ground."

Cadwaladr, continuing his conciliatory ways, hustled to get between Roger and Gareth. Llelo stared at Cadwaladr's shoulders, stunned that he could be so trusting as to put his back to Gareth.

Gareth's hand didn't go to his belt knife, and Cadwaladr said to Roger, "Prince Henry believes the valet is one of four murders. He has a right to be here until it is determined otherwise."

Unmoved by Cadwaladr's pleading, Roger's lips thinned, a match to Gareth's. If six people hadn't died, Llelo could have seen the scene before him as part of a mummer's play, and while Cadwaladr was begging for mercy for Bernard, he was really asking for himself.

Roger's voice, meanwhile, when he spoke again, had no patience in it. "The sooner this is dispensed with, the sooner we can put these events behind us. We have business, my lord, that should not wait."

From behind Cadwaladr, Gareth finally moved, bowing and stepping back into the room to allow everyone else to file inside. "I'm afraid there's been a misunderstanding. We haven't found Bernard's body."

Roger sniffed. "I will be the judge of that. You never even met the man."

Gareth raised his eyebrows. "As you wish. I have only just glanced at the body myself, my lords, but it is difficult viewing."

Despite his own reluctance, Llelo stayed close, his eyes on Roger. With a strange mix of dread and glee, he wanted to see his face when he realized the magnitude of his error. His arrogance would have been amusing if Llelo didn't think the overt display of ignorance was going to make him furious in a moment.

Gareth pulled the cloak off the body, and they all stared at it, though Llelo less directly than the others this time. He had no fear of being judged a coward.

"That isn't Bernard." Roger sounded genuinely shocked.

"Bernard drowned. This man drowned. Hence, this man is Bernard." Fitzharding had been anxious to stop Roger earlier, but once Roger rejected him, he'd kept his distance. Thus, he spoke from the doorway, and from there, with so many people between him and the body, he could see only the shape on the table and not its substance.

Silence greeted this statement, as it would.

"Who-who—" Roger swallowed hard. "Is this who I think it is?"

"Who do you think it is?" Gareth said.

"The servant. Rose."

"What?" Fitzharding swung around the door, gaping. He took two steps into the room, and the others gave way before him.

"Did you know her?" Gareth said, with what Llelo knew to be a studied innocence, since he'd heard Hamelin's story about their argument.

"What?" Fitzharding frowned. "No, of course not. Where's Bernard?"

Fitzharding had just lied with fluency. Llelo met Hamelin's eyes for a moment in joint acknowledgement of that fact before they each looked away.

"Not here." Gareth's voice was steady.

Fitzharding still seemed to be in shock. His mouth opened and closed like a landed fish. "I don't understand why this isn't Bernard."

Roger rounded on him. "Why are you going on about Bernard when it's Rose who's dead?"

"Because he owed me money."

Llelo just managed to swallow down his involuntary gasp. He'd told Hamelin that murder uncovered secrets, and here was another one.

In the face of everyone's stares, Fitzharding put up his hands. "It was nothing."

"It doesn't sound like nothing, my lord. How much money?" Gareth said.

Fitzharding's hands were still up, and now he spread them wide. "He needed a loan to cover other, more pressing debts. I thought as Earl Robert's valet, he would be good for it."

"Did you argue with him about it?" Llelo asked.

Fitzharding looked affronted. "Not argue, so much as discuss forcefully his repayment plan."

"When was this?" Gareth said.

"A few days before he died." Fitzharding shrugged. "I had nothing to do with his death, obviously, since killing him would hardly have allowed me to be repaid, would it?"

"One of the people we've spoken to saw you in an argument with Rose as well," Gareth said.

Fitzharding's expression hardened. "He was mistaken."

Gareth had tried to protect Hamelin, but now Hamelin himself cleared his throat. "Was I?"

Fitzharding folded his arms across his chest in a recognizable gesture of defiance. "If you must know, she had learned that I had developed a bond with Lady Eva, an understanding, even. She was angry about it."

Roger barked a laugh of disbelief. "You are a lord, and she a laundress."

"She had designs above her station." Now Fitzharding gestured to Aelfric's body, which lay next to Rose's. "Instead of questioning me, we should be considering why it is that we don't yet have the man responsible in custody. You've had another murder on your watch, sir."

Llelo was irate for his father, but Gareth answered civilly, "We arrived weeks after the initial deaths, and these two appeared to have died the evening of our arrival. My own efforts have been hindered by the conference, as you know."

It was rare to see his father defending his actions in this way. On the whole, he never made excuses, but Fitzharding's accusation had been absurd—and probably made out of a desire to distract them from his relationship with Bernard.

Roger, for once, put out a hand placatingly. "We know these deaths are not the fault of anyone in your party. If someone is to blame, it is those of us who live here, who have allowed a murderer to walk free."

Llelo cleared his throat. "The murderer is the only one to blame, my lord. He must be very good at hiding in plain sight." More as a distraction from the fact that he may have just spoken out of turn than because it needed doing, he stooped to pick up the cloak Gareth had cast aside. The move put his head close to the dead woman's feet. Her shoes were gone, but he noted for the first time that one of her ankles had the remnants of a rope tied around it.

"Father, look at this." The end of the rope was frayed as if it had been torn away.

Roger frowned. "She was tied to something?"

"A weight, perhaps. The body wasn't meant to be found. Well done, Llelo." Gareth took in a breath. "Because of the conference, I have not yet informed the prince of all else that has come to light, but perhaps I should now. We have reason to believe that Aelfric had something to do with the loosening of the stones on the rampart. We found a hammer and chisel among his possessions."

Roger stared at him. "He was not an initial suspect, was he?"

"He was in the guardroom when Sir Aubrey died, so no." Gareth drew in another breath. "Rose, too, behaved suspiciously in the hours before she died. She spoke privately to my wife and implied that Earl Robert had told William that he was not his son."

"What?" Roger's mouth dropped open. This was an hour for astonishment, it seemed.

Fitzharding snorted. "Any man with eyes can see that's a lie." He was feeling more confident now, perhaps because the truth of his relationships to Rose and Bernard had come to light, and he wasn't in chains because of it.

"So we concluded immediately. We have spent the last two days looking for Rose as a result." Gareth gestured to the two bodies in the room. "They didn't kill themselves, though, did they?"

"If I might put forth an idea …" Initially, Cadoc had stayed outside with Fitzharding and entered the room only at the tail end of the conversation. "We might consider the possibility that Bernard is not dead. In fact, I would suggest that Bernard staged his own death, perhaps for so simple a reason as to avoid these debts he couldn't repay."

Roger wet his lips. "Would you go as far as to say that Bernard is the killer?"

Cadoc spread his hands wide. "I don't know what Rose or Aelfric might have done to incur his wrath, or why he might want anyone dead at all but himself, but to my eyes, in all of this, he seems to be the one man we've not accounted for."

23

Gwen

"I'm Adela. We spoke earlier." The woman appeared to be about Gwen's height and near to her age, with dark hair pulled back so tightly it had Gwen wincing.

Gwen had found a bench in the back of the great hall out of everyone's way to nurse her son. She would have chosen a spot closer to the fire, but she didn't want to call attention to herself. Sitting in the corner, she could watch and wait. Or so she'd thought.

"I remember." And Gwen did, though the specifics of the conversation they'd had were somewhat fuzzy.

It might be wrong to claim that all English people looked the same, but Gwen felt that way much of the time, in large part because their expressionless faces, all grim and dour, made them similar in appearance and so very difficult to read. The Welsh spoke with their hands, their faces, and their eyes as well as their mouths.

Though, as she'd discovered during the course of this investigation, the English—whether Saxon or Norman—were no less full of emotion on the inside, if one could get them to show it. Gwen was willing to bet this woman felt something too. "I'm sorry for your loss."

She'd said it to every person she'd interviewed, but she thought it bore repeating. Adela bent her head in acknowledgement, as had every woman today. But then she went on to add, "Sir Aubrey was my grandfather."

"I-I didn't know." Gwen found herself stuttering her surprise, and it was on the tip of her tongue to ask *why didn't you say so before?*

But she didn't have to because Adela said, "It didn't seem right to claim it in front of Mabs."

"I'm sorry. I still don't understand."

Adela sighed. "Mabs's mother was my aunt, Sir Aubrey's daughter. Mabs is illegitimate, however, whereas my father married my mother." Then she laughed lightly. "You don't need to say it: yes, you are not the only one who finds it odd that Earl Robert named his illegitimate daughter after his wife."

"Did it help?"

Again the low laugh. "As you could probably tell yourself, there's both love and hate there. Mabs's life would have been very different if my aunt had survived her birth, but she did not."

"What was your grandfather's relationship with Mabs?"

Adela hemmed and hawed for a moment. "He tried. He blamed himself for his daughter's death, feeling that he didn't sufficiently discourage her relationship with the earl."

"What could he have done? Earl Robert was your grandfather's employer and possibly the most powerful man in England, next to King Stephen."

"Don't let anyone else hear you say that!" She dropped her chin. "He *was* the most powerful man in England. But if Sir Aubrey had come to him and asked that he put aside his daughter, the earl would have done so. My grandfather feels he should have sent Isabeau away. Or, better yet, married her to someone else. Many men would have accepted her."

Gwen looked Adela up and down. "If you and Mabs are cousins, what is your role in the household?"

"I kept house for my grandfather. Our quarters are above the inner gatehouse." That was typically the location of the steward's apartments. In some castles, they were as well appointed as the king's. Gareth had mentioned a desire to inspect them but, with one thing and another, had not yet gained permission.

"Do you and Mabs get along? She doesn't seem very happy with her lot." Taran had fallen asleep nursing, and Gwen adjusted him and her clothes so they were both more comfortable. Gwen didn't remember Tangwen being so accommodating at this age, but she was grateful that he had so far been a help to the investigation.

Adela sighed. "Mabs is illegitimate, but she is King Henry's granddaughter by blood. She allows herself to be stuck in the middle—too lofty for the likes of me, even if we are cousins, but not high enough to be an equal in the earl's household. She is Earl William's half-sister! But if they have spoken more than a few words to each other in ten years, you wouldn't know it."

"It must be hard for all of you." Not for the first time, Gwen was thankful to have been born Welsh where these distinctions were either less evident or nonexistent.

"It is much easier being me." Adela paused. "I loved my grandfather." Her voice was choked off by rising tears, and she looked down at her lap.

Gwen reached out and took her hand. "Why are you here instead of with your family in their time of grief?"

"I didn't want to be at home anymore. I don't want to cry anymore, and I knew that if I went the tears would fall again." There was as much pain in her voice as Gwen had heard in Lady Mabel's, and she herself unstiffened further, scooting closer and putting her arm around her. It seemed her lot to comfort the mourning women of Bristol Castle.

Eventually Adela calmed and regained control of herself, her face settling back into repose. Gwen had questioned many suspects and witnesses over the years, and while she didn't feel comfortable milking a grieving woman for information, she would listen as long as Adela was willing to stay with her.

"You are very kind to sit with me. With all these other deaths, I think nobody wants to talk to anyone else. We are all tired of tears."

"Since you worked in the castle, you must have known Jenet and Bernard," Gwen said.

"And Rose."

The news that Rose's body had been discovered in the river had spread through the castle like a fire through a stable. People had been openly weeping, so William had left the conference to speak calmingly to everyone, and a priest had come as well to bless and sanctify the hall and pray for a quick discovery of the murderer.

"Bernard was often in our chambers," Adela continued. "He and my grandfather were friends, you know."

"I didn't know," Gwen said. "Weren't they very different in age?"

"Yes. My grandfather was much older, but Bernard amused him. And, of course, they were both companions to Earl Robert. Along with Fitzharding, and occasionally Charles, late in the evening they would sit together and drink good wine." Then Adela frowned. "They had a falling out a few days before he died, however. I heard them arguing."

"Before who died?"

"Bernard. I'd woken in the night and saw a light. I didn't go out into the sitting room, but my grandfather was speaking in a harsh whisper to someone at the door. I realized it was Bernard, and then my grandfather said something like *you made your bed. Now you must lie in it.*"

"Do you know what he was talking about?"

Adela shook her head. "I drew back before he knew I was listening." She paused. "Perhaps you've been told that my grandfather was struggling with his memory? That's why he kept lists of everyone who came and went in the castle. If he didn't, he wouldn't remember."

"We have noticed the lists," Gwen said encouragingly.

"After Bernard went away, my grandfather got very drunk. I helped him to bed, and the whole time he was muttering about his lists. He kept saying there was something he should be remembering about them but couldn't. He even took the name of the Lord in vain."

Gwen allowed a suitably shocked expression to cross her face, though traveling with knights and men-at-arms as she often did, few curses could shock her anymore.

Adela shrugged. "In the morning, as was often the case, my grandfather had forgotten all about it."

"Do you have any idea what he'd been talking about?"

Adela shook her head again, the tears returning, and her words echoed what Gareth and Llelo had concluded. "I've gone over those lists of his many times. There's nothing out of the ordinary in them at all."

24

Dai

The manhunt was in full swing. Dai felt the excitement of it tingling up and down his spine. Last summer at Dinefwr, he'd been abed and unable to participate, but today he'd spent the last hour poking around the castle, his thinking being that castle soldiers would operate by brute force rather than cleverness. If Bernard had been smart, he would have been long gone by now, but then, if he'd been smart, he wouldn't have found himself under a debt so crushing he faked his own death rather than face it.

Why he might have returned to the castle to kill again was anybody's guess. While Roger was ready to blame Bernard for the deaths of five people, Dai was having serious doubts about any assumption. Earlier that afternoon, before the discovery of Rose, he'd exchanged Evan for his mother, and gone with her to the castle healer, a man named Denis. Even to someone as skeptical as Dai, Denis appeared to know more about his craft than any healer Dai had ever met, including his new grandmother, Saran. Denis had come to Earl Robert twenty years ago from France—and before that the Holy Land—which was an adventure Dai wanted for himself one day. Denis had insisted that Earl Robert's death was regrettable but natural, and Dai couldn't help but believe him.

The second person they'd spoken to was the midwife, who had confirmed Jenet's troubled pregnancy. Of all the deaths, perhaps Jenet's was the one least likely to have been murder. They would see what Bernard said about all of that when they caught him. If they caught him. One of the reasons Dai was checking every nook and cranny in the castle was because he was expecting to find not Bernard, alive and well, but his dead body.

Dai stepped past Aron, who was keeping watch outside the door of the laying-out room, and found Aelfric's body gone, Rose's body covered, and his father staring out the tiny window. The plan was to attend the funeral for Sir Aubrey as a family, and now that the day was waning, the designated moment to meet was not far off. Earl William had contemplated postponing the mass but decided in the end to go forward with it. The possibility that they were close to finding Aubrey's killer was all the more reason it should continue as planned.

Gareth turned towards the door as Dai entered. "Your mother was just here. She told me about your day. Were you with her when she spoke to Adela?"

Dai shook his head.

Gareth put his hands on his hips. "Bernard and his debts and these damn lists again."

"Mother shouldn't be wandering alone. That's what I'm for."

"She hasn't gone far; she's just walking Taran."

Dai liked babies, it turned out. He knew his parents had worried he might resent the arrival of a new brother, fearing he would usurp Dai's place as their son, but they worried needlessly. As Llelo had said to him when they'd first discovered Gwen's pregnancy, they would both be knights with families of their own before Taran became a man. They had nothing to worry about.

Dai lifted his chin to point to the covered body. "You're done here?"

Gareth sighed. "She was garroted like Aelfric. I'd even say the same laundry line killed them both and was used to tie her to a weight." He indicated a length of rope trailing from Rose's ankle to the floor. "Unfortunately for the killer, laundry line is not the sturdiest of rope."

"And as we know, it's very hard to get rid of a body." Dai gladly moved with his father back to the doorway and out into the fresh air. It had been a sunny day, and Cadoc promised there would be another tomorrow.

"So it seems." Gareth gave a mocking laugh. "Unfortunately, notes that say *Bernard killed me* are rather thin on the ground."

"A note wouldn't have survived the water." Sometimes jests were the only way to make death bearable. "I am distrustful of this sudden rush to judgement anyway."

Dai was pleased to see his father looking at him with interest. "Why?"

"Two days ago, nobody wanted to believe that even Sir Aubrey had been murdered, and now they are ready to hang Bernard for killing five people, including his own wife and Earl Robert. It's like

Hamelin told Llelo: we need a man with means, motive, and opportunity, and I don't see Bernard as filling those requirements."

"He's good for the first and third, anyway," Gareth said. "It's the one reason I haven't protested openly about the manhunt. Bringing him in, if he didn't, in fact, die in the river, could help the investigation enormously."

"I just hope the men in the search party don't string him up before you can talk to him."

"I did speak to Harold about that, and he promised to put the fear of God in the men not to harm him."

"We know better than to trust crowds." Dai snorted his skepticism. "Where has Llelo gone?"

"I sent him for wine." Gareth gestured towards the room. "Aelfric and Rose are the loose links in the killer's armor, Dai. It may be that Bernard murdered five people, but this late in the day, we still have no proof that Earl Robert and Jenet died by anything but natural causes. I have allowed myself to assume murder, and Hywel would have my head for it." He grimaced. "But Aelfric and Rose? *Their* deaths were indisputably murder. Theirs are the ones we're going to solve."

His father's surety had Dai's spirits rising, despite the fact that they were standing over the bodies of two more people.

A bell tolled above them. And then again, echoed by a dozen others—perhaps all the bells in Bristol. He looked at his father. "The funeral is about to start."

"Find the others. Llelo and I will close up here and then join you at the church."

Dai did as he was bid, walking with dozens of other people through the northern gateway towards St. Peter's Church. Dai hadn't actually been inside the town of Bristol yet, since the priory was located outside the city proper, and the only entrance he'd used so far was the eastern gate. He allowed himself to be swept along in the flow of people and noted again that nobody was writing down names or even checking identities. With the loss of Sir Aubrey and the call of the bell, discipline had broken down entirely.

Then Gruffydd fell into step beside him. He appeared to have been lurking nearby, standing guard as Aron had been, though from a different vantage point. "I can't decide if it will be more interesting to note who isn't at the funeral or who is."

Dai tsked through his teeth. "Everybody who is anybody will be there. They wouldn't dare miss it." Then he stopped in his tracks. "That's a problem, Gruffydd, isn't it? Will they pull the guards off the walls like before? Half of them are already gone searching for Bernard." He lifted his chin to point back the way they'd come. "Did you see that nobody is keeping track of who's going in or out?"

"I did." Gruffydd's eyes went to the ramparts of the castle looming above them.

Dai himself had never seen a castle as tall as Bristol. It was a sight to behold, visible for miles because of the white limestone exterior that shone even when there was no sun. He didn't see any heads moving along the wall-walks, but that didn't mean nobody was there.

Gruffydd set off at a fast walk back to the laying-out room. When they reached it, Gareth and Llelo were just leaving, each with a cup of wine in his hand.

Gareth tipped up his cup and drained it in two gulps before dropping his chin and saying, "You're back."

"We were wondering if the funeral could be used as an excuse to do more mischief," Dai said.

Gareth's eyes looked past him to the throngs of people heading towards the church. The church bell was bonging again, its warning echoing over the whole of the castle and town. "Find your mother, Dai, and attend the service with her. I still want eyes there. Gruffydd, bring everyone else to me in the guardhouse of the inner ward."

Dai was past feeling resentful of being left out of the search. His father trusted him with the safety of his mother and brother. When there was a murderer on the loose, that was no small task.

Once again, they crowded through the gateway with twenty others and then set off at a faster pace for the church. By the time they reached it, the entire Welsh contingent had arrived, the rest having come into the town directly across a bridge near the priory.

"I'm here to watch your back, Mother."

Gruffydd grinned as he clapped Dai on the shoulder. "I'm glad you're so cheerful about it. Remember, all work done in the spirit of service pleases God." He swept out an arm. "Come along, those who are coming."

As everyone else walked away, Dai heard Gruffydd explaining to his fellow Dragons, barring Cadoc and Aron, who'd remained inside the castle with Gareth, what had transpired.

Thus, it was only Angharad, Gwen, and Dai (and Taran, of course) left to attend the service. They entered the church to find the nave packed with people. At the front, Prince Henry, Earl William, Lady Mabel, Roger, and all the high lords who were here for the conference sat on padded benches arranged in rows. Cadwaladr was among them. Other well-dressed people sat in subsequent rows, followed by the castle staff and common folk, who crowded up behind them, standing instead of sitting.

Gwen herself didn't feel like she could stand holding Taran for a whole hour, and she led Angharad sidling along the south side of the church to a stone bench permanently affixed to the wall just behind the seated mourners. Mercifully, the bench had room at the end for Gwen to perch. If it hadn't, Dai might have gone over and asked a well-dressed merchant of the town to stand and give Gwen his place.

Angharad leaned against the wall beside her, but Dai chose to post himself in the porch, to better watch the comings and goings of the congregation. So far, everybody who should be there was there.

Taran was awake but not crying, and Gwen rocked him while the people around her hushed and the priest raised his hands. Dai allowed the Latin mass to wash over him—he knew the words by heart, of course, and even what they meant, as he'd been tutored with Llelo—a fact he mostly resented, though not in this moment.

He crossed his arms, eyeing the people in the nave. He had the sense from the shifting feet and dispersed coughing that they were restless and not able to focus their reverence. There'd definitely been too many funerals of late in Bristol. If anything, with the finding of two more bodies, the wards against evil had increased in the last day.

Whether because the priest realized how nervous his people were or simply because Sir Aubrey hadn't been as great a lord as all that, the mass was simple and relatively short, taking less than an hour. Nearing the end, Taran began fussing and Gwen put him to her breast, which meant that as the mass ended and the people started to disperse, she didn't move.

"It was kind of you to come."

Dai had been edging away from the doorway to allow the wave of people to leave, but now he turned around to find Prince Cadwaladr gazing down at him with what he could only describe as a benevolent expression. Dai had no idea what to say, if for no other reason than Dai's presence at the funeral hadn't been kind at all. He was here to watch the residents of Bristol mourn.

But he managed a slight smile. "You as well. Did you know Sir Aubrey?" The appropriate *my lord* stuck in Dai's throat.

Something in Cadwaladr's expression flickered, like a candle flame in the wind, and then steadied again. "How is the investigation coming? Do you think this valet they're hunting did it?"

Again, Dai almost didn't answer. He knew instinctively that Cadwaladr had sought him out because he was the youngest member of Gareth's party. The prince couldn't ask Gwen or Gareth anything, but he would rightfully see Dai as powerless. "We'll see."

Cadwaladr harrumphed. "Will you? I find the accusation of him a typical rush to judgement."

"Why?"

"Your father claims he never assumes and goes by facts that are known, but as far as I can tell, this investigation is based on nothing but assumptions. I'm surprised he hasn't come for me."

Dai glanced towards his mother, who was gazing at him with a somewhat appalled expression. The church was empty but for her, Taran, and Angharad, and none could help him. It was up to Dai to do his best. "As it turns out, my father and I were just discussing this very thing, and we agree completely. You are right that too many assumptions have been made."

Cadwaladr gaped at him for a moment, and then he straightened, almost preening. "You don't say?"

Dai had assumed that whatever he said to Cadwaladr would be wrong, but he had tried to be conciliatory—it cost him nothing personally—and he had said the right thing after all. At the same time, he was disconcerted to feel camaraderie emanating from the prince.

Cadwaladr looked towards the main gate of the castle, before which a small crowd was gathering. "Hopefully you will find Bernard soon." He sniffed. "Be sure to tell your father that if I can be of any assistance to him, to not hesitate to ask."

Dai bowed. "Of course, my lord." He managed the honorific at the end.

With a satisfied smirk, Cadwaladr strode off, and as Dai watched him go, he had a sinking feeling that, whatever the exchange had really been about, Cadwaladr had definitely gotten the better of him.

25

Gareth

Gareth couldn't be sorry he was missing yet another funeral, especially since it was a known fact that much of the time Gwen was more observant than he was. After examining Rose's body, what he needed more than anything was to move. To breathe. To think about something else.

"William seems like a capable fellow, but Bristol Castle could be better organized," Gruffydd muttered as they picked up the pace, heading towards the inner gatehouse that led to the keep.

Aron shook his head. "You're looking at this from the perspective of a people constantly at war. This castle has never been attacked, much less taken. War is out there—" he gestured to the east, "—not something to worry about here. Or so everyone thinks."

"Stephen hasn't always been the most circumspect of generals," Gareth said, "but with the number of lords and men here today, he would be mad to attack it. Still, I agree with Gruffydd. Despite these deaths and the danger, the response is less measured than frantic. And I don't like all these wards." They'd reached the entrance to the stairwell in the gatehouse that would take them to the battlements, and Gareth touched the limp piece of holly above the doorway.

"Perhaps that's the intent," Iago said, stomping up the steps behind them. "They want us to *think* they have a weakness when they do not. We would then go back to Ceredigion and tell Prince Hywel that Bristol is within the realm of possibility to take, and find ourselves lured into an ambush."

Gareth didn't actually laugh, despite the absurdity of Prince Hywel having designs on Bristol. Rarely did any Welsh lord think of expanding his territory into England itself, despite the fact that all of it had once been theirs. They were too busy trying to hold onto what they had or pick away at the lands the English had already taken away in Wales. That had been the purpose of the campaign against Wiston. It had been a long time since the Welsh were the aggressor as opposed to constantly being put in the position of defending.

They came out on the wall-walk of the inner curtain wall. Gareth first looked northwest, towards the town and the church with its crowd of people around it. Farther on, he could see two separate small groups of men going door to door in the town looking for Bernard.

He looked down at Llelo, who had come up behind him. "Three days into an investigation, and the only suspect anyone can identify related to the deaths of five people is a supposedly-drowned valet with no motive."

"If he really is alive," Cadoc said. "I'm disconcerted that the idea of him as the killer has been latched upon with such enthusiasm.

What happens if we don't find him? Will we be asked to give up the investigation?"

Llelo cleared his throat. "We came here to see if anyone was up to something, but maybe we could get up to something ourselves?"

Gareth stared at his son, who reddened slightly under his scrutiny.

"These lists." Llelo pulled a wad of paper from his pocket and brandished them. "I can't help but think we're missing something about them. I'd like to see the rest."

Gruffydd frowned. "What rest?"

"The ones from before Sir Aubrey died."

Gareth turned to the Dragons. "Feel free to poke your nose into anything that looks strange. Llelo and I will have a look at the steward's chamber. I've been meaning to do it since his death. I never should have put it off this long."

The steward's rooms were located on the floor above the gatehouse tunnel. The door had a knocker in the shape of a lion's head, and Gareth rapped the door with it twice.

"It's always odd entering the home of a dead person," Llelo whispered.

"We've come a long way from old Wena's hut, haven't we, son?"

"A long way," Llelo echoed under his breath. "He would have kept those lists easily accessible, yes?"

"I would think so."

No footfalls sounded on the other side, so Gareth lifted the latch, and the door swung open on greased hinges. He and Llelo found themselves in a large rectangular room, with a long table near the windows for private meals. By the far wall stood a smaller table, behind which were shelves holding rolls of paper.

Or should have been holding them. A number of scrolls had fallen to the floor, and while no cushions were torn apart and no cupboards were open, Gareth's practiced eye told him that someone had gone through the room in a hurry very recently. Most tellingly, whoever that was hadn't secured the trap door in the floor, and a piece of paper had been caught in the join and now stuck up into the air.

Gareth stepped hesitantly inside. "Someone was looking for something."

"Could it have been Bernard?"

"I'm not resting my hopes on him. Let's see what we can see." He bent to lift the trap door by the ring, releasing the paper, which turned out to be a different kind of list, this one of cryptic tasks:

Ewerer hot water

Earl William chamber

Menu for tomorrow

The castle construction was such that there were two layers of flooring here: the stone blocks that comprised the ceiling of the archway below had been topped by wooden flooring in this room above it, leaving a space between the stonework and the wood floor. It was a reasonable hiding place, if a mat had been thrown over the trap door and the ring was flush with the floor, but if Sir Aubrey had used it to hide something, that something was missing, since the space was empty.

Llelo set to work picking up the pieces of paper one by one and setting them on the long table. Gareth, meanwhile, began an inspection of the cupboards. A bottle of wine was still upright and intact, but one of the associated metal goblets had fallen over. Also in the cupboard were three knives in sheaths; two wooden boxes, one large and one small, both containing coins; and a bound manuscript. The purpose of the invasion hadn't been theft.

Curious about the manuscript, since he saw them so rarely, Gareth opened it.

De gestis Britonum, it read in Latin. *On the Deeds of the Britons* by *Galfridus Monemutensis*, or Geoffrey of Monmouth. That was a topic of interest to Gareth, and would be of even more interest to his friend Abbot Rhys of St. Kentigern's Monastery in St. Asaph.

He opened the first page to read the inscription, finding that it was dedicated to Earl Robert of Gloucester. There was irony there: the throne of Britain, which Robert's sister was trying to claim, rightfully belonged to the Welsh. No Norman wanted to hear that, of course.

The book began with the Trojans and Romans and included many chapters about King Arthur. It was a startling creation. And right in the center of the book, hidden between the end of one chapter and the beginning of another, were two folded papers. Gareth pulled them out and was just opening them to read them when—

"What are you doing in here?" Harold, the garrison captain, leapt through the doorway, sword in hand.

Gareth had no patience for being wrongly accused. "Our job, Sir Harold. We had questions about Sir Aubrey's lists, among other things, and came to look for them."

"Oh." Harold lowered his sword and swept his eyes around the room. "I was hoping you were Bernard."

"He isn't here, as you can see. Why aren't you at the funeral?"

"Things go missing when everyone's away, and I was mindful of what your boy said to me about having everyone on duty in the same place at the same time."

"We're here for the same reason," Gareth said. "I suppose you didn't see anything suspicious?"

"One of the guards below heard banging about up here, but we are so short-staffed he didn't investigate."

"Was this just now?"

"Within the hour."

"We arrived moments ago, and saw nobody, though I'm sure that someone else has searched the room."

"Father?" Llelo held a neat stack of paper in his hands. He lifted the top page and held it out, showing Gareth a list of names from the day they'd arrived. His own name was near the top, followed by Gwen's and Llelo's.

"I think this is a list of every person to go in and out of the two main gates every day for the last month." While Llelo had collected the lists from the guardhouses yesterday, they'd been for that day or a few days before. Now, combined with Sir Aubrey's, they told a story of the castle unlike Gareth had ever seen recorded before.

Bernard's name appeared a hundred times, coming and going daily in the days leading up to Earl Robert's death, from every entrance and exit to the castle, including the tunnel. The presence of his name stopped abruptly two days after the earl died. He'd gone to the earl's funeral, also at St. Peter's Church, through the town gate. He had not returned.

"What are you looking at?" Harold leaned across the table, turning one of the papers towards him and then quickly turning it back. "These lists of names again. What of it?"

Gareth was watching Harold rather than the lists and saw the way his eyes had remained unfocused. He knew that look because he'd worn it himself until he was past twenty. "My son is showing you Bernard's name."

Harold understood that Gareth knew he couldn't read and said somewhat defensively, "I can write my name, but a scribe keeps track of the duty rolls for me. Ach—" he threw up his hands, "—why am I apologizing to you? Most men can't read."

"We are not judging you," Gareth said, "but somewhere in here is something that was important to Sir Aubrey. I was convinced of it before, and now I'm sure of it."

Harold scoffed and headed for the door. "The funeral should be over. I must speak to Earl William. We can't catch Bernard quickly enough. He was here an hour ago. He could even be dressed as a guard—" He quickened his pace and left the room.

"What? Wait ... Sir Harold!" Gareth hustled after him, but by the time he arrived at ground level underneath the inner gatehouse, Harold was loping through the outer gatehouse barbican.

From beside him, Llelo muttered, "Why would Bernard turn over Sir Aubrey's rooms? It makes no sense."

"It doesn't." But he had no time to puzzle it out because he saw what Harold was heading for: a disturbance just beyond the main gate to the town, in the clearing between it and St. Peter's Church. A crowd had gathered, forming a circle and pressing on one another to better see what was happening in the middle. That was something Gareth couldn't make out from where he stood, and he started forward after Harold.

He concluded over his shoulder to Llelo, "I'm beginning to agree with your brother that perhaps it isn't Bernard we should be looking for."

26

Llelo

Evan skidded to a halt in front of Gareth and Llelo, more agitated than Llelo had ever seen him. "Something's happening outside the castle. We could see it from the top of the wall."

At a fast walk, they hurried through the gatehouse and out of the castle into the street. The crowd between them and the church was growing by the heartbeat.

Following his father, who edged through the rows of onlookers, Llelo finally reached the center of the mass of people. Most of the great lords were present, lining the inner rim of the circle, along with those in authority at the castle like Fitzharding, Harold, and Charles. These three were huddled on the town side, their heads together. Roger left his mother's side and went to join their conference.

Gwen, Angharad, and Dai were on the eastern side of the ring, by coincidence only a few yards away from the path Llelo had forged through the crowd. He and Gareth made their way towards them, all the while keeping their eyes on Prince Henry and Earl William, who stood a pace apart from each other in the center of the circle. The two lords were focused entirely on each other, apparently oblivious to the hundred onlookers. And both were apoplectic.

"From the start, you have looked for ways to undermine me," William shouted, the first of any emotion Llelo had seen from him. "My father is dead, and I am earl, confirmed by your mother. Why do you take against me so?"

"You are treating with King Stephen! My spies intercepted a message from William of Ypres confirming it!" Prince Henry brandished a piece of paper in the air.

"That you would accuse me of such a thing!" William's outrage matched Henry's. But then, all of a sudden, he deflated. He bowed his head for a moment, and then looked up to pin Henry with his gaze. "My lord, don't you see that our enemies revel in our disunity? That they seek to divide us in order to conquer us? I swear to you on my father's grave that I have no love for Stephen. I have never made any forays in that direction. Never." The last word was emphatic. "This accusation is no more correct than that my father was murdered."

It was the last thing he should have said, because it was the last thing Henry could let go. "I heard it from your father's own mouth. He said he was betrayed! *Je suis fini!*"

"Why does he emphasize that phrase?" Llelo leaned in to his mother, who was looking on with as much interest as he. "*Je suis fini* just means 'I am finished', doesn't it?"

Gwen shook her head. "That would be "*J'ai fini*—I have finished. *Je suis fini* is much more ominous."

"Those are the last words of the Roman general Julius Caesar before he was killed by his friends," Gareth said from Gwen's other side.

Llelo gaped at his father.

Gareth spread his hands wide. "So says Abbot Rhys. I'm just the messenger, but if the abbot knew it, Earl Robert may have as well."

"You've had many conversations with the abbot you have not discussed with me, it seems!" Gwen said, though she was shaking her head when she said it, as if amused.

Meanwhile, there was nothing amusing about the argument. William had been staring open-mouthed at his cousin without replying. Now, he said, "Why did you not speak of this sooner? I tell you, you misheard."

"How do you know? You weren't there!"

The accusation echoed around Henry, full of pain and suppressed grief. There were layers beneath the surface of this relationship too. Henry had loved his uncle, and it stood to reason that he'd loved William too—even worshipped him as he would an older brother. Llelo was an older brother, so he understood that this love made William's betrayal all the more painful.

"You're wrong there too. I was listening in the shadows in the corridor. You really did mishear. My father said, *Je suis beni.*"

Henry stared at William. "That's not true."

"It is."

"You're lying."

An audible gasp went up from every mouth at such an accusation. Henry seemed to realize for the first time that he was surrounded. But despite that fact, and even though his face was red right up to his hairline, he didn't back down. "Why did *you* not come forward sooner?"

There was a moment's pause, and then William said, softly now, but the silence among the onlookers was such that Llelo had no trouble hearing him, "My father was dying, and I was grieving. I couldn't bear to see his end. I had no idea you would take such a simple thing and turn it into murder."

"What about this note?" Henry brandished it again, though his heart wasn't in his accusation nearly as much as before. Gareth had moved a few paces closer to him by now, perhaps in sympathy or because nobody else was doing it. The prince was to the point of embarrassing himself and his House, but he mustered enough anger to shove the paper into Gareth's hand. "The evidence is clear!"

"By my guess, you were meant to intercept it." William's tone was actually wry, as if he was finding humor in the situation.

Llelo had been watching with rapt attention, so he immediately noticed the change in his father. Gareth was standing frozen, staring down at the paper in his hand. Then he pulled out a folded paper from his pocket and compared the two.

Llelo took a step towards him. "Father?"

"William understands," Gwen said.

Llelo looked back at her. "What does he understand?"

"I have thought all along, throughout this investigation, that what people weren't talking about was as important as what they were." Gwen was speaking in an undertone. "We need to examine what the people around us haven't said, rather than what they have. And even more *who* has not said anything at all."

Gareth lifted his head to stare at her instead of at the paper. "We've been so busy trying to put together the pieces of the puzzle that we have gathered, that we haven't noticed the pieces that we haven't."

His parents had lost him, and Llelo was about to open his mouth to say so when yet another shout went up, but this time from outside the circle. The crowd hadn't diminished in the slightest since Llelo's family had arrived, but it parted as the Dragons, led by Cadoc and Steffan, passed through them, holding a struggling man between them.

"Let me go. I've done nothing that you accuse me of!" This had to be Bernard.

"We will be the judge of that." Cadoc's tone was dry, as if capturing a wanted man was all in a day's work to him.

The argument between Henry and William was instantly forgotten. Cadoc forced Bernard to his knees in the dirt inside the circle. The crowd had been both entertained and horrified by the argument between prince and earl, but now there were shouts and fists raised. Bernard was lucky it had been the Dragons who'd captured him. Otherwise he might have been dead already.

"Traitor!"

"Hanging's too good for him!"

"Kill him now!"

These words were shouted in English, and it occurred to Llelo only now that many of the people from the town might not even have understood the fight between Henry and William, since it had been conducted entirely in French.

Charles had been among those shouting. His face was flushed, and he shook a fist in the air. Then he started forward. Seeing his ire, Roger and Harold made a grab for his arms, but he eluded them. As he passed in front of Llelo, he pulled a knife from its sheath at his waist. At first Llelo couldn't believe what he was seeing, and then Charles's steady walk turned into a run.

"Stop him, Llelo!"

The command came from Gareth, but Llelo was already moving. If Bernard really was the killer, then he might view it a blessing to die at the end of Charles's knife rather than a hangman's rope, but that wasn't how justice was done in Llelo's world. His steps quickened, his long legs driving him forward.

Maybe Cadoc would have stopped Charles before he could hurt Bernard, once he'd seen him coming, but it was too great a risk for Llelo to take. As Charles raised his arm to force the knife into Bernard's chest, Llelo hit him from the side, his arms wrapping around the understeward's chest and shoulders in a full-body tackle. They fell together to the ground, Charles beneath and Llelo on top.

Llelo had moved instinctively, without time to think or plan, and while Charles had no time to evade Llelo's blow, he did have time to pivot just slightly. So it was into Llelo's body, instead of Bernard's, that the knife slid home.

27

Gwen

Gwen couldn't hear anything above the rushing in her ears. When Llelo had moved and Gareth had shouted, she had stepped forward as well, pulled along in Llelo's wake by his evident urgency. But when she saw him take down Charles—and then roll off to find the whole right side of his body covered in blood, she'd handed the sleeping Taran to Angharad and fallen to her knees at his side.

"Mam."

"Just lie still. You're going to be fine." She spoke automatically, reassuring him out of habit and because she could do nothing else, though her words were as much for herself as for Llelo. She pulled up his shirt, gasping at the blood and the violent slash through his tissues, and then pressed down hard. Dai landed on his knees beside her, closer to Llelo's head, and she told him to put his hands in the place of hers and press hard, while she whipped off Taran's sling to use as a bandage.

Llelo's eyes had rolled up in his head, which might have been the best thing as far as the pain was concerned, but could be deadly if he went into shock. Meanwhile, his lifeblood was flowing into the dirt beneath him.

"Keep him awake, Gruffydd!" Gwen ordered.

Because, of course, the Dragons had gathered around too.

Meanwhile, out of the corner of her eye, she saw Charles rising to his feet, the bloody knife still in his hand. He looked at it a moment, and then dropped it as if it were a hot coal.

Gareth's hand came down on her shoulder and squeezed as he bent to look into his son's face, and then he stepped towards Charles. "Stay where you are."

Charles put up both hands. "I'm sorry! I never meant to hurt your son. I don't know what came over me!" His voice was high, panicked and contrite.

Gareth didn't have any sympathy in him. "Watch him, Iago. Don't let him out of your sight."

Iago obeyed without asking why, and then Gareth moved back to Gwen. "It's a flesh wound, *cariad.* He's going to be fine."

Gruffydd was supporting Llelo's head, and he growled something back that sounded like agreement. The tiny part of Gwen's mind that wasn't called *mother* acknowledged her husband spoke a possible truth. While there was a terrifying amount of blood, the knife had sliced along Llelo's side, not been driven into the middle of his belly.

Earl William bent forward, his hands on his knees. "A stretcher is coming, and I've sent for Denis. If anyone can help him, he can."

Llelo's eyes fluttered, and Gwen's heart caught in her throat, fearful that her son had already lost so much blood he couldn't waken, but he opened his eyes and looked at her, and somehow his words were clear and sane. "It hurts."

Gareth sat back on his heels. "It would."

Charles's voice could be heard protesting to Earl William at his treatment, but two Dragons were standing on either side of him, and Iago, who was twice as large as Charles, had hold of his upper arm.

True to the earl's word, the stretcher and the healer arrived, and Gareth put his hand under Gwen's elbow to help her up. Dai still pressed hard on his brother's side, and while the cloth was bloody, the rational part of Gwen's mind acknowledged that it wasn't soaked through. The guards began to move away, and Gwen would have followed except Earl William now said, "Charles didn't stab your son on purpose, Gareth. You should not be holding him. He has duties to attend to."

"That's not why I'm holding him." Gareth thrust a handful of paper in the earl's direction as Prince Henry had done to him a quarter of an hour before.

Then he and Gwen started after their son. The castle's infirmary was in the southeastern ward, and that was where the guards were taking him—at a fast walk so they would jar Llelo the least.

Gwen glanced back to see Earl William standing where they'd left him, glancing from one paper to another. Then his long strides ate up the yards between them, and he caught up as they passed through the castle barbican. He put out a hand, and Gwen and

Gareth let the stretcher continue on without them. While Gwen felt the urgency of her son's wound, it was beyond her skill to care for, unless the healer felt that her sewing hand would be better than his. She didn't know if she could sew up a wound on her own son, but she would if she had to.

"What am I looking at?" Earl William said.

"Take note of the writing on the message and then on the list."

Gwen could hear the forced patience in her husband's voice, and she sensed a similar impatience in William's. Roger and Henry had been hovering on the margins of their conversation too, and now they moved beside the earl to look as well.

"Just tell him, Gareth, because I don't understand either," Henry said.

"Look." Gareth took the papers back, holding them in front of him so everyone could see the writing. "The handwriting on King Stephen's supposed message—" he shook the paper, "—is identical to the handwriting on this list." He shook the other. "And then there are these notes, which I discovered in Sir Aubrey's rooms just now." Gareth pulled two more pieces of paper from his pocket. "Are these the two you intercepted before today?"

Henry answered somewhat hesitatingly. "Y-yes. The one today is the third of them. I told you when you arrived that I'd shared them with Sir Aubrey, and he kept them in his chambers."

"You didn't share them with me," William said.

Henry simply looked rueful. "You weren't here at the time, and I feared what you might have done." Then he turned to Gareth. "What are these lists of names? Where did they come from?"

Gareth gave an involuntary scoff, his patience gone, so it was Gwen who answered, "Sir Aubrey instituted a policy of writing down the name of every man, woman, and child who entered the castle. You can see our names clearly on this list from when we arrived three days ago."

"I see that, yes." Henry nodded.

Gwen took in a breath, anxious to get to her son, but knowing how important it was for Henry and William to understand. "Look more closely. The same man who wrote these notes, carried by King Stephen's courier, is the one who wrote our names when we arrived." She paused. "That man is the understeward, Charles."

28

Gareth

What had begun as a funeral service for a staunch companion had ended in chaos and recriminations. Once Gareth was convinced his son would live, he visited both Bernard and Charles in their cells. Bernard was being kept in a genuine dungeon, with iron bars and damp floor, but Charles had a room at the top of the tower, at Gareth's request, with a chair to sit on and a table to eat at. Gareth didn't approve in theory, but he was hoping to lull Charles into thinking they didn't understand what he'd done, and that he could still talk his way out of a hanging.

Gareth began with Bernard, who'd practically prostrated himself at his feet, in relief and gratitude that Gareth was willing to listen. During Sir Aubrey's funeral service, Cadoc and Hamelin, who was the one who recognized Bernard, had caught the former valet exiting the latrine in the outer ward, and as Gareth listened to the tale of woe, made all the worse by Bernard's own mistakes, he felt sullied himself.

"I'm an inveterate gambler. I admit it! But I didn't kill anyone! Earl Robert knew about my gambling. He even gave me a coin at one time or another to keep my creditors at bay. I think if he hadn't been so ill he might have spoken to them himself, but he was nearing the end, and he couldn't help me. I took nothing from him! I swear it!

"When he died, and then my own wife died, it was as if something snapped inside me. I was in more debt than ever, and those Italians don't take no for an answer. Even Fitzharding wanted his silver. I was going to lose my position. I'd already lost my lord, my wife, and my child. There was nothing left for me. They would have killed me if I hadn't killed myself. So, yes, I faked my own drowning. I thought to start over somewhere else."

Bernard drew in a unsteady breath.

"Charles wooed me over a long period of time. I think now that some of my worst debts were by his hand, because the wine he fed me was richer than I was used to. One time he found me in a tavern and plied me with drink—and I ended up losing worse than ever."

"Don't blame him for your gambling," Gareth said. "There's no honor in that."

Bernard scoffed. "I have no honor. I betrayed my lord. I can't come back from that."

"What about Earl Robert?"

"What about him?"

"Did you murder him?"

"Of course not!" Bernard had his hands clasped in front of him like he was before an altar. "In my heart, I knew it was only a matter of time before someone started asking questions, and those questions would lead to Charles, and thus to me. Or maybe to me and then Charles." He pointed with his chin again at Gareth. "You're here, aren't you? And Charles and I are behind bars. I was right to run."

Gareth had thought he understood where this was going, and now he was sure. "To pay off some of your debts, you did favors for Charles. What, in particular, did you do for him?"

"I gathered information."

Gareth didn't think he had to ask *about what*, but he did anyway.

"Everything that I could about what Earl Robert and his allies were thinking and doing. Movements of armies. Our resources. Charles had access to some of it, but I was with Earl Robert all the time, and nobody notices a servant, do they?"

"What did Charles do with it?"

Bernard shrugged. "He sent it to his masters."

"When did you realize that master was King Stephen?"

"It wasn't too hard to figure out." Bernard snorted. "Once, I even saw the great William of Ypres." At the widening of Gareth's eyes, he continued, "Yes, King Stephen's spymaster himself. Charles met with him in an abandoned barn outside Bristol. I went with him to keep watch."

"You say you didn't murder Earl Robert, but in the same breath you accuse Charles of spying for Stephen? It was Charles, then, who murdered the earl?"

Bernard shook his head emphatically. "The earl's death, my wife's death, even Sir Aubrey's, were all accidents. Charles kept his hands clean because he was playing a long game. He has been a spy at the very heart of Bristol for *years*, you understand, never giving himself away by word or deed."

"What changed?"

"Earl Robert's death, I think. It was all coming to a head. William didn't favor Charles, and perhaps he feared for his position. Maybe he was tired of his passive role, or maybe King Stephen wanted more from him. Maybe he'd had people making mischief all along, like Aelfric chiseling out bits of the castle. You should have the mason go over the entire castle, by the way. There are more stones on those battlements waiting to fall."

"Maybe you're the spy and Charles is the pawn," Gareth said. "You're the one who faked his own death, after all."

"No! I didn't hurt anyone!"

Gareth studied Bernard's pleading face. "Why did Aelfric end up dead? Why did Charles try to murder you? That certainly isn't keeping his hands clean."

Bernard became even more agitated. "You were here, asking questions. Charles was worried about Aelfric's loyalties, and Rose had decided she wanted more from her life than spying."

Gareth had been waiting for her name to come up. "Rose ran errands for him too?"

Bernard snorted. "Why do you think he killed her? In speaking to your wife, she'd done her last errand for him. You were getting too close, and he thought she was going to talk. Just like Aelfric."

"So to be clear, you, Aelfric, and Rose all worked for Charles, knowing that his intent was to betray Earl Robert?"

Bernard's hands were clenched in his hair, the very image of regret and despair. "I never meant to hurt anyone, but I needed to pay off my debts."

"Why did Rose do it?"

He sneered. "She wanted silver, so she could rise above her station."

"And Aelfric?"

Bernard shrugged. "He wanted revenge."

"Revenge on whom?"

"Not all Saxons have taken to the Normans, you know. You Welsh aren't the only ones who look to fight back."

That was the first Gareth had ever heard of a Saxon resistance, but he supposed one was bound to turn up eventually. He canted his head as he contemplated his prisoner. "Why *did* you come back, Bernard? You faked your own death perfectly. What possible reason could you have for coming back?"

"I tried not to! But when it came down to it, it's hard to start over with no money, no name, no friends. It had been three weeks of hell, living on the run, and I couldn't take it anymore. Besides, I knew—" he stopped short.

Gareth pounced on the hesitation. "What did you know?"

"What Charles's real plan was, of course! Why do you think Charles tried to kill me just now? To silence me!"

Gareth was skeptical. "Why would he want to do that?"

Bernard's chin stuck out, and even though his life was on the line, he was still reluctant to admit the truth. But then he did—to save his skin rather than his soul. "Because I knew what he was up to. I couldn't—" He looked down at his hands. "Charles's plan was to open the castle to King Stephen's forces on Christmas Day, when everyone was merry from revelry and good cheer. I know what you think of me, but even I am not so worthless that I would allow all of my friends to die."

This was credible and believable, but Gareth tsked through his teeth anyway. "I don't believe you."

"It's true, my lord! You have to believe me!"

"I don't, actually. You may have some modicum of conscience, but I don't believe that's why you returned—" He paused and began to nod as more pieces of the puzzle started falling into place. Everyone had liked Bernard, and he'd found favor with many, but nobody had trusted him—because he wasn't trustworthy. "You came back for money."

Bernard had been groveling at Gareth's feet, but now his head came up. "What? No, I didn't."

"Who did you think would give you money, Bernard?"

Bernard gaped at him and then shook his head vehemently. "No, no. You have it wrong."

Then the door opened behind Gareth, and he turned to see Gwen standing on the threshold of the guardroom with Mabs, of all people. Gareth frowned at them, feeling this was no place for women, even one as daring as his wife.

But Gwen came forward anyway, her arm hooked through Mab's elbow. "Mabs has something to tell you, Gareth."

Bernard gasped. "No." But the word came out strained and didn't carry.

"It's my fault he was caught. He came back for me." Mabs sniffed and wiped away a tear from her cheek with the back of her hand. "I told him I needed a few more days before I could leave. The manhunt caught us by surprise, so I smuggled him into the castle because we thought it would be the last place anyone would look. He was only caught because the latrine nearest my chambers is blocked, so he had to go outside." She looked past Gareth to where Bernard was on his knees on the floor. "We were leaving tonight, as soon as we could get away. We were going to be together forever!"

"I love you, Mabs," Bernard begged. "Don't believe anything anyone has said about me."

"I love you too!" Mabs burst into tears and turned to sob on Gwen's shoulder. "It isn't true. It isn't true."

Gwen looked over the top of Mab's head, neither she nor Gareth having the heart to tell the grieving woman that the only thing Bernard had cared about was her money.

*　*　*　*　*

Prince Henry spoke first, as was his right, silencing the company of noblemen who'd gathered in the conference room. "We have come together this week for a noble cause, but I must speak to you now of the deaths that have occurred at Bristol over the last month, beginning with the loss of my uncle Robert." Here he gestured to William, who was sitting with an elbow on the arm of his chair and a finger to his lips. His other hand tapped out a rhythm on the table. "While the information uncovered recently has shown me that I was mistaken in thinking my uncle was murdered, murder *has* been done." Now he motioned to Gareth. "I give you Sir Gareth of Gwynedd, to explain the hows and the whys—and the danger that lies before us now."

Gareth rose to his feet. At one time, he would have felt intimidated by speaking before this august company, but not anymore. He knew these men now, and he'd been in similar positions before. He also had begun to realize that the sooner he laid these murders to rest, the sooner he could take his family home. Llelo was wounded, but he would heal better if he could see the mountains of Wales from his window.

"If you will indulge me for a moment, I will begin at the beginning." Gareth gestured to Prince Henry. "The prince asked me to come to Bristol because he feared that his uncle had been murdered, and the fears were only heightened by the additional deaths of Earl Robert's maidservant and valet, a married couple. Within an hour of our arrival, we were faced with a fourth death, that of Sir Aubrey, Earl Robert's steward. By this point, it seemed apparent to us that all four deaths not only must be related, but could not be accidental."

He took in a breath. "We were wrong on all counts."

A murmur swept around the room, and Gareth put up a hand. "That is not to say that murder has not been done, and I will get to that in a moment. Let me dispense first with these four: As you know, Earl Robert had been ill for many months. In light of the testimony of various witnesses who came forward during the course of this investigation, both Earl William and Prince Henry feel it safe to conclude that he died of natural causes.

"The second death, that of the maidservant, was a surprise in that she was young. She was pregnant, however, and consultation with the castle midwife revealed that the pregnancy had not been going well." He sighed. "It is not an unreasonable conclusion that she too died a natural death, even if a premature one."

He put out a hand and pointed to the door. "Which brings us to the third death, that of Earl Robert's valet. He, as you must know by now, is not dead."

At a nod from Gareth, Evan opened the door and gestured the hapless Bernard into the room. He stood, hesitating on the threshold, until Gruffydd and Cadoc, who had hold of his upper arms, urged him inside. His hands weren't tied, but with so many men in the room, nobody was concerned that he would get away. Unfortunately for him, admitting to treason was as likely to get him hanged as murder. Possibly more likely. Gareth wasn't sure Bernard had figured this out yet.

Mabs had tried to intervene on his behalf to her half-brother, but William's face had remained stony, and Gareth was uncertain as to whether her attachment to Bernard made the earl more or less likely to hang him.

Bernard was followed by Charles, who was staunchly maintaining his haughty demeanor.

Gareth gestured expansively. "I give you Bernard, our wayward valet. By his own admission, he faked his own death to get away from his creditors. Charles, however, is a spy for William of Ypres."

Both William and Henry had known this, of course, and neither moved even an eyelash. The other lords in the room—Ranulf, the Clares, Cadwaladr too—surged to their feet in outrage.

Prince Henry lifted his hand at the wrist. "Please be seated, everyone. Continue, Sir Gareth."

Gareth obliged: "Charles arrived in Bristol many years ago after Stephen's failed attempt to take the castle by force, with the single goal of insinuating himself into the household. According to Bernard, Charles planned to open the castle to Stephen's men on Christmas Day."

"I have no idea what you're talking about." Charles's nose was in the air. "Everything you've said is a lie."

"Rose and Aelfric are dead by your hand," Gareth said. "You deny killing them?"

"Of course I do." He was standing before them with his arms bound behind his back, but with his legs spread, so he looked like a man-at-arms at rest rather than a prisoner. His shoulders were straighter than Gareth had ever seen them, and he seemed to be wavering between maintaining his mild-mannered persona and defiance.

Gareth turned to the surprised barons. "Charles was also working with the guard, Aelfric. Their goal at first was to collect information and perhaps make a little mischief while they were at it. We've noted the wards against evil spirits about the castle. Charles's intent was to capitalize on the fear the deaths created and to make it worse. These last weeks, he and Aelfric have made little things go wrong, from soured milk to strangely clogged latrines to—" he canted his head, "—broken masonry."

"You're saying that Sir Aubrey's death really was an accident?" Even Cadwaladr was aghast at the villainy.

Gareth frowned as he looked at Charles. "That was a piece of bad luck, wasn't it?"

"Why do you say *bad luck*, Gareth?" Ranulf said. "It paved the way for Charles to become steward."

Gareth's past encounters with the Earl of Chester hadn't always been pleasant, but he was an intelligent man, if amoral. "Charles didn't want the job, and quite liked staying in Sir Aubrey's shadow, especially as Aubrey's mind wasn't as sharp as it had once been. It was the perfect cover for him. That's why he didn't object to Lord Fitzharding's assumption of responsibility for the castle. His intent was to be as plain as the day is long, competent but unassuming.

"Sir Aubrey's death also focused attention on the troubling atmosphere at Bristol and gave credence to the idea that a killer was loose in the castle. It was the last thing Charles wanted—and I believe he panicked. He killed his co-conspirators rather than risk them talking."

"Why did Charles ransack Aubrey's rooms?" William said.

Charles answered for himself with a sneer. "I didn't."

Hamelin cleared his throat and put up a hand. "He's right. That wasn't Charles. I did it."

Even Gareth gaped at him, taken entirely by surprise. "Why?"

"Because I asked him to." Now everyone swung around to look at Prince Henry. "I had given to Sir Aubrey for safekeeping the messages we'd intercepted. I needed them in hand to prove my cousin had betrayed my mother and his father." The young prince looked genuinely sheepish. "He didn't find them, and I was wrong on all counts." He stood and bowed to William. For a future king to bow to one of his earls was unheard of, and yet he did it. "Forgive me, cousin. I was lost in grief."

"It is forgiven and forgotten." William stood and bowed back.

Gareth shook his head in disbelief. "Thank you, my lord Hamelin, for clearing that up. I had assumed Charles realized his mistake and was looking for either the notes or the lists."

"What lists are these?" Ranulf said.

Gareth explained again: "Since Earl Robert's death, Sir Aubrey had been noting everyone who entered and left the castle. According to his granddaughter, Aubrey studied the lists all the time, as he was struggling with the acuity of his memory. In the days before he died, he became convinced that he was missing something important about them. She never figured out what was bothering him— and he didn't either—or if he did, by morning he couldn't remember it."

Henry scowled. "But now we know."

"The lists." William was shaking his head. "You had your finger in every pie, Charles. How did I not see it?"

"Nothing this Welshman—" of course Charles accompanied the word with another sneer, "—has said about me is true."

William looked down at his hands as they rested on the table near the relevant pieces of paper. He shoved them towards Charles. "Don't lie to me anymore. You have literally been betrayed by your own hand."

29

Gwen

Thankfully, Gwen hadn't had to sew up Llelo's wound, but she'd watched with an eagle eye as Denis had done it. If the healer hadn't been English and living in Bristol, she might have suggested to Saran that she learn from him. Saran didn't speak more than a few words of French or English, however, so perhaps it was never meant to be.

Saran wouldn't have liked to leave Wales either—or her new husband.

Gwen herself, if she hadn't been so concerned about Llelo, would have been riveted.

Llelo had been dosed with poppy juice, and he woke to find Gwen and Dai on either side of him. Taran had nursed and was back at the priory with Angharad. Soon, Gwen would need to go to him and Tangwen, who'd been deprived of her mother far too much today.

He blinked at Gwen. "Is it done?"

"You will heal, God willing," Denis said from behind her.

Llelo coughed, and Dai helped him drink a sip of water. "I didn't mean me. I meant the investigation. What did I miss?"

Gwen narrowed her eyes at her son. "You want that now?"

"Of course I want it now."

"You might as well give him what he wants." Boots scraped on the threshold to the infirmary, and Gareth entered the room, followed by Hamelin.

"Why did Charles do it?" Llelo asked.

"Fundamentally, he is loyal to his king. He had principles, misguided as we might think they are, and stuck to them doggedly." Gareth gestured to Hamelin. "Means, motive, and opportunity, you said. He had all three, all this time."

"I don't understand why he showed his hand when opening the castle to Stephen at the Christmas feast was his goal," Llelo said. "He had only a month to wait!"

"He overthought, as many villains do," Gareth said. "He knew that we had been sent for, and he feared his best laid plans were going awry at the last moment. Truthfully, if he hadn't murdered Aelfric and Rose, we might never have caught him, and he would have been able to wait us out."

"There were still the lists." Gwen patted Llelo's shin, fairly certain it was one place that didn't hurt. "Well done, you, on that."

"It was Father who finally saw it," Llelo pointed out.

Hamelin shook his head. "You saved a man's life. How did you know to do it?"

"I didn't." Llelo gestured weakly to Gareth. "From the moment the manhunt started, we had been concerned that someone would kill Bernard before he could talk. So when Charles pulled out that knife, I had to stop him."

Gareth bent to kiss Llelo's forehead. He seemed about to speak, but then he gripped his son's upper arm—on his left side, opposite the wound—tightly. "The risk—"

Gwen patted Llelo again. "We have talked, your father and I, about putting our family in danger. We have sworn not to, and yet here we've done it again." She gestured to Dai. "You almost died last summer at Dinefwr, and now Llelo here. I don't know—" she found herself swallowing back tears as well, but she managed to conclude, "what's to be done."

Llelo was weak, but the growl in his throat was unmistakable. "You speak as if you did this to me. I chose to follow in your footsteps. And you could hardly be blamed for Dai being poisoned at an event where we thought we were at peace. These decisions are our own to make."

Gwen was rocked backwards slightly by Llelo's adamancy. She couldn't believe her son was comforting *her* instead of the other way around. "I'm your mother. I can't—"

Llelo put out a hand, first to her and then to Gareth, who still held him too. "I'm your son, but I'm also a man. You have to let me do what I must."

"He's right, you know." Gareth straightened and came around the bed to Gwen. "Come. Let's leave these young people to reflect on their triumphs."

Hamelin took Gwen's place at the edge of Llelo's bed. Since it would be days before Llelo could travel, they were stuck at Bristol still—time enough to cement a friendship with Hamelin that Llelo would not regret in the future. Gwen herself had never imagined that she could be treated so well in an English castle. These English had turned out to be just *people* after all, with all the same fear, strife, love, and joy that she had.

She would be sorry, if Gareth's assessment turned out to be correct, to find her lord and her country once again on the opposite side of a conflict with the English. Sadly, with the way the war was going in England, it seemed inevitable.

As they left the infirmary for the wall-walk of the outer ward, Gwen took Gareth's hand. "You have pulled me away for a reason, haven't you?"

They were on the western side of the castle. It was raised up above the countryside, so they could see the River Severn from where they stood.

"Other than because you were hovering over your grown-up son unnecessarily?" Gareth grimaced. "*Cadwaladr.*"

Gwen hummed deep in her chest. "What don't I know?"

"The conference has concluded. Henry's plan is to return to France to gather an army—and the support of his father—so he can take back England for his mother. Cadwaladr intends to go with him."

Gwen swallowed down a shocked *what?* "Why would Prince Henry allow it?"

"Because while nobody trusts Cadwaladr, and none of the other barons want him in their court, he has pledged his life to Henry."

"He has no lands of his own outside of Wales. Why would Henry even want his allegiance?"

"Because it's either take him with him or cut him loose."

Gwen's stomach sank into her boots. "At which point, he would return to King Stephen."

"Nobody doubts it. Ranulf, in particular, had a few choice words to say about our treacherous prince. They are relations by marriage, but there's no love lost there."

"And still, as we know, Ranulf isn't above using Cadwaladr."

"Which is why Ranulf chose to speak of his concerns only to me and Henry. Ranulf backed up Hamelin's explanation of Cadwaladr's treachery, by the way, and embellished upon it. We should have no fear that Henry will trust him, but—"

Gwen sighed. "He is not above using him."

"I wish I could kill him."

"Honor is a pesky thing, my love."

Suddenly, Gareth laughed. "I can't be sorry for it." He gestured back the way they'd come. "You only have to look at the men our sons have become."

The End

Historical Background

On October 31, 1147, Robert, Earl of Gloucester, died peacefully in his bed. With his death, Empress Maud's chances of gaining the throne of England received a serious setback. Prince Henry was only fourteen, and since his invasion of England in the spring of 1147 had ended so miserably, it would be several more years before he could muster the support to try again. Maud left England in early 1148, never to return. We'll get to that story in a later book ...

Unfortunately, Bristol Castle no longer exists, other than a few ruins, which include the gate to the tunnel under the keep and the sally port into the dry moat by the town gate near St. Peter's Church. Most of what remained after the medieval period was destroyed during the bombing in World War II.

Robert of Gloucester was one of the most powerful men in England in his time. Certainly he was one of the richest. One of his longest-lasting legacies (other than my birth, as you shall see below) is the sponsorship of the work of Geoffrey of Monmouth, who wrote The History of the Kings of Britain, which he dedicated to Robert in 1136.

Geoffrey is the author who first placed Arthur in the line of British kings, and it is his stories that sparked the growth of Arthurian literature. "Such an action not only asserted the historicity of Arthur but also gave him an authoritative history which included many events familiar from later romance.

http://www.lib.rochester.edu/camelot/geoffrey.htm

As a side note, the story of Sir Aubrey's death is a case of truth being stranger than fiction. While Aubrey himself is fictional, his death is based on the actual death of a real person. While at Montgomery Castle, I noticed a plaque on the gatehouse wall describing the sudden death of a woman from a stone falling from the battlement. She had come to the castle seeking the return of a cooking pot someone in the kitchen had borrowed from her. Her death was deemed an accident. Sadly, Gareth and Gwen weren't available to look into it.

On a more personal note, before researching this book I had already discovered that I am a descendent of many medieval kings, including King Owain's father, Gruffydd, through his daughter Gwenllian. Imagine my delight, then, to learn that I am also descended from King Henry I of England through Robert of Gloucester himself. Robert's illegitimate daughter, Mabel, known as Mabs in this book, married Gruffydd ab Ifor Bach, Lord of Senghenydd. I descend directly from one of their children. As my son is wont to say, how cool is that?

To sign up to be notified whenever I have a new release, please see
the sidebar on my web page:
http://www.sarahwoodbury.com/
You can also connect with me on Facebook:
https://www.facebook.com/sarahwoodburybooks

About the Author

With two historian parents, Sarah couldn't help but develop an interest in the past. She went on to get more than enough education herself (in anthropology) and began writing fiction when the stories in her head overflowed and demanded she let them out. While her ancestry is Welsh, she only visited Wales for the first time while in college. She has been in love with the country, language, and people ever since. She even convinced her husband to give all four of their children Welsh names.

She makes her home in Oregon.

www.sarahwoodbury.com